I0691789

# Skin

First Edition

Published by the Nazca Plains Corporation

Las Vegas, Nevada

2015

ISBN: 978-1-61098-358-7
E-Book: 978-1-61098-359-4

Published by
The Nazca Plains Corporation®
Paradise Rd, Suite 141
Las Vegas, NV 89109-8000

PUBLISHER'S NOTE
*Skin* is a work of fiction created wholly by Greg Bowden's imagination. All characters are fictional and any resemblance to any persons living or deceased is purely by accident. No portion of this book reflects any real person or events.

Photo Copyright
Art Director, Kimm Antell

*For Prime Timers of the Desert, a social organization
"for older men and their admirers." This book is, in many ways,
the result of the encouragement so many Prime Timers
have given me.*

*To all the Prime Timers of the Desert...*

*Thanks guys*

# Skin

First Edition

Greg Bowden

# Contents

# Prologue

"Sam? Please..." Harry's voice came as a whisper, weak in volume but still strong in tone.

Sam Davis, sitting across the room reading a book, looked up. "Yes Harry. I'm here." He marked his place in the book, set it on the lamp table and got up. "Can I get you something? Water? Tea?"

Harry, ninety-two years old and dying of cancer, could still smile. "If it's after five o'clock, I'll have a martini. Otherwise, no. Just you."

Sam sat on the edge of the bed and took Harry's hand in his. He found it dry, the skin papery, hiding the cancer that was eating Harry alive.

"I'm here," he said, his voice thick with emotion.

"You know I love you, don't you Sam?" He tried to squeeze Sam's hand but didn't have the strength. "More than any son, more than any lover." He let out a sigh, weak from the exertion.

"I know you do, Harry. I know. I love you too. I have all this time, ever since I got over being scared of you."

Harry smiled. "Did I actually scare you, Sam?"

"You did. Probably for most of the first year I was here." He leaned down and kissed Harry on the forehead. "Then I figured out you were just an old fraud."

Harry's breathing turned labored. "It's time, Sam. I just couldn't go without telling you I love you." He went suddenly rigid and then relaxed, his last breath taken. He closed his eyes and quietly died.

Sam sat on the edge of the bed for a while, petting the limp hand he held. Then he got up, crossed the room, and telephoned Harry's doctor. "It's over."

"I'll be right there."

A few hours later Harry was gone. His hospital bed and all the other trappings of grave illness were now packed in their boxes, ready for the rental agency to pick them up. Sam sent the staff home and then found himself at loose ends, wandering through the house, looking for... what? He didn't know.

He finally came to rest in the library which was perhaps his favorite room. He lit the fire, poured himself a drink and settled into his favorite chair, a large wingback, covered in a heavy cobalt blue fabric. Harry had been unsure about the chair, but it had grown on him and now there were two of them, side by side with a small table between, facing the fireplace.

Sam drank some of the cold, dark whiskey and settled back, letting his mind wander back to the late spring of 1980.

\* \* \* \*

Just turned 22, he thought. A long time ago. He had been fired from yet another job, this one as a bus-boy at a Denny's. Once he'd been let go he had nothing much to do so he walked over to the unemployment office and stood in the familiar line. When he got up to the counter he found it manned by Mr. Willow, a man he had had dealings with in the past.

Mr. Willow looked up and smiled. "No, wait. Don't tell me. It's... it's... Sam, right? Sam Davis?"

Sam had ducked his head in what he thought to be a proper show of deference. Mr. Willow just thought it was cute. "Yes sir. Sam Davis."

"Well, nice to see you again. So soon." Turning to the counter behind him, he rummaged through a file box, extracted a card and stamped it. "Don't even have to fill out a new one." He handed the card to Sam. "Just sign here, by the new date stamp."

Sam took a pen and said, "That's all? I just sign and the checks will start?"

"Not quite." Mr. Willow smiled. "We have a new regulation which requires you go to at least one job interview before you're eligible." He flipped over a page or two in a ledger. "And I have just the job for you. You won't get it, of course, and if by some miracle you do, you won't last long, so I'll be seeing your handsome face in here again soon."

Mr. Willow made a phone call, filled out a form, stamped it in a couple of places and handed it to Sam. "Get this signed, bring it back, and you're all set." His voice lowered, "And if you need a meal or something I'm probably the dumb ass who'll buy it for you." Louder he said, "Now go. Others are waiting."

Sam checked the map on the wall by the door and found the address to be deep in Beverly Hills. He could have taken the bus but he hitch-hiked instead, both to save money and to see what adventures he might come across. Sam had one simple rule for hitch-hiking: the word No. If they didn't understand no he got out at the first opportunity. It wasn't that he objected to an occasional approach, he simply didn't want to be in a car with a driver distracted by lust.

He walked the last five blocks. When he got to the address on the form, he found himself a little daunted by the size and formality of the house. He became even more intimidated when he rang the bell and the door was opened by a rather haughty man in a tuxedo who looked him up and down with some distaste.

"Your business?"

Sam held out the form. "I'm to see a Mr. McKittrick."

The man looked him up and down again and sneered. "I doubt Mr. McKittrick will find you suitable, but he has instructed me to show you to the garden." He turned abruptly on his heel and it took a moment before Sam realized he was expected to follow.

The house seemed monstrous, with huge rooms, high ceilings and furniture even Sam could tell was expensive. Sam sighed and wondered what it'd be like to live in such splendor.

"This way, this way," the man in the tuxedo said in an exasperated tone of voice. "Don't dawdle, gawking at the furniture!"

They went through some French doors to the outside and down three steps. The man turned and stopped. "Excuse me, sir. Here is the boy the agency sent. Shall I wait to show him out?"

He stepped aside and Sam laid eyes on Harry McKittrick for the very first time. All of Harry McKittrick.

The man rose from his lounge and extended his hand. "Harry McKittrick," he said. "And you are?"

It was almost too much for Sam to take in all at once. Harry, an older man, stood over six feet tall and had white hair, a closely cropped white beard and a bright smile. He was also naked.

Sam gulped but somehow managed to rise to the occasion. "Good to meet you, sir." He shook the man's hand, smiled, and looked him directly in the eye. "My name is Samuel Davis, but everyone calls me Sam. I've come to see about the job opening you have."

"Have you now?" Harry looked past Sam, to the man in the tuxedo. "You may go, Walker. I'll ring if we need you. Oh, and young Sam here might like something to drink." He looked back at Sam.

"Oh, no sir, I'm fine. Thank you."

Walker turned and left, obviously more annoyed than ever.

In the end Sam got the job, after a long conversation with Harry, and after filling out a lot of papers for Harry's lawyer. Then, in just under a week's time, Sam settled into a room bigger than his whole apartment had been and he became the official companion to Harry McKittrick.

His first duty as Harry's companion was to fire Walker. Over the next twenty-four years he fired, and hired, most of the people who made life comfortable for Harry. He served as Harry's traveling companion, majordomo, attendant, and at the end, his caretaker; everything in fact but his physical lover.

Sam and Harry fit well together and after a year or so most of Harry's friends saw them as a couple and always invited them to social events together. The two men never discussed money beyond Sam's salary, which in later years grew to be quite substantial. On his birthday, Christmas, and oddly, on Harry's birthday as well, Sam always received some shares of stock in some company or another, which he put away in an account with Harry's broker.

Money had never been high on Sam's list of priorities and he didn't pay a whole lot of attention to it. His beginning salary with Harry amounted to several times what he had commanded as a bus-boy and his food, clothes, and shelter were all supplied by Harry. Sam never had to ask for anything; it was almost as though Harry had become tuned to him and anticipated his needs and wants. Very quickly it began to work the other way as well.

For his part, Sam ran the household and went everywhere with Harry, helping him more and more as he grew older. He acted as chauffeur, travel agent, arranger, companion, and starting in his first summer, a decorative – and naked – fixture around Harry's swimming pool. The men invited to Harry's parties were quite aware they should never make advances towards Sam; they could, however, look to their heart's content and, sometimes, longing. Not that Harry required Sam to be celibate. Far from it. Sam could freely have whatever liaisons he might want, but they were always kept out of sight, never spoken about, and certainly not allowed to interfere with Harry's life. This suited Sam, and though he sometimes wondered what it would be like having a man permanently in his bed, he found himself satisfied and quite content.

Sam slipped out of his reverie and found his glass empty except for the remains of an ice cube or two. He thought about pouring himself another, but decided against it and went to bed where he slept peacefully.

When he woke the next morning, Sam showered, dressed, and went down to the kitchen. "I thought I told you to take the rest of the week off, Albert." He laughed, helping himself to a cup of Albert's superb coffee. "Yet what do I find? You can't leave your beloved stove."

Albert grinned. "I'd be lonely without it, sir. And I thought you'd be hungry. I see you didn't touch the chicken and mushroom stew I left for you." This last was said with a scowl of disapproval.

Sam gathered him into a hug. "Thank you, Albert. I just wasn't... interested in food last night."

"Well, you have to eat. Good food helps us with our sorrows my mother always said." His face crumpled a little and he looked into Sam's eyes. "I'll miss him too, you know. We all will. He was a good man." He wiped the back of his hand across his eyes and took a deep breath, his voice becoming brisk. "But you must eat, Mr. Sam. How about a nice plate of scrambled eggs with shrimps. You always like that, now don't you?"

Sam knew he had been outranked, outclassed, and out maneuvered. "Yes, Albert. That sounds good. And maybe a slice of sourdough toast?"

Sam found himself to be hungrier than he'd realized and ate everything Albert put in front of him. As he was finishing the phone rang. Alistair Middleton, Harry's lawyer, was calling to ask if he could visit. Sam told him to come for lunch, thinking it would give Albert something to do.

For the rest of the morning Sam wandered around the house and garden, thinking, remembering, missing Harry.

Over lunch in the solarium, Sam and Alistair made small talk and savored Albert's lobster quiche and baby greens. Over chocolate mousse and coffee, Alistair finally got to the reason for his visit.

"The will," Alistair said, with some finality. "Harry left all that he owned to his grand-nephew and grand-niece." Seeing the look on Sam's face he grinned. "You have a problem with that?"

"Only with the fact that Robert actively detested Harry because Harry was gay. And the fact that Melissa found Harry to be socially superfluous and told him so to his face." He looked around the solarium. "I can't imagine either of them living here."

"Stop right there, Sam," Alistair said with a puzzled look on his face. "Didn't Harry discuss this with you? He told me he would, but you know Harry, always putting off things he didn't want to think about."

Sam shook his head. "Harry never mentioned things like that to me. He was a very private person, you know, and it wasn't really any of my business anyway. I just figured that most of whatever he owned would go to some charity."

Alistair set his coffee cup firmly on its saucer and rose from the table. "There's a bar in here somewhere, isn't there? I think you're going to need a drink, Sam."

Sam then learned that Harry owned, in his own name, only one thing: an insurance policy for one point five million dollars. The beneficiaries of that policy were Melissa and Robert, his only living relatives. Everything else was owned by The Harry McKittrick and Samuel Davis Trust for Benefit of Harry McKittrick and Samuel Davis. There were only two trustees for that trust, and now one of them had died.

"The insurance policy and the will," Alistair said, "were to protect you from Robert and Melissa. They each get $750,000, and if they want more, too bad. They can't contest the will and there's no way for them to get at the trust since they have already been provided for. You, Sam, get everything else." He chuckled. "Well you don't exactly get it. You've had it all along. A very neat bit of planning, I'd say."

From the pride in Alistair's voice, Sam figured it had all been Alistair's idea in the first place.

"So what are we talking about here?" Sam asked.

"Well, I haven't had time to order a full accounting, but in general, we're talking about this house, the cars, the stocks and bonds, and a great deal of cash." He cocked his head at Sam. "As you point out," Alistair said with a grin, "Harry could be something of an odd bird. He always felt most comfortable with cash at hand."

Sam laughed. "You mean like the fifty thousand dollars in the library safe? Or the four thousand dollars," he pointed, "in that antique porcelain box?"

Alistair nodded. "Tip of the iceberg, Sam. There are bank accounts, mind you, savings accounts, with something over five million dollars in them. Cash! Doing nothing but garnering a paltry interest." He shook his head. "But that's what Harry wanted and, after all, it was Harry's money, he earned it and could do anything he wanted with it." He paused. "Oh, yes, and the house in Palm Springs. I always forget about that one." He chuckled. "I think Harry did, too, after a while, but every time I mentioned it to him he told me to leave it as it is."

Sam shook his head. "Palm Springs? We went down there a few times but I didn't know…"

"He bought it from some friends. It seems they had some large financial reverses and needed money. Harry, of course, offered to give it to them but they wouldn't hear of it. Instead, they sold their house to Harry for some exorbitant sum and he let them live in it rent free. They both passed away some time ago, let's see, '95 or '96, I believe." He paused for a moment and shrugged. "Perhaps he was sentimental about it."

Sam found himself having a little trouble taking everything in. "So there's this house, a house in Palm Springs, some savings accounts… what's it all add up to Alistair?"

Alistair looked at the ceiling for a moment, estimating and adding in his head. "Oh, I should say, counting the potential sale price of the real property, somewhere on the order of forty-two to forty-five million dollars."

Sam nodded, although the figure didn't really register on him. "And you manage it."

Alistair shook his head. "No, no. I, that is my firm, oversees the actual managers. We make sure Harry's, uh, well, now your, wishes are carried out. We also handle necessary payments and so on. We basically make sure everything's on the up and up and running as it should."

Sam stood, walked around the table and put his hand on Alistair's shoulder. "Thank you," he said, and when Alistair stood, thinking to shake hands, Sam pulled him into a tight hug. "Thank you."

\*\*\*

It took several months for Sam to figure out what to do with himself. Other than that of companion and caretaker he had no actual profession, and no real need of one. He busied himself with a celebration of Harry's life, with seeing to the house and staff, and, ultimately, with nothing.

His friends, Harry's friends, entertained him and did their best to keep him busy. One couple decided he needed a long ocean voyage so he booked a cruise but then couldn't go through with it because Harry wouldn't be there to take care of and it would be lonely. The same thing happened with a trip to Australia. Why be at loose ends in Australia when he could be at loose ends at home?

He hired handsome young men to bring him pleasure, once three at the same time, but found it hardly better than he could do for himself.

Ultimately, he realized his whole life had been devoted to Harry and now it had come up empty. He needed a change, a change of place; a change of people.

He closed up the house, gave generous bonuses to the staff, and asked Alistair to arrange for the place be kept up. He'd decided to go to Palm Springs, live there for a while, and see what kind of a life he might find in the desert.

When Sam went to see Alistair and pick up the keys to the Palm Springs house, Alistair suggested he arrange to stay in a hotel until he'd actually seen the house, seen if it suited him.

"There's a phone in the house," Alistair said, "and electricity, both of which are there to support the security system Harry had put in." He referred to a note on his desk. "There's also a man who cleans the swimming pool. When you get there, you can assess his skills and decide if you want to keep him." He handed Sam an envelope containing the keys, the address, and the alarm code then pulled him into a hug. "We'll miss you, Sam."

And so, around noon on Saturday, February 26, 2005, Sam found himself checking into Some Guys, a gay, clothing-optional resort in Palm Springs.

# Chapter One

Of the more than thirty gay resorts in the Palm Springs area, Some Guys had been recommended by a couple of friends who thought Sam might like the informality and camaraderie of a clothing optional place. Sam, once checked in to the resort, spent the afternoon lying in the sun by the pool. At five o'clock, he joined the other men for the wine and cheese put out by the management. Sam found it a great way to meet the other men staying at the resort.

The evening had grown cool and Sam had put on a pair of shorts and a tee shirt. When he was introduced to a couple named Jack and Pete they asked if he might be cold.

"Yeah," Sam answered. "The afternoon turned a bit cool."

"Boy, not for us" Jack said. He, along with his partner Pete, hadn't dressed after an afternoon around the pool. "We think it's downright balmy! Of course if you were from Minnesota like we are, you'd probably find it the same way."

Sam laughed. "Probably true. But I'm from Los Angeles where I'd be wearing a sweater or a jacket about now. But even here in Palm Springs, I need something to keep me warm…"

Pete looked at him and smiled. "Well, if you need something to keep you warm…" He didn't finish the sentence but Sam caught his meaning.

He grinned. "What say we go to dinner together and see what develops?"

They consulted with Bob, one of the owners of the resort, and he recommended a couple of different restaurants. They chose El Mirasol, a Mexican place where Jack pronounced the margaritas Fantastic!

After dinner they went back to the resort where something did, in fact, develop and Sam spent several blissful hours being kept warm by Jack and Pete.

Sam got up early the next morning and had coffee on the patio with Bob, one of the owners of the resort. When Bob asked him about his plans for the day, Sam explained about the house.

"I've never even seen the place," he said. "I inherited it and thought living in Palm Springs might be a good change for me."

Bob didn't press him on why he felt he needed a change. "Is the house vacant?"

"Yes. It's been vacant since the people living in it died, six or seven years ago. I think that means I'll need to be staying here for a while longer, if you can put me up."

Bob stretched in the early morning sun. "I'm sure we can squeeze you in somewhere, for as long as you need." He smiled when a handsome man came up and kissed him. "Mornin' sleepyhead," he said to the man.

The man leaned across the table and shook Sam's hand. "I'm Roger," he said. "The other naked innkeeper. I think I checked you in yesterday, didn't I?"

Bob grinned at him. "You are getting senile, forgetting you checked in a handsome stud like Sam."

"Oh, yeah. Sam Davis, room 27, open-ended stay, right?"

Sam nodded. "If you can find me a bed."

Roger laughed. "Oh, I'm sure a handsome guy like you will be able to find a lot of beds to get in. Now sleeping, that may be a different matter."

Sam liked the banter. "Not to worry. I've been told I'm very cuddly and that often leads to sleep. Eventually."

Both Roger and Bob laughed. Bob turned to Roger and said, in a little boy voice, "Can we keep him, Daddy? He's just so cute, we can't send him away."

"If you want him to stay, he may stay." Roger turned to Sam. "For as long as he likes." He poured himself a cup of coffee and selected a donut from the box on the bar. "You know, Bob, you really shouldn't buy these things. They're not good for you."

"Me? They're not good for me? I'm not the one scarfing them down! Besides, I didn't buy them. Byron did."

Sam raised a curious eyebrow. "Byron?"

Roger turned, looking glad for the change of subject. "I guess you haven't met him yet. Byron is our son, Bob's and mine, and Matt is his partner. They live just over the wall," he said, nodding behind them. "Byron's offices are there along with the cottage they live in. They like to help us out around the place."

"You'll come to dinner some night, meet them," Bob said. "You'll like them. Now, tell us about this house."

Sam told them what little he knew about the place. By the time he finished, he'd also told them a little about Harry and his relationship with him.

"You know," Bob said, "what you need is to find a man you can settle down with and make a life. And a gay, clothing optional resort probably isn't the ideal place to do that."

"You're probably right," Sam said, standing and folding his towel, "but guys you want to settle down and make a life with don't come around very often anyway so this is better than nothing. See you later, and thanks for the coffee."

Sam got dressed and drove to the house with high hopes, which, when he found the place, began to crumble just like the wall around it. Sam got out of his car and took stock. He saw a block wall with very little stucco left on it, a badly rusted front gate and another at the driveway secured with a newer chain and large padlock. Behind it all was a jumble of wild vegetation. He thought about climbing over the wall but when he stood on tiptoes and ran his hand along the top he found it embedded with sharp rocks.

"Excuse me. May I help you?"

Sam hadn't seen the man approach and jumped at the sound of his voice. "Uh, it's okay. I own the place."

The man, who had evidentially been walking the huge dog standing beside him, stuck out his hand. "Oh, well then…"

Sam went to take the hand but jumped back when the dog began vacuuming him, starting with his crotch.

The man laughed. "He won't hurt you; he's gentle as a lamb. He just wants to see if you have a dog."

"Well, I don't know about the gentle part," Sam said, tentatively reaching out to let the dog sniff his hand, "but he's sure big as a lamb. He's a Great Dane, isn't he?"

"Yep!" the man said. "Biggest, smartest, and gentlest dog in the world." He took the hand the dog was working on and shook it. "I'm Tom Wacker. Live there, next door." He gave Sam a long look. "Don't know how you could have bought the place, though. As far as I know it hasn't been on the market."

"Oh, uh, well, I inherited it."

Tom eyes narrowed. "Who died?"

Sam's first impulse was to tell the man it was none of his business but then thought better of it. "A fellow named McKittrick; Harry McKittrick."

Tom seemed to be thinking for a few moments and the dog went back to vacuuming Sam's clothes. "Then you must be the hunk."

"The hunk?"

"McKittrick's boyfriend. Heard all about you from Jack and Larry. You know, the guys who used to own the place." He stepped back and looked Sam up and down. "They weren't kidding, were they?"

Sam blushed a little and looked off into the distance, trying to remember the men. It finally came to him. "Oh, yeah, tall guys, both of them, one bald, the other with a beard. Nice guys. Stayed with us a couple of times."

"That's the ones. After they lost all that money in the futures market, your Harry bought the place from them, let them live in it free. I always figured he'd sell the place after Jack and Larry died."

Sam smiled. "I think he forgot about it."

Tom's face fell. "I'm sorry to hear about Harry. Only met him a couple of times, but he seemed a pretty good guy. It must be hard on you, after all these years."

"I'm learning to live with it, one day at a time."

Tom brightened up. "Well, I suppose you'll be wanting to see the place. Come on next door. We put the chain and lock on the big gates." He turned to the dog. "Come on Tige, let's go home."

"Tige? That's the dog's name?"

Tom smiled. "Yeah, it's kind of a joke. Before your time, I imagine. Back in my day there was this shoe company called Brown. They had a cartoon kid named Buster and Buster had a cartoon dog. The dog was named Tige and we kind of liked it," He laughed. "They lived in a shoe."

"Don't you think he's a little big to live in a shoe?" Sam laughed.

Tom grinned. "Big shoe. Remember, the kid lived in it with him."

Next door they went through a gate and Sam looked across the lawn to the house. He liked it. "Is my house anything like this?" he asked.

"Not really. Ours is more Spanish in character while yours is what they now call Mid-Century Modern. Or was. Jack and Larry made a lot of changes to it and, in my opinion, not all of them were for the good. Come on in and meet Dan."

Dan Godges turned out to be the exact opposite of Tom Wacker. Where Tom stood tall and had salt and pepper hair, Dan had a shorter stance and a shaved head. Where Tom appeared outgoing and talkative, Dan seemed quiet, almost shy. Sam thought their differences played well against each other.

After introductions, Dan went to find the key to the lock on the driveway. While he did that, Tom showed Sam around their house. Sam found the place beautiful, but the heavy, dark Spanish furniture seemed more than he thought he would be comfortable living with. But it all fit and the windows opening out on the garden brought in a lot of light, which minimized the effect of the dark wood and heavy fabrics.

They were in the kitchen when Dan returned and handed Tom a key.

Tom, in turn, handed it to Sam. "We put the chain on the gates after someone tried to break in the place. The alarm company said they only got notified if someone went inside the house. We gave them a key just in case. Oh, and one for the pool guy, too. Didn't know of anyone else we thought might need a key."

Leaving Tige to have a nap, they went back to Sam's house. The key fit the lock and, to Sam's surprise, the key which Alistair had given him actually unlocked the front door.

The place was a disaster. Everywhere Sam looked he saw a thick layer of dust and grime. The air smelled of mold. One of the windows in the living room had broken and part of it was missing; a pipe had burst in the master bathroom and all the little tiles on the floor were either loose or missing. The toilet had been cracked and came crashing apart when Sam touched it. The kitchen was... well, Sam didn't want to think about the kitchen.

There was an odd collection of furniture scattered around the house and Sam asked Tom and Dan what had happened to all the other stuff.

"Well," Tom said, "Jack and Larry told us to let their friends come in and take what they wanted. So we held a sort of open house one Saturday and their friends came and took stuff away. This is what's left. Not much, is it?"

Sam shook his head. "I wouldn't have wanted any of their things anyway. This," he waved his arm taking in the entire house, "will all go to the dump. Unless there's anything you guys want."

"Well, if you wouldn't mind..." Dan held out a photograph in a dented silver frame, A picture was of Sam when he was twenty-six or –seven. He was standing naked on the diving board at the pool in Beverly Hills.

"I'm flattered," Sam said, rubbing at the tarnish with his thumb. "Of course. Anything you want." He handed the photograph back to Dan and they heard a sudden, very loud bell ringing. "What the hell's that?"

"Phone," said Tom. "They were both a bit deaf toward the end." He crossed the room and picked up the handset to what Sam had thought to be just an interesting antique. Tom listened for a moment and held it out to Sam. "Alarm company. Want to talk to you."

"Damn, I forgot all about the security system." He took the phone.

While Sam talked, a man in a well-fitted uniform walked in, his right hand resting lightly on the butt of the gun in the holster on his belt.

He looked at Sam and growled, "What're you doing?"

Sam grinned. "Talking to your supervisor. Here." He held out the phone.

The uniformed man shook his head. "What's his name?"

"Her name is Cynthia." He listened for a moment. "And the word for the day is wombat." He tried to choke back his laughter but didn't quite make it, "Wombat?"

The man glared at him and grabbed the phone.

It took a while but they got it all sorted out and the man showed Sam how to arm and disarm the system.

# Chapter Two

The next afternoon, over a Coke, Sam told Bob and Roger about the house. "It's a real disaster," he said, "but it looks as if it might be good architecture. It's all cut up and filthy and the garden – or what used to be the garden – is so overgrown you can hardly find the house." He shook his head. "I just don't know what to do with it."

Roger shrugged. "If it was mine, I'd get an opinion from someone who knows about buildings and architecture."

"Yeah," Bob picked the idea up, "how about Bill, that guy who did our exercise room, and Byron and Matt's place? He's straight, but he sure seems to know what he's doing." He looked at Sam. "He's a little on the pricey side, but he knows his business and does high quality work." He grinned. "Has good looking workers, too. Lots of eye candy on the job."

Roger rolled his eyes. "The studliness of his workers is hardly the basis for a recommendation, sweetheart. An added plus maybe, but not in and of itself a reason to hire him." He turned back to Sam. "We can put you in touch with him if you like. Matt said he'll be at their cottage tomorrow and we could introduce you."

Sam nodded. "Might as well get to it. Yeah, I'd like an introduction if you can arrange it." He looked around the resort. "Kind of quiet today."

Bob nodded. "Well, it is the last day of February. And a Monday to boot. It'll pick up mid-week and we're full up for next weekend. Enjoy the peace and quiet while you can."

By five o'clock in the afternoon Sam had grown bored with peace and quiet, so he put on his clothes and went to a bar Bob and Roger had recommended. The bar, called Sidewinders, was a mile or two down Highway 111, in a small shopping center. It turned out to be on the second floor, above a pizza place.

When he got to the top of the stairs and looked around he thought the place was pretty crowded for a Monday evening. After he worked his way through the door he was confronted by a couple of guys sitting behind a table. "Name?" Sam gave it and the man rewarded him with a stick-on name tag. The man also offered a sticker with Single printed on it along with one that said Desperate. Sam took the Single one.

He made his way over to the bar and ordered a scotch and soda. "Hey, what's going on, why the name tags?" Sam asked the bartender when he put down the drink.

"Mixer," the bartender said. "Prime Timers, you know, the guys social club. Do one every Monday, one place or another. Good crowd. Friendly." He pointed to the man standing next to Sam. "What's yours?"

The bartender went back to work and Sam looked around. Over in a corner he spotted Tom and Dan, sitting on tall stools at a table with a couple of other guys, one a striking redhead. He started to work his way through the crowd to them when a slightly stocky guy with a short beard, actually more a heavy stubble than a beard, and a killer smile caught his eye. Nice. I wonder if Tom and Dan know him.

Tom and Dan waved Sam over and introduced him to the other men. The striking redhead, naturally, went by Red and the other one they introduced as William. Sam quickly figured out that they were a couple. Too bad. That redhead looks to be quite a man.

When Tom mentioned that Sam owned the house next door to theirs Sam shook his head. "Yeah, but I'll probably never live in it. The place is a mess."

Tom brushed Sam's comment aside. "It's a good house, Sam. All it needs is a little – well, a lot – of work. But it's still a good, solid house."

William looked up. "You want to get out of it?" He pulled out his wallet and handed Sam a card: Best Reality, Palm Springs. "Give me a call and we'll see what we can do."

Sam put the card in his pocket and grinned. "I just might do that. Just might."

"Well, I hope you don't. It would be nice to have a good looking neighbor for a change," Tom said.

Sam shrugged. "The guys at the place I'm staying are going to introduce me to a contractor tomorrow. I'll just have to see what he has to say." He looked around the table. "You guys ready for another?"

An hour later, Sam picked up a Prime Timers newsletter and application for membership, left Sidewinders, picked up a pizza, and went back to Some Guys. He read the newsletter while he ate and decided to join. It seemed like a good way to get to know the locals.

The next morning Roger introduced him to Bill Flint, the contractor, and they hit it off right away. Bill liked Sam's no nonsense approach to things, and Sam liked Bill's easy attitude. Bill offered to go out to the house and have a look around and Sam said he'd take him to lunch afterword.

When they walked in the gate, not even in the house yet, Bill exclaimed, "Good God!"

"Yeah, it's something of a mess isn't it?"

"Not the word," Bill replied. "It's more of a disaster. Nothing out here has been pruned in years." He shook his head. "Well, let's see the inside."

Sam unlocked the front door and shut off the alarm.

Bill watched and nodded. "Well, that's a good sign. There's power at least."

"Water, too, although it's been shut off in the house, probably because of leaks."

They took a quick tour through the rooms first and then Bill went back, spending time in each space, looking it over carefully.

"Well?" Sam asked when Bill finished. "What'd you think?"

Bill shook his head. "Got to look at the outside first."

Before they started around the house, Bill went out to his truck and returned with some gloves and a pair of pruning shears. He offered a pair of gloves to Sam, pulled on the others and proceeded to hack a path through the tangled growth. "Got to be careful of brown spiders, black widows, and such." When Sam spotted a huge yellowish bug and jumped back, Bill laughed. "Don't mind them, Sam. They're harmless. Ugly, but harmless. We call them Palmetto bugs, but as far as I'm concerned, they're just great big cockroaches."

After making their way around the house, Bill pulled off his gloves and brushed himself off. "You still good for lunch?"

Sam nodded.

"Okay. Let's go over to the Rainbow. It's a gay place, has good food, and we can get a beer. Something stronger if you want." He chuckled. "I suppose I might never have gone into that place if I hadn't started doing work for the gay resorts."

"Why'd you do that, start working at gay places?"

Bill laughed. "Well, Sam, a guy I know needed some work done and I wasn't doing much, so I helped him out. I found out these guys want the best and they're willing to pay for it, not try to do it on the cheap. I like that."

Sam saw that as one more reason to like the guy.

At the restaurant they settled in at a table and ordered sandwiches and a draft.

About half way through lunch Bill ordered them another beer and then said, "Okay, Sam. There's two ways you can go. One, clean the place up, fix what needs to be fixed, put on a new roof and hire some guys to clean up the outside and plant some new stuff."

His tone of voice made Sam think Bill would rather see it done differently. "The other way?"

"Restore it."

"Restore it? To what?"

Bill smiled. "Sam, that place is – or rather was – a prime example of what we around here call Mid-Century Modern. See, Palm Springs was a celebrity hangout in the twenties and thirties. Then it kind of fell out of favor, but in the fifties it blossomed again. Guy by the name of Alexander built lots of houses all over town, inexpensive places for whoever wanted to live here. And they sold, mostly to folks who used them for weekends or places to spend the winter. The designs were clean, uncluttered and what people then thought of as 'Modern.' It caught on and pretty soon some really good architects started doing houses with similar 'Modern' looks. Then some fairly well to do folks came down from the city and built some rather grand places with the same design concepts."

Sam finished his sandwich. "And?"

"And that's what you have. A Mid-Century Modern showplace. Alexander himself didn't build it, but the Mid-Century concept and style of Alexander were definitely used. And used very well, I might add. Oh, it's been fucked it up royally over the years, but you can still see the outlines of what it once was. 'Course it'll be a bit more expensive to restore it. Probably a lot more expensive. But Sam," he reached across the table and touched Sam's hand, "it would be worth it. Trust me on this."

Sam leaned back in his chair and drained his beer. "How much?"

Bill shrugged. "No idea. I'd have to do a lot more looking and talk to some people. But I've got to warn you, Sam. It wouldn't just be thousands. More like tens of thousands. Probably a lot of tens of thousands."

"Okay, then. How long?"

Bill looked up at the ceiling. "A year, maybe a little more depending on how it goes."

Sam put some bills down on the table. "Let's go back. I need another look."

Back at the house, they went through each of the rooms, Bill pointing out things that would have to be done. It was a lot. When they were through and standing in the living room Sam turned to Bill and offered his hand. "Okay. Do it. Make it what it's supposed to be. Make it the showplace it was designed to be."

Bill shook his hand. "Just like that?"

Sam nodded. "Why quibble about doing something that's the right thing to do?" He took out his checkbook and wrote Bill a check for ten thousand dollars. "There's the first of the tens."

"You're really serious about this, aren't you?" Bill put the check in his pocket and then put his hand on Sam's shoulder. "Well, so am I. I've got a couple of loose ends to tie up but I think we can start on it in a couple of weeks, maybe sooner. In the meantime, I think I'll get some landscape guys out here and start clearing outside. I think we should just rip it all out and start fresh. Well, except for the palms and that big ficus tree in the corner. Those should stay. What do you think?"

Sam grinned. "I think you're in charge here, the one who knows what he's doing." He stood back and looked at Bill. "You're getting off on this, aren't you?"

Bill laughed. "Yeah, I guess I probably am. You know, Sam, I've always wanted to do a job like this, restoring a place that's really worth restoring. Ever since I did grunt work for my dad, I've liked fixing things, taking them back to what they're supposed to be." He looked around the room. "I promise you, Sam, you keep the money coming and I'll make you very proud to own this place." They shook hands again and Sam knew they were going to do very good things together.

# Chapter Three

The next morning dawned overcast and cool, with a hint of rain in the air. Sam went out for breakfast and then back to Some Guys to change into long pants and a sweater. Still the only guest at the resort, he found himself faced with nothing to do and no one to do it with. He tried to read, but quickly gave it up as a bad job and sought out Bob to ask him where the sun had gone.

"Oh, it'll be back," Bob said. "It's supposed to get warmer by next week." He looked up at the sky. "I sure hope so. We've got a bunch of rooms filled and the guys won't be amused if the weather's like this."

Back in his room Sam got to thinking. Bill had said restoring the house would take a year or more and he didn't think he could live at the resort for that long no matter how much fun it might be at times. He needed some space he could call his own. He dug out the card the real estate guy had given him Monday evening and called.

William said he had no appointments for the afternoon and asked Sam to drop by the office.

When Sam arrived William smiled, "Ready to sell? That contractor scare you off?"

Sam gave him points for remembering their conversation in the bar. "No, actually, he got me all fired up about restoring the house. Says it'll be a showplace."

William looked quizzical. "So why…"

"Well, see," Sam said, "that's the problem. We're going to restore the place and that's going to take at least a year, maybe more. I don't think I can live at Some Guys for that long so I think I need to find a place of my own."

William raised an eyebrow. "We really don't do much with rentals, Sam, but maybe…"

"No, no," Sam said. "I don't think I want to be paying someone else's mortgage. No, I want to buy a place. I'm thinking maybe a condo. You know, couple of bedrooms, baths, nice grounds, maybe a view of some sort."

William turned to his computer and began typing but before he hit the enter key he turned back to Sam. "You like Some Guys? I mean the atmosphere."

Sam shrugged. "Yeah, it's nice, the men and all. But other than a cup of coffee, I have to go out all the time, and once in a while I'd like to do something for myself. I'm not very good in the kitchen but at least I can make scrambled eggs and toast. Why?"

William leaned back in his chair and put his hands behind his head. "I do have a place you might like. It's in a fairly new development that's all gay, and far as I know, all male. There are maybe fifty units and it's pretty rare to see one of them on the market. And I have to tell you, they're not cheap."

"So what are we talking about?" Sam said.

"The guy is asking four-fifty for the one I have. We might get him down a little but I doubt we'd get to four and a quarter. Oh, did I mention it's furnished?"

Sam smiled. "When can I see it?"

William stood. "Right now, if you like. Come on, we'll take my car."

The development had been named 'Desert Pride' and Sam liked it from the moment they drove through the gates.

William's listing turned out to be a two story end unit. On the first floor it had a combination living-dining room, a half bath, a nice kitchen, a one car garage and a large walled patio with a spa. Sam looked at the spa surrounded by flowering shrubs and a potted palm tree and grinned. "Very nice. Bedrooms upstairs?"

The master bedroom, a suite really, had a large balcony overlooking the patio. Its bath was good sized as well and had a shower that Sam figured to be big enough for two – assuming the two were good friends. It had three shower nozzles, including one, a foot across, squarely in the middle of the ceiling. Sam pointed to it and William said, "It's a Rain Nozzle. Supposed to make you feel like you're out in the jungle or something."

Sam nodded, "I'll watch out for snakes."

The second bedroom had been fitted out as a sort of office but it had a built in wall bed. It also had a full bath and a small balcony.

"What more could I want?" Sam went back to the master bedroom and looked around. "Well, maybe some decent pictures on the walls. Have you noticed? This stuff is awful."

William laughed. "I know. I noticed it when I was here before. I guess the owner just had a penchant for really bad paintings. But come on, I'll show you something you'll really like."

They went outside and walked through the gardens. William pointed up the walk, "There's a second pool over there but the main pool, the reason I thought this place might appeal to you, is over here." He turned down a path flanked by flowering hedges. At the end of the path stood a gate and beyond that a large free form pool.

William used the condo door key to open the gate and the first thing Sam noticed was a naked man lying on one of the lounge chairs.

"This whole area is clothing optional," William said as the man got to his feet. "I thought you might like that."

The man came over and said, "Hey, you're William, aren't you? The real estate guy? Is this," he reached out and shook Sam's hand, "a hot prospect? I heard the old man might be selling."

William laughed. "Word gets around fast, doesn't it, Martin. Oh, Sam Davis, Martin Shields." He turned to Sam, "Martin owns the place next to the one you're considering."

"Nice to meet you, Martin. Isn't it a little cool out here? I mean..."

Martin smiled. "You mean to be dressed like this? Actually, I've been in the sauna in the health club there," he pointed to the glass doors off to the side of the pool area, "and this is cool down time." He scratched at his pubic hair. "Besides, this place is used all year long. See those?" He pointed at several umbrella shaped, stainless steel objects. "Those are heaters. They do a very good job of warming us during those long winter nights."

William turned to Sam. "See? I thought you'd like the place."

Sam nodded, still looking at Martin. "Health club allows naked workouts?"

Martin tugged at his dick and nodded. "Practically requires it. Really. I've never seen anyone dressed in there. Well, except for the guys playing handball. They all wear jocks with cups."

Sam grinned. "My kind of place alright."

After a quick tour of the health club, Sam looked at William. "Four-fifty, huh? What do you think they'll take?"

"Four-thirty, maybe. You want it?"

Sam nodded.

"Okay, you offer four-twenty. They come back with four-thirty. You take it. One thing, though. I think the old boy wants a quick sale." He grinned. "Get the money before he dies so he can hold it over the family's head. You got a lender who can push it through pretty fast?"

Sam smiled. "How about this afternoon?"

"Oh man, you're on. Let's go back to the office."

In the office, William called the owner and caught him just before his dinner. When William made the offer, the man didn't hesitate. He countered with four-thirty and William told him okay. They agreed on a two week escrow.

Sam signed the papers as fast as they came out of William's computer and an hour later William had a check for fifty thousand dollars.

William said, "I'll arrange for a home inspection next week but I doubt there will be any problems. I'll get you a copy of the CC&R's, you know, the home owner's rules and responsibilities, in a day or two.

"Good," Sam said. "Let's seal it with a drink."

\* \* \* \*

After buying the condo, Sam found himself to be pretty much at loose ends. He couldn't get into it until after the home inspection and that wouldn't happen until the next week. He couldn't shop for anything because he didn't know what might be in the cupboards and what he'd want to replace. The resort seemed deserted although Bob and Roger did expect a weekend crowd starting Friday evening. Sam sighed, well it was the desert, a place where people went to relax so he'd better get used to it.

\* \* \* \*

On Saturday morning Bill stopped by the resort. "Hey, Sam," he said, "Today's the day. We're going to start work on the house. I found some laborers who will haul away some of the brush that's choking the grounds around the place. They should get a lot of it done today and tomorrow."

Sam asked, "How come they're working on the weekend, Bill?"

"Oh," Bill explained, "they work for a landscape company during the week and moonlight for extra pay on weekends."

"Well, be sure to give them a little bonus," Sam said. "No one likes to work on weekends," at least no one I ever knew."

\* \* \* \*

Sunday dawned clear and warm so Sam decided to spend the morning around the pool admiring the new guys. By noon though, he'd grown restless. He dressed, had a sandwich, and went out to the house to see what was happening.

Plenty was happening. A big truck sat in the driveway, piled high with dead brush. In the yard there were four men cutting brush and clearing it. One of the men came over to Sam and asked if he could help him.

"No, not really. I own the house," Sam gestured at the structure, "and I just wanted to see what's going on."

The man yelled something in Spanish and the other three turned and tipped their hats to Sam. Looking at them, Sam thought two of them couldn't be much over eighteen and their jeans sagged so far he wondered how they could possibly keep them on.  Both had on colored underwear, one dark green and the other medium blue.  Sam smiled and gave them a salute.

After hanging around watching the men work for a while, Sam went next door to say hello to Tom and Dan.  They were happy to see him and wondered what might be going on.

"We went over and tried to talk to the men but our Spanish is so bad we never did find out anything."

Dan looked up and said, "Except that they're clearing out the garden. You can see that.  What happens after?"

Sam had to laugh.  "To tell the truth I haven't a clue, Dan.  Bill, Bill Flint, my contractor, is taking care of it.  I suppose they'll put in some landscaping; or someone will.  But probably later, after the exterior work is done.  Now I think they're just clearing it out so Bill's workmen can find the outside walls."

Tom nodded.  "You like a bloody Mary?  It's what we're having.  Too early for gin."

Sam nodded and they went out to the patio and sat in the shade.

"Well, I've decided to restore the place rather than just fixing it up," he said.  "Bill said it was once a showplace and he wants to bring it back to its former glory."

"It was a showplace," Tom said.  "I remember when it was built, long before we came out here.  They featured it in the Chicago papers and everything.  That's where we saw it.  'Course we were still in college then, never dreamed we'd be living next door to it someday, you know?"

Sam nodded.  They talked through the afternoon, regaling each other with stories of the past.  Towards sundown they switched to martinis and grilled steak.  Over dinner, Sam told them he had bought a condo in Desert Pride.

Tom laughed.  "Isn't that the place where they have orgies around the pool every night?"

Sam shook his head.  "I doubt they have orgies, but one of the pools is clothing optional.  I guess the health club is too."

"Ah, I've heard tales about cocktail parties around that pool. Pretty wild if you ask me."

Sam secretly hoped Tom was right but he wasn't about to say it. "Cocktails probably, but orgies? I doubt it."

"Oh, I don't know," Dan laughed. "After all, this is Palm Springs."

Sam took his leave after dinner and went back to Some Guys where he spent a couple of hours with the guys in the Jacuzzi and then went to bed. Alone.

Monday came on as a very laid back and lazy day. Sam did go out to the house in the afternoon and found the place nearly bare of vegetation except for the palms and the ficus in the back. The guys had done a fast, and as far as Sam could see, a good job.

That afternoon Sam went to a Prime Timers mixer at the Rainbow, the place he and Bill had had lunch. Even though he'd been with the group only one other time he found himself beginning to feel very comfortable with them. They all seemed to be extremely friendly.

Sam was leaning against the bar when he spotted the stubble-faced young man he had noticed the week before. *Well, the worst he can do is tell me to get lost.* He pushed his way through the crowd and caught up with the young man in front of the piano.

"Hi," he said. "I'm Sam, and I'm pretty new to the club. Like maybe a week."

"Toby," the young man said extending his hand, "Toby Litchfield. Yeah, I don't think I've seen you around before. New to Palm Springs or just to Prime Timers?"

"Both," Sam said with a grin. "I just moved here from L.A."

Toby smiled. "Me, too. From L.A. I mean. I came down here a couple of years ago."

"Were you in L.A. long?" Sam asked trying to prolong the conversation.

Toby sipped his drink. "Twenty four years I guess. I was born there and went to college there."

"How'd you come to be here?" Sam asked.

"My job," Toby said with a shrug.

Sam bought a round of drinks and met several of Toby's friends who stopped to say hello. None of them seemed to look askance at Sam which gave him further encouragement.

"Hey, I've got an idea," Sam said. "You want to go to dinner?"

"Can't," Toby said. "I think it's about time for me to leave. Here," he pulled out his wallet, dug around and found a card which he handed to Sam. "Maybe another time?"

"Yeah, for sure. I can't give you a card," Sam said, "because I haven't had any printed yet. I guess I'll get right on that."

"Probably should," Toby said. "They're pretty handy, especially when you're new in town. See you around."

As soon as Toby was out the door Sam pulled his card out and examined it. He breathed a sigh of relief when he noted that it had a phone number on it.

While he looked at the card an older man came up and introduced himself. "I'm Jay, uh," he looked at Sam's name tag, "Sam. May I buy you a drink?"

Sam looked the man over. He had gray hair, a trim figure, and showed himself to be obviously male. Sam nodded. While they sipped their drinks they gave each other well edited versions of their past lives.

"May I get you another?" Jay asked. When Sam shook his head Jay, with a twinkle in his eye, said, "Well then, may I take you to dinner? It's getting to be that time and I hate to eat alone."

Sam found himself flattered by the invitation and accepted. Jay took him to Spencer's, a very beautiful, very upscale restaurant nestled at the base of the mountains. Jay seemed to be well known there and they were immediately shown to a table on the patio. Jay asked if he might order for Sam.

"Of course," Sam replied, feeling a little bit like he had so many times when he'd been out with Harry.

He didn't know exactly how he felt about that now, however. His life with Harry had been put behind him, finished and gone, and Sam had begun to like the feeling of being the man in charge. On the other hand it felt nice, being taken care of.

Everything Jay ordered turned out to be exactly right and they finished with coffee and brandy. When they had had enough, Jay took Sam's arm and led him to the parking lot. No bill had been presented.

"Will you come to my place?" Jay asked, opening the car door for Sam. "Your car will be quite safe here and I'll see to it that you get back here in the morning."

Before he could think, Sam sank into the pale gray leather of Jay's Bentley. Oh, what the hell. Jay was quite a handsome man.

Jay showed himself to be quite accomplished in bed and seemed to want nothing more than to bring Sam to orgasm with his mouth as often as possible. Sam managed three and Jay looked like a happy man.

True to his word Jay took Sam back to Spencer's after breakfast. Sam thanked him, kissed him, and then drove back to Some Guys where he slept until noon.

* * * *

The home inspection that afternoon went well. The inspector, an overweight man named Clyde, did what Sam thought very thorough job and spent more than two hours turning on faucets, checking outlets, running the air conditioning and heat. When through, the man said he'd found nothing that shouldn't be and everything that should. He said a complete written report would be issued in a couple of days. Then Clyde spent another hour walking Sam through the place, showing him how everything worked and how to operate it. Sam found himself very impressed with the guy and mentioned it to William.

"That's why we always get Clyde to inspect our sales," William said. "You pay for a good job and you get a good job."

* * * *

The next afternoon Sam found Bob sitting on a lounge by the resort pool. "This is one, mind you only one, of the joys of being a naked innkeeper," Bob looked up at Sam with a grin. "Whenever I have a little free time I can come out here and watch the naked men around my pool. And sometimes I even get lucky."

Sam laughed. "I'll bet it's more than just sometimes. I'll bet it's more like whenever you want to get lucky."

"I suppose so. But you know what?" He put his hand on Sam's thigh. "I've got Roger, so I don't much need to get lucky." He grinned again. "How about you? You doing okay?"

Sam nodded, thinking of Jay. "Yeah, I'm doing as well as can be expected." He had a sudden thought and added, "Mostly."

Bob sat up. "Don't tell me someone turned you down! Who would do that?"

"Sweet little guy at the Rainbow the other night. I asked him to dinner and he had 'other things' to do. Gave me his card though, so I guess it wasn't a total rejection."

"Have you called him? Asked him out another night?"

Sam blushed a little. "No."

"Well, you have to do that." Bob reached up and gently batted Sam's dick. "It's no wonder that thing isn't getting its fair share, big and pretty as it is."

"Careful," said Sam. "You'll make it go all hard and embarrass me."

Bob merely laughed.

Sam laughed too but without much humor. Something about that kid that had gotten to him. He excused himself, went back to his room, found the card, and dialed.

When he got Toby on the phone, Sam asked him to dinner Friday but was disappointed again. Toby had something on his calendar for that night. Sam's spirits picked up when Toby suggested that maybe they could do it on Saturday instead. They agreed to meet at a restaurant called The Uptown Grill. Sam was unaccountably excited by the prospect.

\* \* \* \*

The next afternoon Sam, lying in the sun, saw Bill Flint approach. "Hi, Sam. I was wondering if you could come over to the house on Sunday and look at a couple of things. I've got some ideas I need to bounce off you."

"Sure," Sam said. "Around two?" He hoped to be busy Sunday morning.

They settled on the time and after Bill left Sam realized he was naked and Bill had been fully clothed. Sam chuckled but it was also vaguely erotic and his dick began to fill out.

Down, boy, I'm saving you for later.

It seemed a long time but later did eventually arrive.

\* \* \* \*

The evening had turned cool and Sam dressed in heavy twill pants and a pullover sweater. When he got to the restaurant it surprised him to find they had valet parking and he happily left his car to the middle-aged lady attendant. While waiting in the foyer, he idly thought about the parking valets in Los Angeles. The people who parked cars there were always handsome, gung-ho young men. He'd never seen a woman attendant before, much less a middle-aged one. Palm Springs was obviously a very progressive place.

His thoughts were interrupted by Toby's arrival. While Toby made his way through the crowd in the foyer, Sam watched him closely and decided he indeed was something special. The trouble? He was also a kid; a handsome one, especially with that stubble, but a kid nonetheless.

The restaurant was crowded so they waited for their table in the bar. Toby ordered a martini, up.

"I think I'll have one of those too," Sam said to the barman. "It's been a while and I think maybe I've missed them." He turned to Toby. "Martinis your usual drink?"

Toby shook his head and laughed. "Not really. I don't think I could deal with martinis all the time. But before dinner, or on a special occasion… yeah, I can handle one or two of them."

Over dinner, Sam found out Toby worked at the Hyatt Hotel as a junior accountant. He'd gone through Cal State University at Los Angeles with a scholarship and a part time job and, when he'd graduated, had gone to work in the accounting department at the Park Hyatt. After a year, they asked him if he'd consider a move to the hotel in Palm Springs which was having reorganization problems.

"So I said, 'Sure, I'll go. For the right salary.'" He laughed. "And they said okay. Just like that. A big raise, moving expenses, free room in the hotel while I looked for a place to live. Hard to turn down."

Sam nodded. "Obviously, impossible to turn down seeing as how you're here. You glad you did it?"

Toby smiled. "Yeah, I am. The first year was fairly horrendous but we got through it and I really like my job. It's more than that, though. People here are friendly. None of the attitude you find in Los Angeles and West Hollywood."

"You can say that again. You like Prime Timers?"

"Uh huh. All the guys are friendly and it's nice to be in a gay group, especially one that's not so frantic, one that's more mature."

Sam laughed. "That's the word alright. Mature." He took a sip of wine, trying to cover a nervousness he hadn't realized he had been feeling. "You like mature men?"

Impishness flashed into Toby's eyes. "Well, as long as they can fog a mirror. Can you do that, Sam? Fog a mirror?"

"Usually. It's the first thing I check in the morning when I hobble into the bathroom."

Toby laughed. "I can just see you hobbling." His eyes seemed to change to a darker blue. "Besides, you aren't all that mature anyway. How old did you say you were?"

"A hundred and three. Well preserved, don't you think?"

Toby nodded. "You're even well preserved for forty-five." He pushed himself away from the table. "The food's good here but they give you too much."

"Yeah, and dessert is yet to come. A growing boy needs his dessert, don't you think?"

"One who's growing around the middle, I suppose. God, I already need an extra hour in the gym. What'll I need if we have dessert?"

They compromised on a single order of crème brûlée, which they shared.

Over the dessert Toby asked, "What are you anyway? A spy? A CIA operative?"

"I don't think either of those occupations would suit me very well. As a gay man. What brought that up?"

"Well, we've talked all the way through dinner and I still don't know anything about you. You let me babble on, but you never told me anything about yourself. Ergo, you must be a spy."

Sam laughed. "Hardly, my boy, hardly. I'm just interested in you. But I tell you what, have dinner with me again and I'll give you my whole life story, more than you ever wanted to know."

"Promise?"

Sam put his hand on his chest. "Cross my heart."

"Deal. You'll have to call me later though because I don't have my calendar with me."

Sam extended his hand. "Deal."

They left the restaurant in separate cars bound for separate destinations. Sam found himself disappointed, but consoled himself with thoughts of another night – well, another dinner – in the offing.

Back at Some Guys, Sam considered hitting the Jacuzzi but decided on bed instead. Alone. He slept well.

# Chapter Four

Sam met Bill the next afternoon at the house which, Sam learned, stood in an area of Palm Springs called Las Palmas. They took a tour around the outside of the house now that they could see it.

"The guys pulled eleven truckloads of brush and junk out of here," Bill said as they walked. "And all that vegetation growing up against the house didn't do the walls much good." He showed Sam where one of the steel posts showed definite signs of rust.

He gestured at the front of the house. "Okay. The first thing we have to do is get rid of all this nonsense." He pointed at some trellises which blocked several of the windows. "And this for God's sake." He waved his arm, taking in the whole front façade. "Siding? Someone put aluminum siding on it? No, no, no! Stucco, wood, concrete but not aluminum siding! Of any color."

Sam grinned. "Okay, Bill, okay. Whatever you say." He looked at the house again. "Do I get to keep those cute little plaster cherubs up there over the door?"

An expression of horror spread over Bill's face until he realized Sam spoke in jest. "No," he said, "they aren't right up there, over the door. I thought we'd take them inside, mount them over your bed."

They then continued around the house and Bill said, "The structure is supposed to have clean, straight lines. The materials it's built from are supposed to stand alone, speak for themselves." He looked up. "And there aren't supposed to be birdhouses in the eaves.  In the trees maybe, but not in the eaves."

Together, they spent several hours at the house, Bill explaining what needed to be done, which walls should be removed or changed, and which windows ought to be replaced by ones that were more like the originals.  When they got to the kitchen, Bill said it would all have to be ripped out.  "I think it's been remodeled several times and each time made it worse than it was before."

When they were finished, Sam had a pretty good idea of what the house would become and he felt almost as excited about it as Bill.  Sam offered to buy Bill a drink somewhere but Bill declined and instead invited Sam to a family barbeque.  Sam begged off that one but left the door open for another invitation.

When Bill left, Sam thought about checking in with Tom and Dan but then decided just to go back to Some Guys to see what was going on there.

On Monday Sam called Toby and asked him out for dinner.  Toby couldn't do it that night but could the next.  Sam was elated and said he would pick him up.  Toby gave him an address in the Warm Sands district of town.

"It's a kind of court," Toby said.  "I'm in number three, by the pool.  It's my turn to pay, isn't it?  Let's go to The Rainbow."

* * * *

Sam was right on time Tuesday and Toby invited him in while he finished tying his shoes.  It was a small apartment but the sparse furnishings and lack of clutter made it seem bigger.  There were flowers on a table in the living room and a couple of interesting paintings on the walls which in Sam's mind gave the place character and made it feel lived in.

"Nice apartment.  You've done well."

Toby looked around and smiled.  "I guess.  It isn't what I'd like, of course, but junior accountants have to start somewhere.  Come on, let's go."

At the restaurant they ordered martinis.  "So," Sam said when the drinks had been served, "are you out at work?"

"Pretty much, I… oh, no you don't, Mr. CIA Agent."

"Wha… ?"

"It's your turn to talk." Toby dropped his voice into a low register. "'I'll tell you my whole life story, more than you ever wanted to know.' Remember? Well, talk."

Sam did talk and over dinner he managed to give Toby some outline of his life. He didn't want to be secretive; he just that he didn't think of his life as being all that interesting and he didn't want to bore Toby. Especially since he wanted to get to know him better.

After Sam told him a little about Harry, Toby asked, "How old..." he searched for the name, "how old was Harry when he died?"

"Ninety-two. He lived a long and pretty good life. For that matter, so did I."

Toby's eyes dimmed. "Were you his lover?"

Sam had an impulse to laugh but he saw how serious Toby was. "No. But that's not to say I didn't love him. I did. You can't be someone's companion and caretaker for twenty-four years without there being an element of love to it. But no, I wasn't his lover."

Toby sighed and the sparkle came back into his eyes. "Have you ever had a lover?"

Sam thought for a moment. "Maybe once. But it didn't last very long and it was a long time ago. You?"

"No." He paused as if he needed to think about it. "Well, there was this one guy... we were pretty thick for a while, maybe a little more than a year."

Sam had a sudden insight. "Did he break your heart?"

Toby looked up sharply. "No!" There was a pause and then, quietly, "Yes." Another pause, then, "Maybe. I don't know. It happened a long time ago, when I was in college. Anyway, he taught me to be careful where men are concerned." He held Sam's eyes. "Very careful." Another pause, a long one, letting his words sink into Sam's brain.

They ordered ice cream for dessert, vanilla, and with chocolate sauce. While they were waiting for it to be served Toby asked Sam where he lived.

"I just realized, you've been to my place and I don't have a clue as to where you live."

"Would you believe at Some Guys?"

"Really? The resort? Are you rich?"

Sam shook his head. "I don't think so. I guess I have maybe more than a lot of people, but I don't think I'm rich. You know the place, Some Guys?"

"A little. When I first moved here I was kind of frisky and a guy took me there." Toby shrugged. "He had a room there so that's where we went. I went back a couple of times, you know, on a day pass. You can have a lot of fun." He sat back while the waiter served the ice cream. "You like living there?"

Sam laughed. "What's not to like? As you said, you can have a lot of fun." He tasted the ice cream and found it good. "But I don't exactly live there any more, or I won't after Friday."

"Why not?" Toby's eyes sparkled. "They throw you out for being rowdy?"

"Me? Hey, I'm a quiet, upstanding guy. No, I bought a condo and escrow closes Friday." He grinned. "You want to come over and christen the place."

"I'd like to, except I have these meetings I have to go to in San Francisco. I fly out Thursday afternoon and won't get back until Monday."

Sam tried not to show his disappointment. "Maybe later?"

Toby nodded. "Definitely later."

Toby insisted on paying for dinner. "It's my turn. You paid when we went to the Uptown Grill."

When Sam took him home, he didn't ask Sam in, but he did lean over and give him a kiss. Sam savored that kiss all the way back to the resort.

On Friday morning Jay called and asked Sam to dinner. "And perhaps afterward we can manage a reprise of last week?"

Sam smiled. "Three times? I don't know…"

On the other end of the phone, Jay laughed. "You'll do your best, Sam, I know you will. Take a nap this afternoon. Alone."

"Okay. But not your place. I bought a condo and I close on it this afternoon. We'll break it in."

"I can't wait. Shall we say seven? Where shall I pick you up?"

"I'm not sure where I'll be. Tell you what, give me a call when you're ready and we'll work it out from there."

When he hung up, Sam called William to find out when he could actually get the keys to the condo. William said he'd meet Sam at the gate to the complex at two.

Sam went to the resort office and talked with Bob and Roger. It turned out Sam would be doing them a favor by moving out that afternoon. The resort had been fully booked up and they had an old friend, actually the former owner of the resort, who would arrive that afternoon. They had planned to have him sleep on their couch if Sam had to stay on for another day or two.

Sam grinned. "Well, I'm glad I can help out a little. It'll be nice having my own place but believe me, I'll sure miss this. You guys have been so good to me." He chuckled. "And so have some of your guests. Yeah, I'll miss it all."

Sam kissed them both, paid his bill, and went back to his room to pack. At two o'clock Sam, his clothes, his books, and his car were waiting outside the gate at Desert Pride.

William showed up right on time and handed Sam a couple of plastic cards. "Gate cards," he said. "Put one in that slot over there and presto, the gate opens. You only get two, so don't lose them. The homeowners' association gets very huffy if you do, and charges you a hundred dollars to replace it."

Inside, at Sam's condo, William handed him a pair of keys, one for the front door and one for the mail box.

"That's it? Two keys is all I get?"

William smiled. "That's it. And the one for the front door you'll probably throw away when you have the locks changed. Be sure to tell the lock guy the door key also has to open the gate to the pool and gym area. By the way, I went over the inventory yesterday and it all checked out. You need to do it again, just to be sure?"

Sam shook his head. "If you can't trust your realtor, who can you trust? I'd offer you a drink, but I don't think there was any liquor on that inventory, was there?"

"No, you're on your own there. Besides, I'm meeting a client at three." He pulled Sam into a hug. "I know you'll be happy here. Anything you need, just give me a call."

Sam pushed his crotch into William's and kissed him.

"Real estate, Sam, real estate," William said with a chuckle.

"Oh, yeah, I forgot about Red. Pass the kiss on to him, will you?"

It took Sam all of twenty minutes to get his stuff into the condo and put away. Then he went shopping for groceries and liquor.

Jay called around five and Sam gave him the address and gate code. When he arrived he came bearing gifts. He brought a huge bouquet of flowers, two bottles of iced Dom Pérignon, and a half dozen Waterford flutes.

"I knew decent glasses wouldn't come with a furnished place so I got you these," he said, putting the flutes on the counter.

Sam pulled Jay into an embrace. "Thank you," he said, kissing him, "for the glasses and all the rest."

Jay pushed away from him and began opening one of the bottles of champagne. "Don't get me started yet, my sweet. Not until we've sampled the wine." He rinsed out two of the glasses and poured some of the pale bubbly liquid into them.

He handed one to Sam, touched it with the rim of his own and said, "To your new home, Sam. May I visit often."

Tasting his champagne, Sam echoed, "Yes, often." He put the flowers in a vase, sipped his wine and took Jay into his arms again. "You're very sweet, you know that?"

Jay smiled and ran his hand over Sam's fly and then, not finding what he was looking for, moved the hand down, along Sam's right thigh until he did find it.

"No underwear," he murmured into Sam's mouth. "I like that in a man. Tells me that perhaps I might have my way with him."

Sam began to harden under Jay's hand and Jay pulled back to look at him. "Is that for me?" he asked, "or just a reaction to the wine?"

"Both I guess, but mostly for you."

Jay grinned, deftly opened Sam's pants and let them drop to his feet. Putting his hands on Sam's butt, he indicated Sam should sit on the counter. When Sam complied, Jay had his way with him.

They went to Le Vallauris and ate lamb with garlic herb sauce and finished with chocolate soufflés and more champagne. Afterward they went back to Sam's and initiated the living room, the bedroom and, in the morning, the shower.

After a breakfast of coffee, scrambled eggs, and sausage – which Sam cooked – Jay had to leave. He was flying to Boston that afternoon and would be gone for a couple of weeks.

He kissed Sam at the door and patted his crotch. "Save some of that for me, okay?" Another kiss and he was gone.

Sam puttered around the condo for the rest of the day, washing the sheets from the night before, scrubbing out the spa on the patio, filling it, moving some of the furniture around. When the doorbell rang at four o'clock he was happy to quit.

At the door, he found two very attractive men. "Hi," the blond one said, handing Sam a bottle of wine. "I'm Mark and this is my partner, Jeff. We thought we'd come around and welcome you to Desert Pride. We live down there," he pointed, "building three, better known as Boys Town Three."

Sam accepted the wine and shook hands with both men. "I'm Sam and thank you very much, both for the wine and for the welcome. Come in."

"Oh, we don't want to bother you," Jeff said. "We know how busy it is, moving in."

"No. Please. I'm looking for an excuse to take a break and have a drink."

The young men came in and Sam settled them in the living room. Then he served some of the Dom Pérignon which Jay had insisted Sam open for breakfast. Mark and Jeff seemed suitably impressed.

They made small talk for a while and then Jeff said, "Listen, uh…"

"Sam."

"Sam." He smiled sheepishly. "Sorry, I've never been good with names. Anyway, we'd like to invite you to an informal little cookout we're having tomorrow. Just some steaks and salad and stuff. Down at the pool."

"Well, thank you. I'd like very much to come. What time?"

Jeff grinned. "Oh, any time. We'll probably eat around six but it looks to be a warm day so a lot of the guys will no doubt spend the afternoon swimming and sunning."

"Yeah," Mark broke in, "even if it is bad for you, you gotta have a tan." He glanced at Jeff who nodded. "You know about the pool don't you? The one by the West Clubhouse? The one with the gym?"

"What do you mean?" Sam said.

"You do know it's clothing optional, right? One time a new guy didn't so we just want to make sure… I mean, you can wear clothes if you want to."

Sam chuckled. "I can see where it might be something of a surprise to find a bunch of naked guys standing around, eating steak while you're all dressed up. But I'll tell you what. For the past three weeks or so I've been living at Some Guys, you know, the resort?" He laughed. "I guess you could say I'm pretty comfortable around a bunch of naked guys. Yes, I'll be happy to be there."

Mark and Jeff stayed another half hour and took their leave. Sam had a sandwich for dinner and went to bed early. He hadn't gotten a lot of sleep the night before.

The next morning Sam took the pictures off the walls in preparation for a trip to the thrift shop. All of them looked like they were done by machines or retarded artists-in-training. One even had a Art-Mart price sticker on the back: $21.99. He thought even the thrift shop might not take that one.

He also went through the various linens in the cupboards and made three piles, rags, thrift shop and maybe okay, this last being the smallest of the piles. Then he went out and bought a case of a good red wine.

Around four, he showered, put on a pair of loose shorts, grabbed three bottles of wine and made his way down to the pool where Mark greeted him.

"Hi, Sam, glad you could come. Looks like everyone turned up, it's such a nice day." He accepted the wine and put it on a counter along with several other bottles and led Sam over to the door to the gym. "Find a locker for your stuff and get natural like the rest of us. Then we'll introduce you around."

Sam found the locker room easily enough and went in to remove his shorts. He found a couple of other men in there, doing the same.

"Hey, you must be the new guy," one of the naked men said. He shook Sam's hand and then stood back, looking him over. "Nice to have a new face around here."

The other man smiled. "Yeah, not to mention the rest of him!" He came forward and offered his hand. "Martin Shields. Your next door neighbor. We met briefly when the real estate guy was showing you the place but your name got by me."

Sam smiled, frankly looking the man over. Nice. Maybe a year or two older than me, but in awfully good shape. Nice uncut dick, too. "Oh, yeah," he said, "out there at the pool. The name's Sam, Martin. So we live next door to each other? At least now I'll know who's banging on the wall when the opera's playing too loud."

"Won't be me," Martin said with a laugh. "I like opera. Well, not at three in the morning." He looked Sam up and down. "On the other hand... maybe."

The other man grinned. "Don't mind Martin. He's always a little horny. I'm Pete Addison, by the way." He put a hand on Sam's shoulder. "Come on, let's go meet the other guys. And don't worry, you probably won't remember who's who but that's okay. There won't be a test later. Besides, most of us answer to 'Hey, you.'"

"Among other things," Martin added with a roll of his eyes.

Sam was usually pretty good with names but after fourteen or fifteen, it would take more than just this one meeting to get them all sorted out in his mind. It was a very diverse group, too. Most of the men were in some semblance of good shape, although a couple could certainly stand to lose five or ten pounds. Most were in their late forties to mid sixties except for Mark, Jeff, and a kid named Duane something. He looked like he might be in his teens although it turned out he was twenty-five. He had come with his partner, a man named Howard who looked to be in his mid-fifties.

They spent the late afternoon in and around the pool, mostly discussing the affairs of the day – and of life. A few guys in the water played grab-ass off and on and a couple, Sam noticed, disappeared into the gym. They reappeared some time later, looking very satisfied with themselves – and each other. Sam smiled. This was shaping up to be his kind of place.

When the sun went down, the air cooled quickly and someone lit the heaters in the covered area. The wine was opened and several tables were set. Shortly after that the steaks and salad were served, along with some very potent garlic bread. It turned out that the party was to celebrate the anniversary of one of the couples in the complex. Sam didn't get anything but their first names – Charlie and Ben – and never did figure out which was which.

All through dinner Sam was aware of Martin, his next door neighbor, looking at him. Might be worthwhile, he thought but ended up leaving the party with Pete, the other man he'd met in the gym. They went to Pete's place for drinks and ended up on Pete's living room rug, in front of the fire. All in all, a very pleasant and satisfying evening for both of them.

Very early the next morning, Sam's phone rang, waking him out of a pleasant, but dimly remembered, dream. He thought later it might have had something to do with that Duane kid from the night before – or maybe Toby – but he couldn't be sure.

On the phone, his contractor said, "Sam? Listen, I wondered if you'd like to be on hand for the start of the demolition this afternoon. We're finally going to start on that aluminum siding."

Sam said, "Okay Bill, I'll be there around one o'clock."

After the call, he turned on his back and took himself in hand but found he really wasn't very interested. Man, that Pete last night turned out to be really something. He smiled. But not like Jay. Now Jay is a man with a mouth! Further reflection, however, made him decide Pete was more fun. He was not only an enthusiastic cock-sucker, he was a wild man when someone reciprocated. The more Sam thought about it, the more excited he became, finally throwing off the cover and taking hold of himself again. This time it resulted in a long, slow – and very explosive – session.

Later he went to a couple of thrift shops and dropped off the stuff he'd set aside over the weekend. That done, he had a light lunch and went to the house to meet Bill.

"Hey, Sam, you're just in time to see the first piece come off," Bill called when he spotted Sam coming through the gate. "Now we'll get to see what's under that stuff. By the way," he pointed to the two well built men standing to one side with crowbars in their hands, "I don't think you've met these guys. They're going to be doing a lot of the work on your house." He waved the men over.

"Steve, David, this here's Sam, the owner, so be nice to him. However, you don't take orders from him, understand? He wants something he'll go through me." He turned to Sam. "Okay, Sam? Believe me, it really does work better this way."

Sam smiled at the two workmen and shook their hands. "Sounds good to me, right men? I give you orders, you just remind me of what Bill said." He caught the eye of the one called David and thought he might be open to taking an order, but only after work hours. He gave the man a very quick wink and David smiled back.

They pulled off the first of the siding and found that the concrete block under it had once been painted a sky blue. "Does it have to be that color?" Sam asked no one in particular.

"Ask Bill that one," the workman called Steve said, bending down and looking closely at the exposed blocks. "Wasn't always that color though.

Look here, where the crowbar scraped a little. Before it was blue, it was yellow."

They called Bill over and together they examined the blocks. "Yup," Bill said, scraping the block with his pocket knife. "When they built it they painted it yellow. See here? There's nothing but unpainted block under the yellow." He straightened up and looked at Sam. "You mind a yellow house?"

"I guess not," Sam said. "But maybe put a little more brown in it, make it darker?"

Bill nodded. "Yeah, I guess we could stretch things that far. Okay guys, back to work. Let's see how much of that ugly siding we can get off today."

While the men were working, Sam went next door to Tom and Dan's. They were sitting on the front patio taking the sun, and happily greeted Sam.

"Want some iced tea?" Tom asked. "Fresh made in the sun."

Sam declined. "Can't stay long. Prime Timers mixer at Toucan's at five. Can't miss that." He hoped Toby would be there. "I just came over to ask if you knew when the house got painted blue. It was yellow to start with, so the contractor says. Who changed it?"

They both shrugged. "It's always been blue, far as I know," Tom said. "At least until Jack and Larry put that siding on it." He laughed. "Would you believe they bought that stuff from a traveling salesman? We made a lot of jokes about that. You know, like all the old jokes where the traveling salesman gives certain, shall we say, incentives to buy his stuff?"

Dan looked up. "Never did believe that, though. Don't think they ever did stuff like that."

Tom nodded. "Yeah, they were kind of like us, pretty thick with each other but nobody else. Least not that we knew." He shrugged. "But, as they say, to each his own. Might have been kind of fun the other way. I don't know."

Sam nodded. "Fun when you're single." He saluted them and turned to go. "I want to keep an eye on what's going on over there. See you later."

He watched the workmen for a while and then took his leave so he could go home and shower before going to the mixer.

# Chapter Five

The mixer, held at a bar called Toucans, turned out to be a lot of fun. The place carried a kind of ersatz South Seas motif with lots of plastic flowers, plastic banana trees and plastic fish in a plastic fountain. Beyond that, the bartenders were friendly and could only be described as hunky. One of them wore nothing but a short grass skirt and a lei around his neck. As he moved around behind the bar there were little flashes of flesh which only served to prove that he wore only the grass skirt. Everyone loved it.

Sam scanned the room and spotted several guys he could identify as living at Desert Pride although he couldn't think of any of their names. Since everyone wore a name tag, he made it a point to greet each one of them and mention the man's name at least once in conversation.

Over the shoulder of one of his neighbors, he saw Toby come in and go to the table to get a name tag. Sam excused himself and worked his way across the crowded room. He caught up with Toby just as he pasted on his name.

"Buy you a drink?"

Toby glanced over at the bar and grinned. "No thanks. It's always more interesting to get your own drink when Frank's behind the bar."

Sam laughed. "You're right about that. Come on, you order, I'll pay and we'll both get to look."

They stood at the bar for as long as they could, until they had to give up their places to some newcomers. They moved across to the fountain with the plastic fish in it and Sam asked Toby about his trip. Toby seemed pretty happy about it. "The only thing I hate about these meetings is I have to shave," he said.

Sam looked at him critically and realized Toby's cheeks were clean. "So I see. Too bad, I kinda liked it."

Toby grinned. "Not to worry. It'll be back in a couple of days."

Sam nodded. "I'll bet you grow it pretty fast." He reached out and ran his thumb across Toby's jaw. "It's already making an appearance. I'll tell you what, why don't you let me take you out for a dinner to celebrate its re-emergence."

Toby smiled. "I guess it is your turn to pay, so yeah, I'd like that."

Toby suggested they go to a place called Plum where they sat out on the patio, under the heaters and ordered martinis.

"One only," Toby proclaimed. "Any more and I'll never make it to work tomorrow." He grinned. "So, what have you been up to while I sat all cooped up in a meeting room in San Francisco?"

"Not a whole lot. I moved into the condo, which took about three minutes."

Toby nodded. "I remember you telling me you bought it turn-key. How is it? Nice stuff?"

Sam laughed. "Mostly junk. I took a bunch of it to a thrift shop this morning. You should have seen the stuff on the walls that tried to pass itself off as art. The kitchen stuff looks okay though. At least from what I can tell. Most of the linens are rags so I'll be spending some time replacing sheets and towels."

The waiter, a boy about Toby's age and almost as good looking, came to the table, pad in hand. He recommended the salmon with roasted garlic and dill or the leg of lamb with mint sauce. "Not the beef," he said in a conspiratorial whisper. "It's a little on the fat side. I think the chef is going to make them take it back."

They ordered the salmon. When the waiter left, Toby asked Sam if he had met any of his neighbors.

Sam grinned. "Some. Two of the residents had an anniversary barbeque for a couple and invited me. Turned into quite a party. They had it out at the clothing optional pool so I got to see quite a lot of my neighbors."

Toby laughed. "I've heard stories about that place. Nude swimming, naked cocktail parties, midnight orgies around the pool. Sounds to me like you got yourself into another hotbed of naked frolicking."

"Wow! You think stuff like that really goes on?" Sam asked.

"So I hear tell. One of the guys in the office lived there for a little while and loves to tell stories about it. I'm not sure how many of them are actually true, but they're fairly entertaining," Toby said

Sam smiled. "I'll keep you posted."

After the salmon had been served and sampled, Sam looked at Toby, "Now, what about you? What did you do in San Francisco besides go to boring meetings?"

"Not actually a whole lot, although one night some of us went to a concert. It was pretty good," Toby said.

"Oh? Where was it, the Opera House? Davies Hall?" Sam asked.

Toby grinned. "No, Sam. It wasn't that kind of a concert. It was called Naked Boys Singing and they performed in a converted store front."

Sam laughed. "Oh, yeah. They're really good, I've heard. And really naked, too. Sounds like fun, I'm envious."

"They were good." A twinkle came into his eyes. "Good and naked. That pretty much describes them. Other than that it was work, work, work."

When the server appeared offering dessert, they ordered the cheese cake, but only one piece, to be divided between them. The waiter grinned and went off to fetch it.

"You know," Sam said, "this has been fun. Why don't we do it again Friday evening?" He held up his hand, deflecting Toby's response. "No, no. My treat. Really, I want to and I can afford two dinners in one week. Okay?"

Toby seemed hesitant. Finally, he said "Okay. But you can't keep taking me out to dinner all the time. I mean, sometimes it'd be nice if I could do something."

Sam shrugged it off. "It's not important who pays, Toby. Let's just enjoy it, okay?"

Afterward Sam took Toby back to Toucan's to get his car. Then he went home, to bed. Alone, he thought. How come it's always alone?

\* \* \* \*

Sam spent the rest of the week shopping for things for the condo and watching the siding being stripped off the Las Palmas house. Things were going well, but they had to be very careful not to damage the walls. By week's end, though, the guys had the siding off and stacked up in the driveway.

Sam also decided he needed to drop a few pounds and maybe shape up a little, so he started going to the gym at the complex. He actually found it kind of fun, exercising in the buff, especially when someone else happened to be doing naked exercises at the same time. On Wednesday, he got to play with a guy in the steam room. Nothing serious, but enough fondling to make them both breathe just a little harder. When they quit and went to the showers, the guy introduced himself as Nick Avery. He said maybe they could do it again, maybe more, if he could get out of the house without his lover. Sam simply nodded. He figured a guy who needed to get out of the house without his lover might be a good guy to stay away from.

\* \* \* \*

Friday evening finally came and Sam knocked on Toby's door promptly at seven. Toby seemed a little out of sorts, but Sam passed it off as the result of an overwhelming amount of work at the office. Sam kissed him lightly and suggested Toby might feel better with a martini in his hand. Toby agreed.

They went to Spencer's, the restaurant that had impressed Sam so much when Jay had taken him there. He'd even arranged for no check to be presented.

They were seated quickly and the maître d' took their orders for very dry martinis. Toby ordered a double, which Sam found a bit out of character.

When the menus came, Toby saw his didn't have any prices on it. When he mentioned it, Sam just smiled and said it was that way so Toby wouldn't be distracted by anything and would order whatever really appealed to him. Toby rolled his eyes but didn't say anything more.

When they ordered, Toby also asked for another double martini which Sam took to be a bad sign. When the shrimp cocktails came, Toby picked at his a little, drained his martini in one gulp, and threw down his napkin.

"I can't do this," he said slowly, looking at Sam. "I cannot sit here eating a shrimp cocktail that cost God knows what and wondering how you are going to want me to repay you."

Sam looked up sharply. "Toby, easy. I don't want you to repay me. Your company is enough. I just like..."

"What?" Toby asked, looking down at his shrimp cocktail, his voice becoming sharp. "What do you like? You looking for a toy? Well, I'm not your man. Try one of the busboys."

"Toby, no. I just wanted..."

"I know what you want and I'm not it. You're looking for a... a thing you can have for a hundred dollars and the price of dinner."

That stung Sam so hard he lost all control of his civility. "Is that what you think I want? A common whore? Someone I can buy?" His voice grew low, menacing. "Well, if that's the case," he pulled out his wallet and threw a bill on the table, "there's your hundred. I guess you've earned it. Now eat your dinner."

Toby looked at the money on the table for what seemed a long time before he wadded it up and threw it into the shrimp cocktail. "I'm not hungry. Goodnight." He walked slowly and carefully to the door and out.

Sam pushed his chair back and stood, thinking to go after Toby.

A waiter suddenly appeared at his side, "It's alright, sir, it's alright. There is a taxi outside which will take him."

Sam's sudden anger quickly turned to embarrassment. "Will you see if you can..."

The waiter spoke kindly. "I've taken care of it, sir. The wine had not yet been opened and was canceled as well. Will you come to the bar and perhaps have a drink?"

Sam hung his head. "No. Thank you, no. I'm way too embarrassed for that. I'll just leave. Quietly."

The waiter patted him on the shoulder. "Don't be embarrassed, sir. This... ah, this sort of thing has happened before. Please, promise you will come back another time." He handed Sam a card. "Ask for me. It will be my pleasure to serve you."

Sam dug out his wallet and handed the man a hundred dollar bill. "Thank you, uh..." he looked at the card, "Henry. You're very kind."

Driving home Sam ran the gamut of emotions, from angry to hurt to confused. He couldn't figure out what he'd done to set Toby off and found he desperately wanted to know. Without Sam even thinking about it Toby had somehow grown on him in the past three weeks. He'd even begun to think of him as potentially more than a friend. And now this.

Over a cheese sandwich at home, Sam decided to dump the whole thing, forget about Toby, and just get on with life. He knew he wouldn't do it, but he felt better pretending he would.

He took his second scotch on the rocks up to his bedroom, stripped off his clothes and went out on the balcony where he could look at the stars. When he saw a couple of guys walking by holding hands he drained his drink, said 'shit' and went to bed. It was not a good night.

When he woke on Saturday morning Sam did what he could to get on with his life but by two o'clock he felt terrible. He'd hoped Toby would call and apologize, but when it became obvious Toby wasn't going to do that, Sam called him.

Toby sounded very non-committal on the phone but agreed to meet Sam for a cup of coffee. They went to a little shop on Palm Canyon Drive called Koffee, where they could sit outside and enjoy the early spring weather.

When they'd gotten their coffee – each paying for his own – they sat at a little white table under a tree and looked at their cups. After a few minutes of uncomfortable silence Sam quietly said, "I'm really sorry for last night, Toby. The trouble is, I haven't any idea what I did wrong."

Toby stared at the cup in his hand and then took a long drink. When he looked up he seemed so miserable that Sam hurt for him.

After a moment Toby took a deep breath and shook his head, as if to clear it. "May I tell you a story, Sam?"

Sam nodded and tasted his own coffee, not trusting himself to say anything.

"Once upon a time," Toby started, in a quiet and dreamy voice, "in a far away land called Los Angeles, there was an eighteen year old college boy. The boy lived with his parents because, even though he had a scholarship and a part time job, he couldn't afford to live any place else.

"One day, in the college coffee shop, he met a man who swept him off his feet. That very night he took the boy to dinner and, afterward, to bed. It was the biggest bed the boy had ever seen and from it he could see for a hundred miles across Los Angeles and, if the night were clear and he looked carefully, he could see the lights on Catalina Island."

Sam swallowed hard, thinking he had an idea of what was coming. He was wrong.

"The boy spent that night, and many others, with the man. He learned to do things that brought the man – and himself – incredible pleasure, things he'd heard about and some he hadn't, but all wonderful.

"There were other pleasures too. The man gave the boy things the boy could never have bought for himself. And experiences. They actually went to Catalina Island once, for a weekend, and looked back with a telescope, trying to find the bedroom with the big bed." Toby looked at Sam and laughed, but the laugh had no joy in it.

"So the boy fell in love." He shrugged. "Who wouldn't? The boy loved, trusted, and adored the man and would do anything to please him. Anything. Even go to bed with his friends."

Sam sucked in his breath. "Toby, no."

Toby smiled. "Oh, yes, Sam. Anything. I loved him." His tone changed and he became very controlled, almost business like. "I think I knew pretty quickly, but when you love someone the way I loved him, it became easy to ignore. Well, that was until a man I'd spent the night with – an unusual occurrence, by the way. Jack, that's the man, Jack liked me home at night, in his bed, in his arms. He was very sweet that way." He shrugged and looked away from Sam, as though talking to the tree they sat under.

"Anyway, I spent the night with this man and in the morning he pressed a hundred dollars into my hand and told me it was just for me and not to tell Jack about it." He paused and looked back at Sam. "By the way, it took me the greater part of the trip back to Jack's before I realized that he intended it as a tip. That's how dumb I was. So you see, Sam…"

Sam shook his head. "So what happened?" He felt half afraid to hear the answer.

"The usual. A loud scene, some things were broken…" Sam started to speak but Toby waved it away. "No, no parts of me – or him – got broken. Except maybe for my heart. And then I ended up where I'd started, back in my parents' house."

Sam wanted to cry and take Toby in his arms but he knew it would be the wrong thing to do, at least just then. He sat back and rubbed his eyes, searching for the right thing to say.

Toby solved his problem. "So now you know why last night happened."

"Yeah, I guess I do." They sat in silence for a while. Then, quietly, Sam said, "I'd still like to get to know you, find out who you are, let you find out who I am. Can we do that? Try to be friends? No strings, no expectations, no obligations. Just… just friends?"

Toby spent a long time thinking before he nodded. "I need a little time, Sam. Mostly I guess to get over my embarrassment about last night but… yeah, we can try being friends."

Sam reached across the table and offered his hand. Toby solemnly shook it, sealing the bargain.

# Chapter Six

The next day, Easter Sunday, Sam slept very late. After breakfast – lunch really – he couldn't find anything to interest him so he decided to go out to the Las Palmas house and see what progress had been made. He found all the siding gone, which surprised him. He'd expected to find it still neatly stacked in the driveway but there wasn't a sign of it anywhere. He made a mental note to ask Bill what it'd cost to have it all hauled off.

About to let himself inside to see if anything had been done there, he glanced up to see Tom from next door come through the gate.

"Thought it might be you," Tom said, extending his hand. "You or that contractor guy. You know, he's here at all hours, sometimes at night, too, checking up on the workmen and pitching in to help. You got a mighty good deal with that guy." He grinned. "Can't say the same for most of the men who worked over here before. All a bunch of crooks, Jack and Larry were always saying. 'Course, they tended to complain about most everything, so who knows. Come over for a bloody Mary? Seems appropriate to the season, doesn't it?"

Sam smiled. The more time he spent around Tom and Dan the more he liked them. "Sure, Tom, be glad to. You guys make the best bloody Mary's around."

They sat outside and talked for a while but moved inside as soon as the sun started to sink behind the mountains. A little breeze had come up and it got to be quite cool.

Inside, Dan lit the fire and they switched to what Dan called 'proper' cocktails, in this case Manhattans for Tom and Dan, a martini for Sam.

"You know, Sam," Dan said when they were settled in front of the fire, "You really need to find yourself a man, a... what do they call it now? A boyfriend. Someone to take care of you, keep you warm at night."

Tom laughed. "You're not available, Dan."

Dan pretended to pout. "I know. But if this were thirty years ago..."

Tom looked at Sam. "He's right, you know. You really need someone to... I don't know. Someone to spend your life with, I suppose. Everybody does."

Sam nodded. "Yeah, I know you're right. As a matter of fact, I thought maybe I was working on one but... well, we'll see." He felt the need to change the subject. "Hey, you guys want to go to dinner? It's Easter and I've been thinking Italian all day, you know? Serious pasta. You know a place?"

"We do," Tom said with enthusiasm, "Boscoso. Really great pasta."

Dan chimed in. "Yeah, let's go."

Boscoso turned out to be exactly what Sam had in mind. The food proved to be wonderful, the place quiet, and the staff very friendly. The three of them shared an appetizer of fried calamari and Sam indulged his passion for pasta while Tom and Dan both had veal, each dish prepared differently. Conversation ranged all over the place and it turned out to be a fine evening for all of them.

The next night Sam went to a Prime Timers dinner at Lyons Restaurant. During the cocktail hour, he kept an eye out for Toby but he never showed up. His name tag lay on the table so Sam knew he'd planned to be there. Sam almost left when it came time for dinner but then he thought, what the hell I'm here now and I'm not going to let that kid control my life. He went into the dinning room to find his assigned seat.

He was seated at a table for six with two couples and another single man. The couples were both retired and, based on their conversation, seemed to spend a great deal of time traveling. The single man, although past the age of retirement, still worked.

"Yeah," he said to the others over dinner, "after my partner Charlie died, I found myself pretty much at loose ends so for something to do I went and got myself a job with the county."

When one of the men asked him what he did, he laughed. "File clerk," he said. "It's what spending your whole life teaching school prepares you for. On the other hand, they're very impressed, down at the Coroner's Office where I work, that I don't need what they euphemistically call a 'Help Card.' That's a little three by five card with the alphabet printed on it." When everyone at the table laughed, he said, "No, really. Lots of file clerks at the county have them. There's a guy in the supply room who makes them up."

One of the men at the table grinned and said, "Hey, aren't those file clerks the very people you taught in school?"

"May be, may be. But I mostly taught P.E. and coached the baseball team. Kids didn't need much in the way of the alphabet for baseball. The bases are numbered and most of the kids could manage that." He laughed. "At least up to three."

"P.E., huh?" a man on the other side of the table, Paul something, said. "I'll bet the shower room was interesting." He winced and Sam figured his partner had kicked him under the table.

Matthew, the man with the story, laughed again. "I have to say, adolescent boys have never been my thing, but even so, yeah, it was interesting watching their hormones kick the guys around and embarrass them."

Over dessert, the conversation turned to cruises and Sam lost interest. He'd been on a lot of cruises with Harry, and had enjoyed them, but they weren't something he wanted to think about now. He did prick up his ears when the discussion turned to gay cruises. He thought he might like to try something like that someday.

After dinner, he stopped in the bar and had a drink with Matthew, the man who worked in the Coroner's Office. They spent a companionable half hour and Sam learned a lot about local politics, something that seemed to interest Matthew a great deal.

The next morning Sam woke to clouds and light drizzle. After his coffee, he thought some exercise might make the day a little brighter, so he grabbed a towel and set off for the gym. He'd been right; the day did look better from the seat of the rowing machine. It looked even better when Martin, his next door neighbor, came in and started on one of the treadmills. Sam wondered if Martin knew that he was presenting a perfectly framed view of his dick, swaying as he moved on the treadmill. When Martin pulled his foreskin back like a turtleneck sweater, uncovering the head, Sam decided he was well aware of the picture he presented. The foreskin wouldn't stay back and kept slipping down over the head so Martin had to adjust it constantly. His dick seemed to like all the attention.

After a half hour or so, they each moved to a different machine, from which each also had a good view of the other.

Another half hour and Martin sighed, "That's it. I've had it." Looking at Sam he added, "You up for some steam?"

Sam nodded, glad for the excuse to quit.

In the steam room, Martin came up hard almost immediately. "The steam always does this to me," Martin said, flexing his dick.

Sam chuckled. "It just wants to look its best. Mine does that too sometimes, although it's not as cooperative as yours." He reached towards it. "May I?"

Martin stood and took a step towards Sam. "Any time you like."

Sam took Martin's dick in his hand and moved the loose skin slowly back and forth, wishing his mother had left him intact. He pushed the thought away. What's gone is gone. Just enjoy what you have.

Martin sat down and gently fondled Sam's balls. "God, I wish I had your balls. I've always loved big balls."

They played with each other for a short while before Sam stood and said, "Too hot. Got to cool off."

Martin kissed Sam's dick and nodded. They went out to the showers.

"Wash your back?" Sam asked after they'd adjusted the shower temperature.

Martin handed him the soap and said, "Wash whatever you like, Sam."

Sam washed Martin's back, clear down to his legs, and then pressed himself against Martin's slippery back; reaching around to work on his chest. Martin liked to have his nipples played with and every time Sam touched them Martin pushed back against him.

By the time Sam got to Martin's dick it was nearly ready to explode. Sam pulled back for a moment, soaped his own dick and then pressed himself against Martin again, letting his dick ride in the valley between Martin's buns. It was very pleasurable for both and didn't take long before each fell into in the throes of orgasm.

"That was something," Martin said, kissing Sam. "We need to do that again."

Sam kissed back and said, "That we do. Your dick is great fun to play with."

A little later, in the locker room getting dressed, Martin said, "You know, when you pressed against me I thought maybe you were wanting to fuck me."

Sam shrugged. "No. Not my thing."

"How about the other way?"

Sam shook his head. "Not my thing either. Sorry."

Martin smiled. "Not a problem. You're fun to play with just the way you are."

An hour later, at home, sitting in his chair with a book and a cup of coffee, Sam found he couldn't concentrate. The little exchange in the locker room kept floating to the surface of his mind. What he'd told Martin hadn't been exactly true. He loved fucking, both ways, when he felt an emotional connection to the man. He just couldn't do it with a casual trick. He sighed. And they've all been casual tricks, haven't they? Since Joel.

He took a deep breath, put down his book and allowed himself to think back to Joel. He hadn't been able to do that for several years afterward but now the pain had mostly gone, replaced with a kind of vague longing. His mind drifted, going clear back to the beginning.

He'd been with Harry for just over seven years when Harry got it into his head that he needed a chauffeur. A couple of his producer friends had them and it became a sort of status symbol, riding around in a Cadillac limousine driven by a good-looking guy in a snappy uniform. After a while, nothing would do until Harry had one, too, so Sam set off, making the rounds of the domestic agencies while Harry made the rounds of the car dealers. They both struck gold.

After a number of tries which resulted in exactly zero candidates, Sam, as a last resort, checked with an agency that specialized mainly in kitchen help but sometimes had leads on other types of domestic workers. The particular day he dropped by, they just happened to have taken an application from a young man who recently had gotten out of the army where he'd worked in the motor pool. He'd come to the agency in response to their advertisement for a waiter but really wanted something, anything, to do with cars. The guy at the agency frankly admitted they had taken his application mainly because the interviewer had liked him so much and found him both handsome and personable. The man's name was Joel and Sam hired him that same day.

Harry was quite happy with Joel and put him in the little apartment over the garage. Two days later he came home with a yellow and brown classic Rolls Royce limousine. Harry had done his producer friends and their Cadillacs one better. Sam did them several times better with Joel and some uniforms specially designed for him by one of Harry's friends, a costume designer at Paramount.

For his part, Joel fell instantly in love with the Rolls Royce – he always called it by its full name, never just the Rolls. He cared for it as any lover would care for his beloved, and Sam thought he probably slept in it sometimes.

The perfect chauffeur, Joel also kept all the cars in perfect repair and was always ready to drive them anywhere at a moment's notice. He was respectful, both to Harry and to Sam, but there was a slight edge of playfulness with Sam that wasn't there when Harry was around. And, of course, he always kept the proper distance between himself and his employers. At least he did until one night, six or eight months after he'd come to live in the house.

Sam was sitting in the library having a scotch and soda and watching the late news when he glanced up to find Joel standing in the doorway. He smiled and asked if Joel wanted something. Joel nodded but didn't enter the room until Sam beckoned him in.

My God, he was a handsome thing, standing in the doorway to the library, Tall, confidant and yet a little hesitant, too.

He laughed and said aloud, "The swain, come to claim his beloved."

Sam got up, went into the kitchen, and poured himself a scotch and soda, just as he'd had that night. What the hell, it's after five o'clock somewhere. He looked out the window and saw that the drizzle had turned to rain and it seemed a bit colder in the room. He lit the gas log in the fireplace and then settled back in his chair, knowing he was going to go back through it all.

Joel's eyes went around the library, looking everywhere but at Sam. Finally, Sam stood, went over to the bar and asked Joel if he'd like something. Joel nodded and smiled, as though thinking that alcohol might give him courage. But he didn't need it because when Sam stood in front of him and offered the glass Joel leaned in and kissed him on the lips. When they broke, Sam, without a word, turned back to the bar, set the drink on it, went back and gathered Joel into his arms. Without a word they stood in the middle of the library, hugging each other and kissing.

When they broke they each took a step backward and looked at each other, each with a sort of insane grin on his face. Then Joel took Sam by the hand and led him to his room over the garage.

That night Joel introduced Sam to the joys of making love. Sam had had his share of sex in the past but that night he found that he'd never been made love to. The two things were, he realized, completely different. Sex was fun and gave him good feelings, but being made love to took him somewhere he'd never been, somewhere that another person actually became part of him, part of his being.  He loved it and found, after a while, that he loved Joel as well.

Sam drank some of his scotch and, finding that he was hard, opened his jeans to relieve the pressure.  I can't believe you can still do this to me, Joel. He took hold of his erection, not to masturbate, but to feel good, having his dick in his hand and just holding it.  We used to do this.  Just hold on to each other sometimes.  It connected us like nothing else could.

Joel taught Sam to make love to him as well and then Sam taught Joel about sex games, sex for the fun of it, and about quickies, too, up and off fast, just for the jolt of it.  Joel learned that one well and liked to catch Sam just before something was about to happen and bring him to an explosive orgasm just before they would surely get caught.

Harry, of course, knew what was going on but never said a word about it.  As long as Joel made Sam happy and it didn't interfere with Harry's life, it was okay.  It went on for almost three years, until one summer when Harry and Sam went to stay with friends in France for a couple of weeks. When they came home Joel wasn't there and neither was the yellow and brown Rolls Royce.  The police report said Joel had been carjacked and died trying to protect his beloved automobile.  The thief died several hours later on Pacific Coast Highway when he ran the car head on into a bridge abutment at one hundred and five miles an hour.  The car, like Joel and the thief, was a total loss.

Sam, staring off at nothing, dry-eyed.  He'd long since stopped crying when he thought about Joel and their time together.  Now he mostly remembered the good things they had together and how grateful it made him to have been taught about love by a man like Joel.  You are such a cliché, Sam Davis.  A love affair with the chauffeur?

He laughed out loud.  But I still can't do it, fuck or be fucked, unless I'm connected to the guy, and that sure doesn't happen much.  I wish it did.

The ringing of the phone brought him out of his reverie.

"Hi, it's Bill, your trusty contractor.  I just wanted to know what I did on Friday."

"Hi, Bill. I was going to call you with a question although for the life of me, I can't remember what it was now. What'd you do on Friday?"

"I managed to get rid of all that stupid siding stacked up in your driveway, that's what."

Sam took a sip of his drink and found he didn't want it anymore. Cocktails in the afternoon are only good when you're socializing. Or remembering.

He turned his attention back to Bill. "Good man. That's what I wanted to ask you about. What'd it cost to get that stuff hauled off?"

Bill laughed. "That, my man, is the beauty of it. I didn't get it hauled off, I sold it. For six hundred dollars. Some Mexican guy came around and looked at it. Said it was in pretty good shape and he thought it would look good on his house, a sort of present for his wife. He offered five hundred for it and I talked him up to six. He got a crew of guys out and they took it away that same day. So here I am holding six hundred dollars of your money. In cash. What do you think of that?"

Sam nodded to himself. "Good show, Bill. But I tell you what, why don't you divide that money up among the guys who did all the work, make it a sort of bonus for being so careful with the siding."

"Boss, that is one great idea. Reward the guys for good work and they'll keep doing good work, my dad always used to say."

"That right?" Sam chuckled. "Then I guess I'll have to match that money in a little bonus for you. You've been doing a hell of a job and I want you to keep doing it. Go buy your wife something pretty. Maybe she'll make you happy."

Bill laughed. "Your wish is my command, boss. Got to go. Anything else?"

"Nothing except to say thanks. I figured the siding was going to cost a bundle to have taken away. Now get to work and make me some more money." He hung up, went to the kitchen and poured out his scotch.

That evening, Mark and Jeff stopped by for just a moment and asked Sam if he was going to be around the next Sunday

"Sure I am. Why?" Sam asked.

"Well," Mark said, "we generally have a bit of a cocktail party around the pool on Sunday afternoon. You know, around four or so. We just wanted to make sure you would come and meet the guys."

"After all," Jeff added, "it is in your honor."

Mark laughed. "Don't be too impressed, Sam. That just means everyone will wear a name tag or have his name written on his chest. We don't usually bother with that but it seems a good idea whenever we have a new guy. So you'll be there?"

Sam assured them he would and invited them to stay and have a drink, but they had plans with another couple. A quick kiss and they were out the door.

\* \* \* \*

A couple of days later Sam had a call from Jay, asking him to dinner. He thought about it but turned him down saying he had something else on but leaving it open for the next week. Jay promised he'd call back.

Sam wasn't exactly sure why he hadn't wanted to go to dinner with Jay and the more he thought about it – and what Jay no doubt had in mind for the rest of the night – the more horny he got. By early evening, he could hardly think about anything else so at five-thirty he went next door and rang Martin's doorbell.

"Hi, guy," Sam said when Martin answered, "I was just wondering if you'd like to go out and share a pizza with me."

Martin slowly looked him up and down and wet his lips. "How about we order in? I've got some beer in the fridge and we can put on a movie or something."

They ordered a large with everything and when the man delivered it, Martin asked him if he'd like to stay for a while. The guy said he couldn't but it was obvious he wanted to. He gave them each a card and told them to call any time and that he usually got off work around midnight. Sam paid for the pizza.

While they ate, Martin thanked Sam for paying. "It's been a little hard, the last few months."

Sam raised an eyebrow.

"Financially, I mean. The company I worked for went belly up – with a bang! – and left us all without anything. Since then I haven't been able to find a job that interested me." At Sam's look of concern, he added, "Oh, I will. I will." He shook his head. "I may have to go up to L.A. for a while to find something, but I'll be okay. I'm a survivor, always have been."

After the pizza, Martin put on some porn and they spent the rest of the evening commenting on it and playing with each other.

"Look at that guy," Martin said, "isn't that sexy?" He turned to Sam and tugged Sam's pubic hair. "This is nice," he said, "but look at that guy! Look at his pubic hair."

Sam looked. "You into red pubic hair Martin?"

"More than 'into.' More like obsessed with. You know my secret lust? It's a man with a big dick and that coppery red pubic hair. I tell you, Sam, I'd bury my nose in that bright copper hair and never come up." He demonstrated just what he'd do. A little later Sam returned the favor.

By the time they kissed goodnight, they were both happy men.

# Chapter Seven

On Friday, Sam called Toby at work and asked him out to dinner. A long pause followed which Sam took to mean Toby was thinking about it. He then experienced the disappointment of being turned down.

"But wait," Toby said quietly, "we can do it tomorrow. At your place. I'll cook. Okay?"

Sam nodded, wondering if this signaled some sort of change in their tenuous relationship. "Yeah," he said into the phone, "that sounds good. What do you want me to get?"

"Nothing. I'll bring what I need. Oh, do you have a grill?"

"Yeah, there's one out on the patio. You want me to get some charcoal?"

"No, I'll bring it. About seven?"

"About seven. I'll have the martinis chilled. That'll be my part."

Sam spent the rest of the day cleaning the condo, just why he didn't know.

On Saturday the phone rang at exactly seven o'clock. Sam answered and then pressed the buttons to open the gate. "Left on the first street, then right. Park in the driveway. I'll be on the porch."

Toby arrived with several bags of groceries, a bag of charcoal, and two bottles of red wine. Sam helped him carry the things into the kitchen and asked him if he'd like to see the place.

"Yes, very much," Toby said, "but wait until I put the ice cream in the freezer. Vanilla okay? I wasn't sure so I got both chocolate and butterscotch sauce to go with it." He grinned and held up the bottles.

"Either one," Sam said. "Or maybe both?"

Toby seemed quite impressed with the condo. He thought the patio would make a great dining area as soon as the evenings became warmer. He also admired the potted palm tree but made no comment on the spa. Upstairs, he seemed to really like the balcony off the bedroom.

Looking at the blank walls Toby asked, "What happened to all the pictures? There must have been some here somewhere."

Sam laughed. "There were. And they're all now at a thrift shop. They were delighted to have them. I have no idea why."

"So what now? Empty walls?"

"Not if I can get someone to go picture shopping with me." He grinned at Toby. "You, for instance."

Toby surprised him by agreeing. "We'll hit the galleries and see what's out there. But for right now, I'd better get into the kitchen or we'll be sending out for pizza. And wasn't something said about cold martinis?"

They had a good time and Toby turned out to be pretty handy in the kitchen. He'd brought some wonderful steaks which he cooked on the charcoal grill and served with baked potatoes and a green salad. There was, of course, ice cream with sauce for dessert after. Everything, in Sam's opinion, was perfect.

While eating the steaks, Sam asked Toby if he was out to his parents. "I mean, if you lived with them before you came down here…"

Toby put his fork down and held out his wine glass, asking for more. "Except for that not too brief period when I lived…" he shook his head as though pushing memories back. "Well, anyway, to answer your question, yes, I was pretty much out to them. Since high school really," he shrugged, "when I came out to myself."

"Were they okay with it?"

"After a fashion," Toby said with a sigh. "Mom figured that at least I wouldn't go around getting girls pregnant and causing trouble."

"And your dad? Fathers sometimes have a hard time with it."

"Poor Dad. I think he somehow conjured up a picture of me with a dick in my mouth and then had a lot of trouble getting past it. He still has problems but at least he can look at me now."

Sam laughed. "Well, I suppose that is a difficult image to get past. But he's okay with it now?"

Toby shook his head. "I don't suppose he'll ever be exactly okay with it, but I'm still his son and he's okay with that. He still loves me. How about you? When did you come out?"

Sam pushed his chair back and started to clear the table. "No," he said, "I'm not avoiding the question. But I have to think about it." He turned and grinned. "After all, it was a long time ago."

They cleared the table and put the dishes in the dishwasher. Toby, besides being a good cook, turned out to be a very neat one and clean-up was a snap.

Armed with fresh glasses of wine, they went into the living room and Sam lit the fire before settling into his chair. Toby sat on the couch, opposite him.

"Okay," Toby said, "your turn. How'd you come out?"

Sam frowned and shook his head. "You know, I don't think I ever did, at least not to myself. I think I always knew. As a kid I didn't think a whole lot about it, but I knew I wasn't the same as the other boys, I just didn't know exactly what the difference might be."

"When did you figure that one out?"

"When I learned to masturbate." Toby raised an eyebrow. "No, really. You know how guys talk, especially when they've just learned to masturbate. The guys all talked about their fantasies and they were different from mine." Sam stopped and thought about it for a moment. "Well, not exactly different, they just involved different people. Mine were all with guys instead of girls but we all did pretty much the same things in them."

"How about to your family? Other people?"

Sam frowned. "My family? I didn't have much family, just my mom and she pretty much stayed drunk when she wasn't working, so the subject never came up. She died when I was seventeen so she never really had time to bring up the grandchildren thing. As to everyone else, I was just... just me, the gay boy. Nobody paid any attention to me except to yell at me when I did something wrong – which seemed to be most of the time. That is until I went to work for Harry. Things picked up after that." Sam grinned. "We gonna have ice cream?"

Toby stood and started toward the kitchen but stopped and turned to Sam. "What did people say? When you told them."

"You know, Toby, I can't remember ever telling anyone I was gay." He stared off into space for a moment. "No, I can't think of anyone." He shrugged. "I guess I just was, and everybody who needed to know, knew it."

"God, I wish it'd been that way for me. You going to help?"

They went into the kitchen and Toby got the ice cream out of the freezer. "Telling my folks was hell. Mom went all 'what will the neighbors think?' and Dad, well Dad just sat in his chair and looked like I'd hit him with a two-by-four. He never said a word, just sighed and nodded." Toby portioned out the ice cream into the bowls Sam had taken out of the cupboard. "I really wish he'd yelled or cursed or hit me or something, but that's not him I guess. He generally just holds it inside and broods on it." He looked at Sam. "Chocolate, butterscotch, or both?"

"Both, please." Sam wanted to hug him but hesitated. By the time he'd thought it through it was too late.

"You know?" Toby said, handing Sam a bowl, "he's never said much of anything about it. He's hardly even acknowledged that I'm gay."

They took their ice cream into the living room and sat on the hearth, their backs to the fire.

"What'd he say when you went to live with, uh..."

"Jack? He made up some fantasy about me working for him. A sort of live-in houseboy." Toby laughed without humor. "Little did he know."

This time Sam didn't pause to think. He rose, pulled Toby up from the hearth and wrapped him into a bear hug. They stood that way, arms around each other, for a long moment.

Then Sam pulled back. "You poor kid," he said. "Parents can be so damn stupid."

The moment passed and they went back to their ice cream. When it was finished Toby told Sam what a good evening it had been and went home.

     \* \* \* \*

Sunday started out sunny and warm and then got warmer, just as the guy on TV had predicted the night before. It hit the mid-nineties just after noon and the heat lingered, making the early evening comfortably balmy. Sam dressed in loose shorts, a tee shirt, and sandals and right at four o'clock went down to the pool.

Sam estimated there were forty or fifty men standing around, most with cocktails in hand and those without at the bar trying to get one. Most of them were naked.

Just by the entrance gate Ben stood at a small table, writing people's names on their chests. "Hi Sam. If you're going to get rid of the clothes you might find a place for them in the locker room. Come back here when you're ready and we'll put your name on you." He reached out and put a hand on Sam's shoulder. "Glad you came. You'll like the guys. We're a pretty tight knit community around here and I think you'll fit in nicely."

Sam pulled him into a hug. "Thanks Ben. I know I'm going to like it here. I knew that in the first ten minutes of that anniversary party." With a little wave he turned and made his way through the crowd of men and into the gym locker room. He was stopped several times by guys who shook his hand and welcomed him.

The locker room was a sea of clothes, most of them in bags or neatly folded on the floor. He figured all the lockers were full so he followed suit, folding his shorts and shirt and putting them on top of his sandals. There were several other men doing the same, including Pete Addison, the man he'd gone home with after the anniversary party. Pete came up and hugged him, making sure their crotches were pressed together and then ran his hand down Sam's back to pat his ass.

"Glad to see you again, Sam. Maybe one day we can do a repeat…"

Sam lightly squeezed one of Pete's nipples. "I'd like that, Pete. Soon. But right now I'm supposed to go and get my name written on me somewhere."

They went to the table at the entrance and Ben lettered Sam's name on his shoulder. He wrote it in red, with yellow underlining. "So everyone will know you're the guest of honor," Ben said. "Now go mix."

They made their way to the bar where Sam poured a light gin and tonic and Pete had vodka on the rocks. "You know," Sam said, "it just occurred to me to wonder. Who pays for all this stuff?"

Pete sampled his drink. "Well, in the end, you do. That is, all of us do. It comes out of the Home Owners Association fees. It's one of the perks of living here."

They circulated, Sam trying to put names and faces together and Pete giving a running commentary on the men they met. After Sam had been introduced to a couple called Nick and Walt, Pete warned him, "Stay clear of them. Or rather of Nick. Walt is so jealous of Nick that he can't think straight."

Sam smiled and put his hand on Pete's shoulder. "Too late."

Pete gave him an inquiring look.

"We fooled around in the steam room one morning. Nobody got off or anything but he sure liked playing. He mentioned that he had a lover." They stopped and Sam turned to face Pete. "I figured his lover would be some old guy nervous about his territory. Didn't realize he'd be the same age and very good looking to boot. Nick is probably the one who needs to be jealous."

They circulated back to the bar and refreshed their drinks. As they were leaving, Pete nodded to their left. "There's your next door neighbor, Martin Shields. I must say I'm surprised to see him here seeing as how he hasn't paid his dues for several months." He waved at Martin, making sure Martin noticed him. Martin didn't react.

Sam turned to face Pete. "How is it that you know so much about everybody?"

Pete smiled. "People talk to me. I guess I'm a good listener. It doesn't hurt that I'm on the board of the Home Owner's Association either. Actually, I do most of the money stuff, you know, pay the bills, collect the dues, that sort of thing. So," he shrugged, "I know stuff."

Sam laughed. "Oh great, now I suppose everyone will know all about me."

"Not unless you do weird stuff. If you do, then it's sort of everybody's business. Otherwise," he looked demurely down at the deck, "I'm the soul of discretion."

They stopped at the hors d'oeuvres table and helped themselves to several of the delicacies. "Where do you find this stuff?" Sam asked, "it's delicious."

Pete looked around for a moment, searching for someone. "See over there? The short guy with the spiked hair and nice buns? His name is Scotty Helms and he does this for us. He's a caterer by trade, a damn good one, and gives us a very good price. He doesn't live here but he loves to come around on Sunday afternoon to show off that slab of meat he carries between his legs. Come on, I'll introduce you, and you can see for yourself."

It seemed undoubtedly to be the biggest flaccid dick Sam had ever seen and the man carrying it looked, to Sam's eyes, to be a sweetheart. Probably thirty-five, with an infectious smile, beautiful dark green eyes and spiked hair which looked good on him. Sam found himself immediately taken with the man, especially when he hugged Sam, pressing his dick firmly into Sam's crotch.

Every once in a while, as they talked, Scotty seemed to unconsciously scratch his pubic hair, making his dick flop. It didn't take Sam long to realize, though, that he was actually doing it on purpose, reveling in the other men's reactions to it.

As they were returning to the bar, Pete said, "See? I told you he likes to show it off." He shrugged. "I suppose if I had one like that I'd do it too. And you know what's funny? To my knowledge he's never gotten it on with any of these guys. He just comes, puts out the food, struts around and then leaves." He thumped Sam on the back. "Weird, huh?"

It was Sam's impression that Pete said this with a hint of disappointment.

When things began to wind down, Sam and Pete went to the locker room to retrieve their clothes. While getting dressed, Pete introduced Sam to Mike Armstrong and then suggested they all go back to his place.

"I made some beef stew yesterday and I'd appreciate you guys helping me get rid of it," he said with a laugh. "And maybe we can find something to do after dinner, huh?"

The stew turned out to be excellent and, sure enough, they did find something to do after dinner. Sam went home and to bed a happy man.

On Tuesday, the Prime Timers had a mixer at a place called The Desert Palms Resort and Sam went, hoping Toby would be there. He still couldn't put a name to whatever was going on between himself and Toby, but he did realize it made him happy to be around the boy. But that was part of the problem, he considered Toby to be a boy and had no idea what a forty-five year old man would do with a twenty-six year old boy. He just knew Toby wouldn't play the same role to him as Sam had played to Harry. Toby had made that abundantly clear by his actions.

It was a good mixer and Toby came in around six. Sam let him get to the bar and buy a drink before he made his way over to him. "Hi, Toby," he said, putting a hand on Toby's shoulder. "How's it going?"

Toby surprised him by giving him a quick kiss on the lips. "Good, Sam, good." He took a sip of his drink and sighed. "It's been hell in the office, one crisis after another, but this," he held up his drink, "makes it all better. You?"

"Not bad. They had Sunday cocktails in my honor at the complex. Slept late yesterday. Today I did a bit of shopping and that's about it." He touched his glass to Toby's. "Good to see you."

Toby smiled. "Sunday cocktails at the complex, huh? Did it turn into an orgy?"

Sam laughed. "No, Toby, it didn't turn into an orgy." He waited two beats and then added, "Too cold."

Toby nodded. "Too bad, Sam. Maybe this summer. I mean, can all those rumors be wrong?"

Sam shrugged his shoulders. "I couldn't say. But hey, over there is a man who might. Come meet my real estate guy."

They made their way through the crowd and stopped in front of William and Red.

Sam made the introductions and then, looking at William said, "Guys, Toby here wants to know if all those rumors of orgies around the pool at my complex are true."

Red put his arm around Toby's shoulder. "An orgy, my man, will happen anywhere there are a few guys and sufficient energy to sustain it. I've been in that pool and there's certainly enough energy there to sustain quite a nice one, should one get started."

William laughed. "That's certainly the long way around to 'yes.'"

Sam shook his head. "Really? I've never seen one. Of course, I've only been there a couple of weeks."

"Wait," William said. "Wait for the warm evenings. It's pretty well documented in the community that stuff does go on there on hot summer nights. That going to bother you guys? I mean…"

"Hardly," Sam laughed. "I don't think anyone here is bothered by a little sex just for its own sake." He turned to Toby. "Are you?"

Toby grinned. "Not hardly."

They all laughed and the conversation turned to the weather.

After another drink, Sam asked Toby to dinner but Toby had other plans. "But how about Friday?" Toby asked before disappointment could set in. "Someplace simple and cheap, okay?"

Sam hugged him. "Yeah, I'll think of something. Pick you up around seven?"

Toby nodded, gave Sam a quick kiss, and left.

The next afternoon Sam went out to the house to see what might be going on. As it turned out, plenty was going on. Several people, mostly neighbors, were standing around in the driveway and Bill, the contractor, was pacing back and forth at the curb.

"Hey, Bill, what's up?"

Bill looked at him and growled, "The fucking pool, that's what's up. God Damn thing blew up on us."

Sam put his hand on Bill's shoulder in an effort to calm him. "Bill, it's okay. But would you please tell me how, exactly, a swimming pool can blow up."

"Gas," Bill snarled. "Heater. Blew sky high."

At that moment David, one of the workmen, drove up in his truck. He hopped out and hefted a large pump out of the back. "Right where I thought it'd be," he said to Bill. "Hose too."

Bill seemed to pull himself together now that he had something to do. Sam followed along as Bill and David unrolled the hose back towards the pool. When they got there they attached the hose to the pump and carefully lowered it into the deep end of the pool. Then David plugged the pump into a heavy duty extension cord. The hose suddenly filled out as the water surged through it.

"Got to thank your neighbors for the power," David said. "Everything's shut off here."

"Okay, okay, David. You go make sure the water's going where it should and I'll try to explain this to our boss." David left and Bill turned to Sam, visibly calmer.

"Well, it's like this," he said, pausing to organize his thoughts. "Your pool was built when they could put the equipment, the filter, the heater, the pump, stuff like that, down in a pit. That's the pit," he said, pointing to a dark hole in the deck. "Normally it has a grate covering it and a stack for the heater." They walked over to it but couldn't see much because the hole was nearly black and full of water.

"We should have checked. I know we should have, but it never occurred to any of us that the gas was still on. I mean, a place empty as long as this one, everything should have been shut off." He gave a deep sigh. "So we didn't check. Since you said we should let that crook of a pool guy go, the pool was starting to grow algae so I thought we should run the filter for a while and then dump some chlorine in it. When we turned on the pump the pressure evidentially triggered the heater to turn on and then ruptured a water pipe. The heater safety valve didn't kick in, it's probably rusted all to hell, so the gas came on and a spark from the motor set it off." He suddenly grinned. "You should of seen it, Sam. That grate came off of there like it was shot from a cannon." He shrugged. "I guess, really, it was. Landed on the roof."

Tom from next door joined them. "Made a hell of a noise, too. Thought a truck had hit the house. Tige was running around barking his head off and Dan dropped the cupcakes he was putting in the oven. Quite a mess."

"Well, we'll get you all the cupcakes you want," Bill said. "And pay for the electricity you're being kind enough to let us use."

Sam looked at him. "Electricity?"

"Yeah, that big power cord there," he said, pointing. "Blew out every fuse from here to Thursday. And we gotta get that pool empty now. God only knows what else ruptured when the thing went. My worry is that it's draining into the sewer, which screws everything up for the water people."

"Not to mention the folks who live around here," Tom added.

"Yeah, them, too. So David went back to the shop for the pump and Mr. Wacker here let us tap into his power."

Sam shook his head. "So now what do we do?"

Bill smiled. "Well, it's not as bad as it might seem. We were going to have to re-plumb the pool anyhow. They won't let you have the equipment underground any more and from the looks of things," he gestured, taking in the whole pool, "we're going to have to re-plaster the pool. At the very least."

Sam squinted at him. "And at the very most?"

"Jackhammer the whole thing out of there and start over." Bill laughed. "I told you this wasn't going to be cheap."

They took a last look at the pit and walked out to the driveway. Bill wanted to make sure the water was running properly down the gutter and into the storm drain. While they were talking and explaining to the few neighbors who were still there a police car pulled into the driveway and the driver got out, pulling on his cap as he did so.

"Okay, who's in charge here?" the policeman barked.

Sam stepped forward. "I'm the homeowner, officer." He extended his hand and said, "Sam Davis, sir."

The officer ignored the extended hand. "Well, Mr. Davis, just what the hell do you think you're doing here?" He gestured at the water running down the gutter.

"Uh, draining my pool?"

Bill stepped between the officer and Sam. "I'm Bill Flint, Mr. Davis's contractor. Can I help you?"

"This your idea?" Bill nodded and the officer sighed. "Don't you know, Mr. Contractor, that in this town you need a permit to drain a pool? That you have to post that permit? Where I can see it? And," his voice was heavy with sarcasm, "under no circumstances are you to do this during the day?"

Bill gritted his teeth. "As it happens, Sir, I do know that." He smiled, lowering the tension level a little. "I also know that if I go down to City Hall, stand in line, get a permit, file it with the Police Department, post a copy of it here on the wall and wait until after six p.m. the entire pool will most likely have drained itself into the sanitary sewer and there will be no need for the permit in the first place."

"No, no, you can't..."

"Exactly." He went on to explain the situation and what had happened. By the time he finished both of them were smiling. The officer shook Bill's hand and each of them apologized to the other.

Turning to Sam, the officer introduced himself as Officer Andrew Koyle. He looked around and said, "So what're you doing to the place?"

Sam found himself warming up to the guy and explained about restoring the house. Then he took him on a tour and explained as best he could what they were doing. The policeman was very interested and asked Sam if he might stop by from time to time and watch the progress. Sam said he'd be welcome any time.

# Chapter Eight

Two days later, on Friday, Sam was still chuckling over the exchange between Bill and the policeman but when he related it to Toby it came out rather flat. "Well," he said, "I guess you had to be there. You know, you really ought to come out and see the place someday."

Toby nodded distractedly. "Yeah, I guess I should. Where are we going to dinner?"

Sam smiled. "I told you I'd think of something. It's just down the road, in Cathedral City. Place called The Red Tomato. I've never been there but it was recommended as cheap and simple."

Toby brightened. "Good food, too. It's been a while since I've eaten there but the pasta is terrific. Good choice, Sam."

Toby had been right. The pasta dishes all looked wonderful on the menu and they both had a hard time making a choice. When the food came, it was even better than described and a comfortable quiet settled over the table for a while as they savored it.

After a bit Sam put down his fork and said, "Say, Toby, don't I remember you saying you would give me some help finding some pictures for my bare, lonely walls?"

Toby smiled at him. "Yeah, I think I did make some rash statement about that. Why? You getting tired of large, blank, off-white spaces?"

"In a word, yes. What say we go hit some of the galleries tomorrow?"

Toby seemed to look inward for a moment before he nodded. "Sure. Tomorrow would be good. You just going to look or are you going to buy?"

Sam shrugged. "Why put it off? If we find something we like, we'll buy it."

"Hey, what's with this we stuff? They're going to grace your walls so you better pick out stuff you like. I'm just going along to keep you away from the fake Tom of Finland drawings."

"There's little chance of that," Sam laughed. "Not my thing. But now that I think about it, the bathroom could use something…"

"No, Sam. Not even in the bathroom."

Sam pretended to pout. "Not even one naked man?"

"You can have all the naked men you want only they have to be originals or excellent reproductions. No fakes, no bad copies. Okay?"

Sam nodded. "Okay. No bad copies of hugely endowed naked men. I tell you what, we'll start early with breakfast somewhere and then hit the galleries. Okay?"

"Well, if you're really serious about buying, why don't I pick you up in my little truck? There'll be lots of room for those monumental Tom of Finland originals."

"Done. And you can take me to breakfast."

"Eight o'clock sharp. Bring your check book."

And so it happened that a few minutes after eight on Saturday morning, Sam and Toby were on their way to The Country Kitchen for a hearty breakfast.

"I wanted to start early," Toby said after ordering eggs, sausage, biscuits and gravy, "because I thought we'd start at the consignment stores. Sometimes you can make a real find at one or another of them. Besides, the galleries downtown don't open until around ten."

Sam, who had decided on an omelet with bacon, goat cheese, and spinach, nodded. "I've heard of the consignment stores but never been in one. It'll be an adventure."

The first thing Sam saw when they walked into his first consignment store was an enormous chandelier made completely out of some kind of antlers.

When he pointed it out, Toby just laughed. "Oh yeah, always look up. I once came across one made entirely out of Ray Charles CDs."

"You hang around these places a lot?" Sam asked.

"Not really," Toby replied, "but when you're trying to furnish your first apartment these places are a treasure trove of goodies at generally reasonable prices. Come on, the pictures are in the back."

At first glance, Sam saw little of interest, but after some explanation from Toby and taking a single picture out of the sea of others around it, Sam began to see possibilities. In the end, he bought three and charged twenty-eight hundred dollars on his Visa card. Toby blanched but didn't say a word.

They visited two more consignment stores but didn't find anything that really spoke to either of them. They then went to the downtown galleries which turned out to be very different from the consignment stores. For one thing, the pictures were pleasantly spaced so each one could be viewed without competing with five or ten others. For another, the prices were triple what they'd seen at the consignment stores. On the other hand, they were given cups of very good coffee and offered plates of small pastries.

Sam found one painting in the Early California style he liked, so he put a hold on it. The gallery manager gave him a postcard sized picture of the painting, complete with a biography of Case Paul, the artist, on the back. The gallery would hold the painting three days, no more.

Altogether they went to a half dozen galleries, but didn't buy anything, although Sam also put a hold on a near life-sized sculpture of a nude man. Afterward, they wandered around town a bit, looking in the stores, and stopping at Starbucks for coffee. Around two o'clock, Sam found he was hungry and suggested lunch. They went to the Rainbow because they could sit outside on the patio.

Once they were served, Toby grinned, "You know what I'd do if I had a million dollars? I'd buy that sculpture right out from under you. And then you know what I'd do? I'd do the same thing with that Case Paul painting."

Sam's initial impulse was to say, 'Well, let's go get 'em,' but he stopped himself. This sounds like some sort of test, he thought. Careful, Sam. You want to pass this one., He said, "I don't know. I'd probably let you do that. But I need to think about them for a while. I'm just not sure."

Toby smiled. "Well, you don't really have to worry about me snatching them away so take your time. Keep in mind, though, that each of them would also be a very good investment."

After lunch they went back to the consignment store and picked up Sam's paintings and took them home. When Sam invited Toby in, he declined, saying he had some things to do. After Toby left, Sam called both the galleries and told them he wanted the things he had put a hold on. He also asked them if they would keep them for a while and both galleries agreed.

Sam spent the rest of the day hanging the pictures he'd bought and then sitting with some iced tea, studying them. The longer he looked at them, the happier he became. I gotta take that boy shopping with me more often. I never would have bought these on my own.

* * * *

On Tuesday, Prime Timers had a lunch at a restaurant called The Deck. Sam almost skipped it, knowing Toby would be working, but decided at the last minute to go since he'd already indicated his lunch choice on the check he'd sent with his reservation. It turned out to be a good decision because the guys never let the conversation lag, both at the cocktail hour and at lunch. Matthew Stevens was there, entertaining a small group of guys with his tales of the Coroner's Office and Sam thought again what a nice guy he seemed to be.

As he was getting ready to leave, a hand grasped his shoulder. Turning, he found Martin, his next door neighbor. "What are you doing here, Martin?" he asked. "Didn't I hear you'd dropped out of Prime Timers."

Martin nodded. "I did, but my friend Chuck couldn't make it and gave me his place. He'd ordered the hamburger and it turned out to be a damn good one."

"Yeah, I had that too," Sam said. They sure don't stint on the meat."

"Hey, Sam, if you're going home, could you give me a ride? My car's on the blink again so I had to walk over. Probably should walk back too, after that lunch, but…" He shrugged.

"Sure, Martin, glad to. I'm in the garage downstairs."

When they got home, Martin invited Sam in. The look in his eye made clear the sort of invitation he had in mind and Sam thought what the hell. He accepted and his dick stirred in his pants at the prospect.

Martin stopped at the little rock garden by his front door and picked up one of the stones "Gift from a friend," he said as he turned it over and opened a little door set in the bottom. "I'm forever forgetting my key and my friend thought this would be a good place to keep an extra one."

Sam thought so too. Placed in the garden among the other rocks it wouldn't be easy to spot as a fake.

Once inside, Martin lost no time in getting Sam out of his clothes. They ended up on the living room floor in a classic sixty-nine position where they brought pleasure to themselves and each other, slowly, without any sense of urgency or competition.

At one point Martin caressed Sam's ass and slid off his dick to say, "That sure is a fine ass, Sam. Pity I can't have it."

Sam let Martin's balls slip out of his mouth and replied, "Breaks of the game, fella. You can't have everything."

Martin smiled up at Sam and patted the ass in question. "That's okay. But it sure is a pretty one."

Later, after they'd satisfied each other, they lay together in companionable silence, enjoying the afterglow.

After a short while Sam got up. "Hard floors and I don't mix for too long anymore." He stretched, arching his back. "I guess I'm getting old."

Martin got to his knees and fondled Sam. "Well, you may be getting old but this thing sure isn't. Look at that."

Sam looked down at his dick which was rapidly growing hard again. "I guess it likes what you're doing." He ran his fingers through Martin's hair. "I know I sure do."

Martin got to his feet. "Let's find a more comfortable place and see if I can make that big ole thing throw up again, huh?"

They went outside, to a wide lounge, and brought each other off again. Later, sitting in the hot water of the spa, Martin put his arms around Sam and kissed him. "You're very talented, Sam. We have to do this again. Soon."

Sam went home with a vaguely uneasy feeling. He had enjoyed the sex with Martin but there'd been something missing. There was always something missing these days it seemed. Just what, he couldn't put his finger on.

He heated some soup and made a sandwich for his evening meal and then called Toby and asked him to dinner the next night.

Toby said he was involved in a series of meetings and dinners at work and couldn't get away for an evening until Saturday. "Okay," Sam said. "I'll make reservations somewhere for Saturday."

"I have a better idea," Toby said. "I'll come over and mess up your kitchen again. Lamb chops okay?"

"A favorite," Sam said "I'll get a nice, mellow red wine."

* * * *

On Saturday, Sam went to Jensen's and found they still had a few bottles of Beaujolais Nouveau from last year's harvest. He bought six bottles and made a mental note not to let Toby know how much he paid for them. Then he went to a florist and bought some flowers.

By the time Toby arrived that evening the table had been set, the flowers arranged and the gin put in the freezer. After a tight hug and a kiss from Toby, Sam helped him carry in the groceries.

"It seems silly, you know, that you have to bring all this stuff. Why don't you just give me a list and I'll..."

"Because this is my dinner."

The lamb chops turned out to be racks of lamb which Toby had already covered with a garlic-rosemary crumb crust. There were also tiny Yukon Gold potatoes which he would sauté in butter, and green beans which would be steamed and seasoned with dill. He was delighted with the wine Sam had bought.

"Trenel et Fils," he exclaimed. "Wonderful! But it must have cost you…" He let it drop and then insisted that they have glasses of wine instead of martinis.

Sam found out just how good the wine really was. "You know this stuff?" he asked when they were sitting in the living room sipping at their wine.

"You bet," Toby said. "One of the bartenders at the hotel gave me a glass of it when he was trying to get in my pants."

"And?" Sam asked.

Toby grinned. "It worked."

Maybe there's hope for me. The unbidden thought flashed through Sam's mind but he didn't say it. Instead, without comment, he asked how Toby liked the placement of the pictures they'd bought.

"Nice," Toby said. "Just where I thought they should go." He turned to Sam and winked. "You've got really good taste."

The evening progressed smoothly and the food Toby prepared was wonderful. After dinner and over chocolate ice cream they sipped more of the wine. Toby left around ten, leaving Sam to deal with the kitchen.

When the cleanup was finished Sam took a last glass of the wine and went upstairs to sit on his balcony and enjoy it. He saw a number of guys out walking, probably on their way to the pool area. He briefly considered joining them but decided against it in favor of his own hand when he went to bed.

\* \* \* \*

On Sunday Sam went over to the gym and worked out. He found himself happy with the way his regular sessions in the gym were going and felt that he was really increasing his stamina. The mirrors showed that he was building a bit of muscle, too.

Sam liked the gym on Sundays because there were always other guys there, working out and sharing an easy comradeship. The chance that he might find a bit of casual sex in the steam room or the showers added to his enjoyment. And in any case there were always other men to look at.

After the gym he went to the house in Las Palmas, mostly in hopes of finding Dan and Tom home with Bloody Marys. He didn't and ended up at home with a good book.

\* \* \* \*

On Monday, he went to a Prime Timers mixer at a restaurant called Blame It On Midnight. He hoped to find Toby there but was again disappointed. He went home early.

Sitting on his patio with a glass of wine, he found himself both lonesome and horny. He decided to see if Martin wanted to share a pizza or some Chinese food and, hopefully, something else. Putting on some shorts, a tee shirt, and some sandals he went next door.

Sam rang the doorbell several times but got no answer. That seemed odd because he could hear the radio inside and he knew Martin's car was still not running. He called Martin's name several times and, getting no response, tried the door. It swung open.

It seemed very unlike Martin to leave the house unlocked, with the lights and radio on, so Sam went through the condo to see if Martin might be ill or hurt and unable to call out.

He found him in the bathroom, in the tub, laid out under pink tinged water. Sam simply stood for a few seconds, studying the man and not fully comprehending what he was seeing. When realization finally came to him, it stunned him and he had a strong impulse to pull Martin out of the tub and try to revive him. But he saw the slashes on Martin's wrists and knew nothing would bring him back. He went down to the living room and numbly dialed 9-1-1.

Sam described the situation to the operator who told him to stay where he was until the police and paramedics got there. He started to say the paramedics were not necessary but stopped himself. They'd find out when they got there.

When he hung up the phone he noticed a stiff white card lying on the desk. In a very controlled handwriting it read:

That's it. I cannot – and I will not – endure this any longer. Whoever finds this, please, go away and leave me be. I'm in a happier place and a happier state and I want to be alone.

Sam stepped back so the tear forming in his eye wouldn't fall on the card and mar it. He stood in the middle of the room, staring at nothing until the police arrived.

The police and the paramedics arrived at the same time and general chaos quickly ensued. Sam led them up to the bathroom and then stood back and watched while the paramedics looked Martin over. They didn't touch him, except to check for a pulse, until after the photographers arrived and took pictures of the scene from every conceivable angle.

While the photographers were doing their work, the police, in the person of a Sergeant Elgar, questioned Sam about his relationship with the dead man and what he was doing in his house. Sam explained it all to their seeming satisfaction. Then he watched while Martin was lifted out of the bathtub, covered with a sheet, put on a gurney, and taken downstairs.

And that did it. The police locked up, put some yellow tape across the door and left. Just like that.

Sam spent the next hour explaining what had happened to the little crowd of guys standing around on the sidewalk in front of Martin's condo. They all seemed to accept it without much surprise.

"He was in big trouble financially," Pete Addison said. "I imagine everyone knew about it. He'd borrowed money from most of us."

"Yeah," Nick said. "Even me."

Walt, Nick's lover, turned to him angrily. "When? What were you doing with him that you'd give him money?" He glared at Nick for a long time and then turned on his heel and left, calling over his shoulder, "I'll see you at home, slut."

Nick trotted after him.

There was silence for a minute and then everyone started talking at once.

Charlie and Ben came up to Sam. "Don't let them bother you," Ben said. "They do this all the time. I think it makes their sex better or something."

Charlie nodded. "We hear them sometimes. But what about Martin? Is there anything we should do or anyone we should call?"

"I don't know," Sam said. "Did he have any family? Or close friends?"

Ben shook his head while Charlie asked the general group. It appeared no one knew a whole lot about Martin, his family, or his friends outside of Desert Pride. Finally there seemed nothing more to talk about and the group began to disperse.

Pete Addison stopped Sam and asked him if he wanted company. "That must have been a hell of a shock, finding him like that. Shall I come in, maybe fix you a drink?"

Sam smiled "No, I'll be all right. But it was a shock. I've never known anyone who killed himself." He put his hand on Pete's shoulder. "But no, I'll be fine. I probably will have that drink though."

Sam did have one – and a couple of others – before he went to bed. He didn't sleep for several hours until finally the combination of the alcohol and the lack of food got to him. He slept badly, dreaming of Martin, lying in the bathtub. Sam would wake up, not wanting to go back to sleep and see the scene all over again. When at last he did exhaust himself, the dreams went away and let him rest. He woke a bit after ten and lay in bed for a while, trying to get the ghost of poor Martin out of his head. He felt he needed to talk to someone and the first person he thought of was Toby. He reached for the phone.

Toby didn't ask questions. He told Sam to meet him in the Blue Bar at the Hyatt.

When Sam got there Toby was waiting for him, nursing an iced tea. "Sam. You okay?"

Sam nodded, sat on a stool, and ordered scotch. When his drink, a double, arrived, he took a swallow from it and started talking. The telling took nearly an hour and another scotch. When he finished Toby asked the bartender for the house phone. He called his office and said he would be taking the rest of the day off. Then he ordered two more scotches – one for himself – and led Sam to a table.

"You shouldn't take the afternoon off just for me, Toby. I'll be okay. I'll just go home and…"

"Shut up, Sam," Toby said gently. He signaled one of the waiters and ordered rare steaks and garlic bread. "This has really gotten to you, hasn't it?"

Sam admitted that it had. Somehow, it seemed the most senseless thing he'd ever known to happen. "And, it's all about money – or the lack of it. God, Toby, if only I'd known…"

Toby caught his gaze and held it. "But you didn't know, Sam and he did what he felt he had to do. It's a damn shame but that's the way it is." A waiter served their steaks. "Now eat."

Sam began to feel better as he ate and by the time they were finished he was almost back to normal. Toby signed the check and suggested they take a walk. Sam agreed, mostly because he wanted to spend some more time with Toby.

They walked eight or ten blocks down Palm Canyon Drive, looking in the shops and commenting on things in the windows, then crossed the street and walked back to the hotel.

"You want to have dinner with me, maybe take in a movie?" Sam asked, not wanting the day to end.

Toby looked at his watch. "Sure. But it's too early for dinner. Let's do the movie first then get something to eat."

They went to a film about Maria Callas, which they both enjoyed immensely, and then had a light dinner at a little Chinese place. Sam felt sorry to see the evening end and almost asked Toby to come home with him but resisted the impulse. His gut told him the time wasn't right. Instead, he asked Toby if he could take him to dinner on Friday night, someplace special to show his appreciation for the way Toby listened to him and shored him up that afternoon.

To his surprise Toby nodded and said, "Seven-thirty, okay? And no place where I need a tie. Please?"

Sam nodded, thinking at least one good thing had come out of the day.

# Chapter Nine

They went to Shame on the Moon, a place one of the guys at Desert Pride had recommended to Sam as elegant, casual, and good. When they arrived they were greeted by Ginger, a warm, friendly woman who escorted them to their table. No sooner were they seated than a very handsome young man came over and introduced himself as Dennis, their waiter, and offered to take their drink orders. Sam ordered Beefeater martinis for both.

"This is a good choice," Toby said, looking around the room. "The concierge at the hotel recommends it a lot."

"Well, so far I can see why." He picked up the card which sat in the middle of the table and welcomed them by name. "Nice touch," he said, handing the card to Toby.

The drinks were served and were perfect.

"You know," Toby said with a smile, "I could get used to this in a hurry."

"Well, I don't know. Let's wait until we see how the food is."

The food looked wonderful and tasted better. It was so good, in fact, that they both ordered dessert.

On the way out, they received a hand shake from Dennis and a hug from Ginger.

In the car Sam said, "That was a keeper. We'll definitely go back."

When they got to Toby's place, Toby turned in the seat and gave Sam a long kiss. "Thank you, Sam. It was the perfect evening." He didn't, however, invite Sam in.

Well, Sam thought on his way back to Desert Pride, almost perfect. He went to bed a happy – but unfulfilled – man.

The next morning Sam went out to the house. He found Bill standing at the boarded up front door, yelling into his phone. From what Sam could tell, the glass company on the other end of the phone had greatly overestimated their ability to fabricate the windows and glass doors Bill had ordered. Bill was attempting to hammer out a new delivery date. Sam left him to it and went next door

Tom and Dan were lounging under an umbrella, by the pool, a carafe between them. They made Sam welcome and handed him a cup of coffee. Tige, who had been shooed off a chaise longue so Sam could sit, promptly went over to Dan and climbed up to lie next to him.

"Haven't seen you around for a while," Tom said. "What've you been up to?"

"Not much. Except, we did have a little excitement at the complex." He went on to tell them about finding Martin's body.

He didn't get nearly as emotional telling the story this time. Sam thought he might be getting used to the idea.

"So he committed suicide," Dan said, patting Tige's head. "Why ever would he do something like that?" Tige looked up at Dan and drooled a little.

Sam shook his head. "Money, maybe. Everyone seems to think he was in some sort of financial trouble. I know he hadn't paid his Home Owner's assessment for a while, and his car wasn't running." He shrugged, "I don't know, but it just seems such a silly reason to kill yourself."

"That's because you have money, Sam. It's different when you're poor."

Sam shook his head. "I've been poor and he wasn't that. Poor people don't live in Desert Pride, don't have two year old Cadillacs they bought new and they don't dress the way Martin did."

"Maybe he had it and lost it," Dan said with shrug. "Maybe he spent it all."

Sam thought for a moment. "Yeah, he did tell me once that he'd lost his job a while back. But he seemed pretty okay with it. Said he could get a job in L.A. any time he wanted." He frowned. "I guess he could have been kidding himself. But he was in TV. TV guys can always get jobs up in L.A."

"Or maybe he got into the market," Tom said, refilling their cups. "Like Jack and Larry," he pointed towards Sam's house. "They lost a bundle in a very short time. If it hadn't been for your Harry, they would have lost their house, too. Maybe... I don't know, but maybe, for this Martin guy, suicide was preferable to whatever was going on in his life."

Sam made a mental note to see if he could find out the status of Martin's condo. Maybe he had been on the brink of losing it.

Aloud, he said, "I don't know either, but something about this is bothering the hell out of me and I wish I could figure out what it is."

When he finished his coffee, Sam excused himself, saying he'd better go next door and see what Bill was up to. "If he keeps working Saturdays then I'm going to be the one with no money."

Bill greeted Sam with an easy hug. "All taken care of," he said with a grin. "We'll get our windows in a couple of weeks, along with an additional three percent discount. Now, how are you, Sam? What've you been up to?"

Sam shrugged. "Just the usual. Hey, how come you're working on Saturday? You running up the bill?"

Bill laughed. "Not hardly, Sam. The wife's off with Alice, our youngest, shopping for God knows what. My boy Davy is working on a science project that I want to be all his and if I hung around there I'd be giving him all kinds of advice he neither needs nor wants. I just ducked out while the ducking was good."

"Well, don't run it up too far. We're not in that much of a hurry around here."

"That's not actually true," Bill said. "We need to get the new roof on before it gets to be too damn hot to be working up there and there's lots to do before we can tackle it." He smiled and they began walking back to their cars. "But don't worry, Sam. I'm just the contractor. I do the thinking and planning but I don't get overtime. The guys who do what I tell 'em to do, they get the overtime." He scratched his head and laughed. "Doesn't seem quite right, does it."

Sam nodded. "Yeah, but you're the guy who gets the big bonus at the end when you pull this thing off. Think about that."

Bill nodded. "Nice to hear that, Sam. Don't think I won't hold you to it."

"That I believe. Now why don't you get on home and annoy that kid of yours."

"Not me." He waved at a set of golf clubs in the back of his truck. "I'm gonna see what I can do on the driving range for a couple of hours. By the time I do that and have a little refreshment with the guys in the clubhouse, the shopping will be done, the project will be finished, and good smells will be coming out of the kitchen." He climbed into the truck. "See you next week?"

"No doubt," Sam said with a wave, "no doubt."

Back at Desert Pride Sam decided he needed some exercise so he changed into loose shorts, a tee, and sandals, and headed for the pool.

There were a number of guys at the pool enjoying the sunshine, some of them swimming laps and all of them naked. Sam found a locker, stripped, and joined the lap swimmers.

An hour later he'd had enough and went to the locker room to dry off. He saw a little good natured ass grabbing going on in the shower but didn't join in. He'd seen Howard, the older guy with the very young lover, lying on a lounge by the pool. He thought a talk with him might help him learn how an older/younger relationship worked.

Sam stretched out on empty lounge next to Howard. "Hi, Howard." He turned to the man and offered his hand. "Sam. Sam Davis."

Howard shook his hand and nodded. "Oh, yeah, Sam. I've seen you around. Didn't you buy ol' Tom Avery's place?"

Sam nodded. "It's a nice condo and it turns out this is a great place to live."

Howard nodded. "We think so."

"That's right. You're partners with that young guy, what's his name? Duane, isn't it?"

"That's him. He had to work today, but," he looked at his watch, "he should be along pretty quick."

"What's he do that he has to work on Saturday?"

"E.R. nurse, over at the hospital. The hours can get pretty long but the pay's good and he loves the work." He grinned. "Besides, he's got lots of stamina. He's still a kid, not an old guy like us."

Sam smiled back. "He did look kind of young when we all met at that party out here."

"Twenty-five." Howard nodded. "Been together seven years now."

Sam did the arithmetic. "He was eighteen? There has to be a story there, right?"

"I suppose. He was in my English class his last couple of years of high school. He waited until he turned eighteen and graduated before he told me how he felt." He shrugged. "I felt the same way. I'd had an offer from College of the Desert here, so we came. He decided to try the nursing school and found that he was a natural. So, here we are. End of story."

"And quite a story it is, too. I admire you, keeping up with a twenty-five year-old."

Howard smiled. "It's not that difficult, actually. Except for his hours we live a fairly normal, routine life together. We're pretty much equals in the relationship and that helps keep it stable. We didn't make the daddy-son mistake so many older-younger couples do and we try to keep it simple." He looked directly at Sam. "You ever been in a relationship with someone older or younger than you?"

"I guess I have to answer that one both yes and no." He went on to tell Howard about Harry and how he and Harry had been a couple – just not a sexual one – and how well it had worked for them.

Howard laughed. "Sex is the least of the potential problems. You'll have to ask Duane sometime how we handle the sex thing." He shook his head. "No, the real problem is being equals, taking equal responsibility for things and especially for each other. It's hard, you know, when you're well along in your career and he's just starting out. Or when you make a lot more money than he does. That can really be a problem. No matter how much you love him, you can't let him feel like you're buying him."

A light went on in Sam's head but he didn't have time to think about it because just then Duane came up to them.

"Hi, guys," he said, giving Howard a quick kiss.

"Hi, honey. How'd it go today?"

"Not as bad as a lot of Saturdays." He shrugged. "The usual cuts, scrapes and broken bones."

"You remember Sam?" Howard said.

"Oh yeah. Hi, Sam. You bought the end condo, right? Next to Martin?" Duane said. "Terrible thing, Martin's suicide. I heard that you were the one who found him."

"Yeah, I was," Sam said grimly.

Duane changed the subject and asked, "You like it here?" He answered his own question, nodding at Sam's nakedness. "I guess you do. You fit right in with the rest of us. Speaking of which, if you'll excuse me, I'll go and get into the uniform of the day." He chuckled and headed off to the locker room.

"Nice guy," Sam said. "Good sense of humor. You're a lucky man, Howard."

"Yeah, he makes my life pretty bright. How about you? You going to stay single forever?"

"Not if I can help it. There's a guy I find myself very attracted to. Young guy, about Duane's age." He shrugged. "We'll see."

"You brought him around here yet?"

Sam shook his head. "Didn't want to scare him off. He's been to the condo a couple of times but not out here." He looked around at the naked men. "But I guess I'll have to, one of these days. See how he reacts."

"Good idea. Some guys, especially young ones, get kind of nervous around a bunch of naked older men."

"How'd Duane react?"

"Oh, he jumped right into the big middle of it. Loves the whole concept."

Sam nodded, wondering if Toby would have the same reaction. He sighed, thinking he probably would. After all, he'd liked Some Guys. Sam wondered if he'd be jealous when Toby went to the showers.

When Duane came out Sam thought again how lucky Howard was. Duane was a very handsome young man but didn't seem to be at all aware of it.

As Duane approached Sam got up from the lounge and said, "Here, take this. It's time for me to go in. Good talking with you, Howard."

Howard nodded. "Let's get together for dinner sometime. Get to know each other better."

Duane nodded. "That'd be fun, Sam. Howard's a fantastic cook." He glanced at Howard. "How about next Sunday? Not tomorrow, a week from."

Howard nodded. "Sam?"

"I'll be there. Thank you."

He went into the locker room to retrieve his clothes but got sidetracked and ended up spending a pleasurable half hour in the steam room.

When he got home the message light on his answering machine was flashing. It was Jay, inviting him out for dinner 'and things.'

Sam called him back. "Thanks for the invitation, Jay, but I think I'd better not. I just got back from the pool and I... uh, I..."

Jay laughed. "Oh, so Sam's been a naughty boy, has he? How many times?"

Sam had to smile at Jay checking the odds. "Uh... a couple."

"My, my. I wish I'd been there. Tell you what Sam, why don't we make it for brunch tomorrow. Surely you'll be recharged by then."

Sam laughed. "I think so."

"Good. Get lots of rest tonight and be sure you keep your hands outside the covers. I'll call you in the morning."

Sam spent the evening reading and went to bed early. He thought about what Howard had said about making a partner feel like an equal and decided it was excellent advice. He also thought back to that disastrous evening at Spencer's and cringed at the way he'd handled it. It's no wonder Toby reacted the way he did. You were insensitive Sam, and stupid. You've got to do better and do it soon. He fell asleep with a picture of Toby in his mind, thinking how much he liked being around him.

True to his word, Jay called at ten and said he'd be over in a half hour.

When Sam asked him about the dress of the day, Jay replied, "It's brunch, Sam. Wear anything you want. Go naked if you like." He laughed. "Yeah, naked would be good. See you soon, Sam."

When he hung up the phone, Sam broke out in a mischievous grin. He went into the bedroom, laid out the clothes he'd wear to brunch and then stripped. When Jay rang the bell, a very naked Sam opened the door. Jay's eyes lit up.

"Care to come in for a moment?" Sam asked, gently tugging on his pubic hair. "Maybe have a drink or… something?"

Jay laughed and pushed Sam back into the room. "I think I'll have the 'something'," he said, pulling Sam by the dick over to the couch. "Sit!" He then proceeded to kneel and give Sam a world class blow job.

It took a while – which made it all the better for Jay – because Sam couldn't seem to concentrate on it properly. When he finished Jay rocked back on his heels. "Good, Sam, very good." He stood and gave Sam a quick kiss and a smile. "Now then, you going to go to brunch that way? It'll wow them at Spencer's."

Sam shook his head. "I don't think Spencer's is ready for the naked me. Give me a minute, huh?"

After brunch, when they got back to Sam's place, Sam asked Jay if he wanted to come in.

Jay answered, "I don't think so, Sam. You seemed just a bit distracted this morning and I think maybe you need a nap or something. Oh, and by the way, I'm off to Paris tomorrow, maybe for as long as a month. I'll call when I get back, okay?"

Sam nodded, gave Jay a kiss, and went inside. He found himself a little chagrined that Jay had noticed how he couldn't concentrate that morning on the couch. It also bothered him that he himself didn't know why he was that way. Jay was very talented and had brought Sam great pleasure in the past. What the hell was going on with him now?

Nothing came to him so he pushed it to the back of his mind and went to the pool to swim laps. After an hour in the water he got out, put on his shorts and went home to shower. After the events of the morning he just wasn't in the mood for any locker room play.

That evening, Bob from Some Guys called and asked him to dinner on Thursday. "Our son Byron and his partner Matt want to show off their new kitchen and Matt plans to do something wonderful with a tenderloin of beef. And if you have a friend you want to bring along, please do."

Sam asked, "This going to be at Byron and Matt's home? We going to wear clothes?"

Bob laughed. "Yeah, we do that sometimes. Why? You got a shy friend?"

"Um... well, maybe. Can I let you know, later this evening or tomorrow?" Sam stammered.

"Sure. We're flexible. Is he cute?" Bob asked.

"Yeah, like a puppy. We just don't... ah... know each other that well yet; what can I tell you?" Sam said.

"Tell us you'll bring him along. We promise not to scare him off." Bob said.

After he said goodbye to Bob he called Toby, who answered on the second ring. When Sam told him about the invitation, Toby hesitated until Sam said the dinner would be at Byron and Matt's, not at the resort. Then he agreed. Sam called Bob back and accepted the invitation.

That night, just before going to sleep, Toby's hesitation kept floating around in Sam's mind. He can't be that shy. He's been around and he said he liked Some Guys. Maybe it's me. Maybe he's shy about being naked around me. No, that's silly. But I asked Bob where we'd be. Am I shy to be naked around Toby? He drifted off to sleep telling himself he'd never been shy about being naked with anybody. Still… something was going on.

* * * *

Sam went to a Prime Timers dinner at The Cedar Creek Inn on Tuesday. He went because he was really enjoying the group. It was kind of like being in an extended family and meeting new relatives at every meal and mixer. So far they'd all seemed like really nice guys.

When he got to the restaurant he looked over the name tags and saw Toby would be there as well. He smiled and headed for the bar.

When Toby arrived, Sam was well into his drink. "Hi," he said when Toby spotted him. "I wondered if you were going to make it. Rough day at work?"

Toby just rolled his eyes. "I think I need a drink."

Sam caught the attention of one of the waiters and he came over to take orders. Toby ordered a martini and Sam asked for one also. When the drinks came, Toby paid for both.

Sam smiled and said simply, "Thank you."

When it was time for the dinner to be served, Toby asked Sam to accompany him to his assigned table. When they found it, Toby went over to a red-headed guy with 'Zach' on his name tag and whispered something to him.

Zach looked up and grinned. "Sure," he said to Toby. "He's hot. No wonder you want to sit with him."

He got up, leaving two places together. Zach looked at Sam's name tag, saluted him with a knowing smile and went off to find the table Sam had been assigned to.

"You must know him," Sam observed when they were seated.

"From work," Toby replied. "He's fun and we sometimes come to these things together."

"He's also very good looking." Sam wondered if the odd feeling in the pit of his stomach might be jealousy.

He also wondered if Toby had ever slept with Zach but decided not to go there.

Sam and Toby found the dinner to be very pleasant and the other men at the table proved to be very interesting. Two of the guys still worked and one, who was a hair stylist, had some very funny stories to tell making the evening pass quickly.

After dessert, Sam mentioned the dinner on Thursday with Matt, Byron, Bob, and Roger.

"Yeah," Toby replied. "Sounds like fun. I've never met any of them but I do remember seeing Matt at the resort." He laughed. "But then, I imagine every man who's ever been to that place remembers Matt."

The little ache in the pit of Sam's stomach returned but he tried to ignore it. *This is getting ridiculous. I am not the jealous type!* He held Toby's chair for him and asked if he wanted to have a nightcap in the bar.

Toby looked at his watch. "Can't. Zach's riding with me and he goes in to work even earlier than I do." He smiled and gave Sam a quick kiss. "But I'll take a rain check."

Sam hugged him and sent the two of them on their way. Then he went into the bar where he found Matt Stevens entertaining several guys with stories from the Coroner's Office.

\* \* \* \*

Thursday was a beautiful day, bright, sunny and very warm. Sam spent a lot of it by the pool, reading and talking to whoever was there. He did almost an hour of laps in the afternoon, decided to shower at home and called it a day. Promptly at seven, armed with several bottles of excellent red wine, he and Toby pulled up in front of Matt and Byron's.

Sam introduced Toby and there were hugs all around. Once settled in the living room with drinks, Matt excused himself to tend to something in the kitchen.

"I understand you restored this," Toby said, indicating the entire house with a wave.

"Don't be modest, Byron," Bob said to his son "why don't you give them the fifty cent tour?"

"Well, if it won't bore you, sure, I'll show you around."

Sam and Toby both nodded. "It sure won't bore me," Sam said. "I'm in the process of restoring that place of mine. It'd be great to see one that's already been done."

"Oh yeah, Pop mentioned that. Bill Flint's doing it, right?"

"He's the one. He did this place too, didn't he?"

"Oh, yeah. He's some sort of genius magician. Expensive, but a genius magician nevertheless. Come on, I'll show you."

The house was exquisite. They were shown where the workmen had had to piece together bits of the old molding and then carve new molding to match. They also saw where, in the den, the men had taken seven coats of paint and varnish off the walls and found beautiful inlaid walnut paneling beneath it.

"Did you restore the bathrooms and kitchen?" Sam asked, thinking about his own house.

Byron laughed. "We love the old Craftsman style here but we like our comfort, too, so the answer is, no. The bathrooms and kitchen are modern and functional but we did attempt to blend them into the house as a whole. Come see."

They went into the master bathroom and it blew Sam away. The room had been paneled in marble of the same color as the light oak paneling in the den and the sinks had been set in a cabinet of the same design as the window seat in the bedroom. The shower was large enough to accommodate three or four men and had heads and nozzles everywhere.

Pointing to the shower, their host said, "Matt and I shower together and let me tell you, the shower in our room at the resort was a tight squeeze. This is wonderful and it even has an instant steam unit. Come on, I'll show you the kitchen."

As soon as they walked into the kitchen Toby said, "Oh, wow. This looks like a smaller version of the kitchen at the hotel!"

Matt looked up from the range and laughed. "Yes, and if I'd had the space we'd have the full sized version."

The room looked to be functional but handsome as well. The counter tops were white marble with oak-colored veining. The stove had six burners, four gas and two electric and a real charcoal grill stood to one side. There were also two large sinks for cleanup.

Dinner turned out, of course, to be marvelous: artichoke soufflés, tenderloin of beef with red wine sauce and fruit and custard in meringue shells.

After dinner, sitting in the living room with coffee and brandy, Roger asked if Sam had known the man who had committed suicide at Desert Pride. Sam admitted he had and, in fact, was the one who found him. "It was pretty awful, finding him like that. Now I can't seem to get the image of him out of my mind." He hesitated for a moment and then went on. "I also have the feeling there's something that isn't quite right about it all."

"What's that, Sam?" Roger asked.

"I don't know." He sighed. "I've thought and thought about it and I just can't put my finger on it. But something's gnawing at me. I suppose it'll come to me, eventually. Things like that usually do."

Later, taking Toby home, Sam couldn't stop talking about Matt and Byron's house and how well it had been restored. "I sure envy them that bathroom," he said. "The kitchen's nice too, but those bathrooms..."

"You know," Toby said, turning in the seat, "maybe it's time you took me out to see that house of yours. Maybe I can... I don't know, maybe I'll see something differently than you do."

Sam felt a swell of happiness but knew he needed to go slowly. "How about Saturday? You could take me to lunch at Tyler's and then I could play tour guide. Only don't expect anything like Sam and Matt's."

"I know. It's a different period, a different style." He hesitated for a beat. "Okay, it's a date. Come by around eleven and maybe we won't have to wait so long for a table at Tyler's."

To put frosting on it, at least in Sam's mind, Toby kissed him before getting out of the car.

# Chapter Ten

Sam didn't think Saturday would ever get there but, as it always did, it came right on schedule after Friday. Sam, of course, arrived early to pick up Toby, but found him ready. They arrived at Tyler's in time to find two tables left. They took the one by the railing even though the view was only of the parking lot. They had hamburgers, French fries and shared a chocolate milkshake.

"Thank you," Sam said, after Toby had paid and they were walking to the car. "I really enjoyed that," he grinned, "even if you did hog the milkshake."

Toby smiled, reached over and patted Sam's belly. "Just saving you from yourself, that's all."

"No fair," Sam whined. "I take care of myself. I go to the gym most every day."

Toby laughed. "Yeah, to play grab-ass in the showers. I know about that place."

Sam stopped and looked Toby in the eye. "I may play a little," he said in a very even tone of voice, "but I don't play that way. I…" his tone softened. "I have to be in love with a guy to do that."

Toby held his eyes. "I'm the same way, Sam." He shrugged. "Let's just leave it at that for now, okay?"

Sam nodded and unlocked the car.

At the house, the first thing they noticed was the wall. The workmen had started chipping off the plaster and it looked worse than it had before. Sam wondered if Bill's crew would have to replace the whole thing. Toby didn't think they would; if it was structurally okay they'd just give it a new coat of stucco.

If the outside looked bad, the inside of the house looked worse. A thick coating of plaster dust covered everything including the debris scattered on the floor. The new windows and doors had arrived but hadn't been installed yet and were stacked against one of the living room walls. There were tools strewn all over the place.

"Kind of a mess, don't you think?" Sam said. "Maybe we should come back, after they get the place cleaned up."

Toby shrugged. "A job like this is messy, especially when they're just tearing stuff out. It'll be better when they start putting it back together. Come on, let's look around."

When they got to the master bedroom, Sam took in the space with a wave of his arm. "I wish this was bigger," he said. "I want a king sized bed and I think that's going to make it kind of crowded in here. I'd also like space for a chair so I could sit in front of the fireplace and read."

"Why don't you tell that to the contractor?"

"Well…" Sam hesitated, thinking. "He seems so intent on restoring the place, making it the way it was when it was built. It would spoil it to change things around."

Toby disagreed. "Not if it's done right. For example, if you pushed that wall out six or eight feet, but did it the whole length of the house and then did it across the back too, you wouldn't change the aspect ratio of the house at all. It'd be just like it was – only bigger."

He took Sam by the hand and led him outside through a large hole in a wall where a door was being replaced. "See out here? You wouldn't lose anything, there's nothing out here but empty space."

Sam cocked his head, listening to Toby. *He's really getting excited about this. Maybe…* His thoughts were cut off when Toby started describing how the bathroom could be enlarged, too.

"It'd give you room for a huge shower. You could have one bigger than Byron and Matt's, and have one out here, as well." Toby grinned. "You'd love having an outdoor shower in the summer time."

He went on, leading Sam back into the house, showing him how the space created could be used to make the rooms bigger and more usable.

Finally Sam said, "Enough! Enough already. You've convinced me. Do you suppose you could convince Bill?"

Toby shook his head, "The contractor? Oh, no. That's your job. After all, it is your house and your money. And doing what I've suggested would not be cheap!"

"Okay, okay. But if it's possible and if he'll do it, will you talk to him? I won't be able to explain it the way you can. Please?"

Before Toby could say anything a shout came from the front door. "Sam? That you?"

Sam recognized the voice. "Yeah, it's me. Come on in, Andy."

Officer Andy, in uniform, picked his way through the living room. "Hi. I'm on patrol today and thought I'd stop in and see how things are coming along."

"As you see, things are a bit of a mess." He grinned. "We weren't expecting company." He turned to Toby. "Toby, Andy Koyle. Andy, my friend, Toby."

The two men shook hands and looked each other up and down.

Toby smiled, "Oh, yeah, I've heard about you. Didn't you once arrest Sam for draining his pool?"

Andy laughed. "Well, not quite but almost. Just trying to teach him to respect the law."

"Good luck!" Toby said.

"Toby's here to give me some ideas on the house," Sam said, ignoring both Andy's and Toby's comments. "And he's got some good ones, too."

Andy looked at Toby. "What sort of ideas?"

Toby briefly described what he and Sam had been discussing. Andy nodded thoughtfully and turned to Sam. "Sounds like he's on to something, Sam. He talked to your contractor?"

"Not yet. But he's promised to."

Toby gave Sam a sharp look but let it go. The men took a quick walk around the place and then Andy had to go. "I am, after all, on patrol, protecting the other folks around here, too."

As soon as Andy had gone, another shout came from the front door.

Tom from next door poked his head in. "Saw the police car out front. Anything wrong?"

"No. Just Officer Andy, checking on how things are going. How're you, Tom?"

"Good. Say, why don't you and your young friend come on over and have a drink with us. I know Dan would like to see you and he's probably looking for another excuse not to clean the garage."

"Oh, sorry, Tom. This is my friend, Toby. Toby, this is Tom, my next door neighbor." He turned to Toby. "Okay? You have time for a drink with the neighbors?"

Toby nodded and they went next door after locking the chain on the gate. When Tom opened the front door, Tige came bounding out, greeting everyone with doggie sniffs and requests for ear scratches.

They went through the house to the patio and the pool where Dan was halfheartedly steering a push broom around the deck.

After introductions had been made, he put the broom in a corner and said, "Got some special iced tea today. Orange flavored. You guys up for it?""

While Dan made the drinks Toby went over to the pool and put his hand in the water. "Oh, man, that's wonderful. You run the heater all winter?"

Tom shook his head. "Not on your life, young man. Couldn't afford that. No, we have solar heat so it's up to around eighty what with this warm weather. Dan's been in it already but not me. Not until the water gets up around eighty-five or ninety."

Toby tested the water again. "You going to have solar heat, Sam? I mean, if they ever finish your pool."

Sam laughed. "I never thought about it but seeing this, I guess I will. Have to talk to Bill about it."

When the tea was served, they sat in the shade, enjoying lazy conversation. Tige, who obviously had fallen in love with Toby, spent much of the time with his head in Toby's lap. Dan said Tige thought of himself as a lapdog but couldn't figure out how to actually get into somebody's lap. Toby laughed said he was thankful for that.

Around five, it grew cool so they went inside and Tom put out some snack mix and scotch. At six, Sam suggested they all go to Boscoso's for dinner.

Later, after he had taken Toby home, Sam thought he'd spent one of the most pleasant days he'd had so far in Palm Springs. He also thought that being with Toby had had something to do with that.

                    * * * *

Sunday, after lunch, Sam went to the gym for an hour and then sat by the pool with a book. He hadn't read much before Pete Addison joined him.

"Pretty dull in the locker room this afternoon," Pete said, settling down on the lounge next to Sam. "No one to play with and no playing to watch." He sighed. "Guess I'll have to go spend some time on OlderButBetter and see if I can dig up someone to play with." He looked pointedly at Sam's dick. "Unless maybe you..."

Sam smiled. "Sorry, Pete. I have to go in pretty quick and clean up. Got invited to dinner."

"Lucky you. I've got no plans and a horny dick," Pete said.

"Hey, what's this 'Older but Better' place? New bar in town?" Sam asked.

Pete laughed. "The Internet, Sam. It's an Internet site. You should check it out. There are lots of guys our age – and some younger ones looking for guys our age."

"Really? Poor me, I'm not the least bit Internet literate. Don't even have a computer."

Pete looked surprised. "Horny guy like you? Without a computer? Sam, you need to come into the twenty-first century."

"So what goes on out there?"

"You look at pictures of guys, talk to them maybe, and if they're from around here and you like them, you make a date. Martin told me about it. He put his profile and some pictures on that site and Bingo! He had more bed partners than he knew what to do with. And that's saying something about Martin. But even a guy like me, looking for maybe more than just a guy to play with, can still get a date or two out of it and meet some nice guys."

"Well, good luck with it, Pete. I don't know that I'd ever get the hang of using a computer. I've always been pretty unhandy with technical stuff and frankly, never needed much of it. Not my thing."

Later, while Sam dressed for dinner with Duane and Howard, he wondered if Toby knew about OlderButBetter and if he'd ever looked at it or… he put the thought out of his mind.

Duane answered the door and gave Sam a hug. "Howard's in the kitchen working his magic on some stuffed pork chops. Let's go and keep him company."

Howard greeted Sam with another hug and waved him over to a couch that had been installed in what had been a breakfast nook. Duane made drinks for them and then sat next to Sam.

Sam toasted him. "Hey, this is really good, having a couch in the kitchen."

Howard nodded at Duane. "It was his idea. He wanted to keep me company while I cooked. We never used the table and stuff that was there and it made a perfect place for that sofa."

Duane looked up and grinned. "I once thought I might learn to cook by watching Howard but nothing much happened except that Howard got watched a lot and I got horny. Sometimes so horny that dinner got burned."

"Duane! You don't have to give away all our secrets."

Duane winked at him. "Well, didn't it?"

Howard laughed. "Yes, but we don't want Sam here to think we're perverted or anything."

"Not on your life," Sam said. "I think it's wonderful. I wish I had someone who'd burn dinner for me once in a while."

The dinner – unburned – was excellent and the conversation lively. Both Howard and Duane were interesting people and had great stories to tell; Howard about teaching and Duane about the emergency room. They drew Sam out, asking about his life with Harry and what it was like working for an important Hollywood producer. Sam said that it had mostly been a job but he did manage to conjure up a few stories.

Over dessert Duane looked at Sam, "Howard said you might be interested in how we handle sex in our relationship. Right?"

"Uh... well... look, I don't want to pry or anything but yeah. I guess I am interested in how you guys handle the sex thing. I mean..." Sam shrugged and grinned at them. "Oh hell, look, I'm interested in a guy, a young guy, about your age, Duane, and I haven't a clue what he thinks about sex, what anyone your age thinks about it."

Duane laughed. "What does a guy my age think about sex? The same things you think about it. It's fun, it's sometimes serious, and it always feels really good."

"Well, yeah, that's what I think, too, but how..."

Duane interrupted. "I'm sorry, Sam. That was kind of flip but it actually does summarize how we deal with it. You know, everyone thinks an older man like Howard somehow doesn't need – or want – sex as much as a guy my age. Not true, Sam. Not true at all. Think about yourself. Don't you need or want sex fairly often? We do. Howard and I have sex more often than lots of guys my age." He laughed. "We talk a lot down at the E.R. when we're not busy. Mostly about sex."

"But what do you do about other men? Guys who come on to you, like over in the gym. What do you do about them?"

Duane chuckled. "So that's your worry. Well, I'll tell you Sam, we have a philosophy about that. First of all, neither of us was a virgin when we got together even though my experience was fairly sparse compared to Howard's. But high school boys do get around and I had had probably more than my share of sex. In our first year together, Howard and I realized there are three kinds of sex. Well, actually five or six kinds, I guess, but we don't have anything to do with the more violent types or with sex as punishment."

"Thank God," Howard said quietly.

"Anyway, there's sex for fun, sex for relief, and sex for making love. And we do all three."

Howard spoke up. "They're all kind of intertwined, Sam. For example, jerking off in the shower brings relief but it's fun as well. Making love is often all three rolled up into one."

"But what about other guys. Like Mike Armstrong who always wants to blow guys in the shower?"

"Our rule," Howard said, "is once with anybody, twice maybe. Three times and you'd have to be pretty special. Mike falls into the last category."

"And one other thing," Duane said, "and this is a pretty important part of dealing with other guys. It's always a package deal."

"What do you mean, package deal?" Sam asked.

Duane sipped at his wine. "Just that. Mike is out of luck if one of us is in the showers alone. If he wants to blow one of us, he blows both of us. If I meet up with someone at the hospital and we're hot for each other, he comes home with me to Howard. We're a team and we always play as a team."

Howard grinned. "It keeps life interesting, Sam. Neither one of us wanted to give up playing, and this solves the problem for us. Don't get me wrong, it won't work for everyone. Take Mark and Jeff for instance. They're all they need. Oh, they look, but I've never heard of them touching. That's what works for them. It probably wouldn't work for us."

"The most important part?" Duane put down his cup. "The most important part is talking about it. Figuring out what works for you and your partner."

"And things change," Howard added. "Never be afraid of things changing. Just make damn sure your partner knows they're changing and can agree with where they're going"

"Okay, that's enough philosophy for one night," Duane said, getting up from the table. "Bring your wine glasses, gentlemen, and keep me company while I do the dishes." He grinned at Sam. "That's another one of our compromises. He cooks, I clean."

Later, home in bed, Sam wondered if he could work out a relationship as good as Howard and Duane's. With Harry he'd never had to worry about such things. To start with, he'd been just an employee of Harry's and he did what Harry wanted. Later, well, later Sam did pretty much as he wanted. He guessed Harry had trained him well and he wondered how it would have worked, putting passion into the mix.

# Chapter Eleven

Sam went out to the house on Monday to talk to Bill about Toby's ideas. Bill seemed open to the changes but a little skeptical. "We can do whatever you want, Sam, but I'm not real sure about just what it is you're getting at."

"Yeah, Bill, I know I'm not making it very clear. It all sounded so easy when Toby talked about it."

"Who's Toby? An architect?"

"He's an accountant, Bill. But he has an eye for things, I think. Tell you what. Maybe I can get him out here to explain this stuff. But he works, so it'd have to be on Saturday. That okay?"

"Sure, but it'll have to be soon. I've found some landscapers who really seem to know their stuff and I want to get them started on layouts."

"This Saturday, I promise."

"Make it in the afternoon, will you? I'm playing ball with my boy in the morning."

That evening, Sam called Toby and asked him if he could spare the time on Saturday.

"I suppose I can," Toby said with an edge of dubiousness to his voice. Then he brightened. "If you don't have anything else planned, how about afterwards I come to your place and maybe cook dinner for us?"

"Wonderful," Sam said. "I'll lay in a supply of gin."

The next day Sam went shopping for some good martini glasses. He found small Baccarat tumblers that seemed perfect and bought a dozen. Then he went to Jensen's and found some very good caviar. What the hell, if you're going to do it, do it right. He also bought eggs and sweet onions for garnish.

By Thursday however, Sam started to have second thoughts, and on Friday he put the glasses in the back of the cupboard and gave the caviar to Duane and Howard as a thank you gift. Then he went out and bought some crackers and herb cheese.

Toby arrived at Sam's a little after one on Saturday. They took the groceries and clean clothes for Toby in and put them away before leaving for the house. Bill was already there when they arrived.

"Hi, guys," he said when they got out of Sam's car. He offered his hand to Toby. "You must be Toby," he said. "Sam's been carrying on about your ideas but, being the strong, silent type, he can't seem to articulate them." He laughed and turned to Sam. "I brought Mary along to make some drawings. She's out back taking some measurements." He turned to Toby. "Mary's my wife. She's got a real knack for drawing; does all the plans I have to give City Hall."

Toby nodded. "Well, I hope she doesn't mind a novice. I think maybe Sam has blown this thing all out of proportion." He shrugged. "It's just a couple of ideas."

Bill put his hand on Toby's shoulder. "Hey, we're open to anything so long as Sam approves. Come on, let's go see how the measuring is coming along."

They went around the house and Bill introduced them to Mary who turned out to be a slender, wiry woman somewhere in her late thirties. If she had makeup on they couldn't tell and her hair had been cut short, in a sensible, easy style. She had a bright smile of greeting and Sam liked her immediately.

When Toby suggested the back and side walls could be pushed out by eight feet Bill scratched his head and made a tour down one side and across the back. "Could be," he said. "Could be. It wouldn't really change the house, would it? Just make it bigger."

"Toby's words exactly," Sam said with a smile.

Mary looked at her clipboard and made a couple of quick calculations. "So what do you plan to do with roughly 850 square feet of new space?"

"Well, for one thing," Toby said with a wink at Sam, "put in a bigger shower."

Mary laughed. "That's one hell of a shower, my friend. You going to bring in a twelve inch water main?"

Toby shook his head. "I don't think he needs a shower quite that big. But it would give him a bigger kitchen and dining room as well as some closet space. Come on, I'll show you."

For the next couple of hours Toby described his ideas, Mary made sketches and took measurements and Sam and Bill listened, nodding their heads and keeping quiet. When they were finished, they went inside and stood where the larger kitchen would be.

"So what do you envision doing in here? It's not particularly well designed as it is and you'll have to be careful not to waste the new space."

Toby shook his head and deferred to Sam who said, "Oh, no you don't. You cook, I don't." He turned to Mary and Bill. "Whatever he wants is what we'll do." He smiled. "Maybe I'll get a few home cooked meals out of it."

Toby looked dubious but went on to point out some things he thought needed to be included looking at Sam for confirmation with every suggestion. Finally Mary, realizing the situation, said, "Okay guys, that's enough for now. Why don't you spend some time together on it and we'll look at it again in a couple of weeks."

They agreed and called it a day.

\*\*\*\*

Back at the condo, they each had a shower and got into clean clothes. Sam mixed martinis while Toby washed lettuce.

"You know," Sam said, handing Toby his drink, "it sure would be nice to have a sofa or at least an easy chair in here." He went on to describe the way Howard and Duane had arranged their kitchen. "It was really nice, you know?

Howard did what he had to do and we could still be with him, keep him in the conversation."

"Sounds like a nice arrangement, Sam, except you don't cook. What was it you said, 'I can boil water but have no idea what to do next?'"

"Aw, come on, I can scramble eggs, I make a mean piece of toast, all that stuff."

"You're going to invite someone over for scrambled eggs and toast?"

Sam twisted his face into a leer. "Well, maybe they stayed over."

Toby dried his hands and tasted his drink. "If they stayed over, you should take them out to a fancy breakfast. It's the least you could do," he said with a grin.

Sam winked. "Hey, I'm so good maybe they should take me out to breakfast."

The dinner of grilled salmon with horseradish, blue cheese potatoes and a salad made Sam very happy.

"That was really good, Toby," Sam said, clearing the table. "You want to do it all over again tomorrow night?"

Toby shook his head. "Sorry, Sam, not only would you be tired of it two nights in a row, but I'll be in Denver tomorrow night."

"Oh, no, not another one of those conferences. What do they talk about at those things, anyway?"

Toby put ice in their glasses while Sam loaded the dishwasher. "You want another one?" Sam nodded. "What they talk about are very important, if somewhat esoteric, accounting issues. And at this one, I'll have you know, I'm giving a presentation."

Sam turned from the dishwasher. "Hey, I'm impressed," he said seriously. "What's it about?"

Toby laughed. "You don't want to know. In the living room, Sam?"

Sam looked up. "Yeah. I'm almost finished here."

Sam lit the fire and sat on the opposite end of the couch from Toby.

After a few moments of silence, Sam sighed. "I think, Toby, it's time we talked about the elephants in the room. Both of them."

Toby looked suddenly wary. "What elephants?"

Sam took a deep breath. "One of them is money. My money. Look, Toby, we all have things we bring to a relationship. In my case, mostly, it's money. I know it bugs you when I do things you think are extravagant, especially when I do them for you."

"No, Sam," Toby said quietly, "it's just..."

"Hear me out, Toby. I know that Jack used money – and a handsome boy's inexperience – to buy you."

Toby looked up sharply, but didn't say anything.

"Or at least try to buy you," Sam went on. "But I'm not Jack, Toby. I'm me and it would never occur to me to try and buy someone. If they don't like me for me, they don't, and nothing's going to change that, especially not money."

He suddenly thought about what Howard had said and shifted his approach somewhat. "Consider today, Toby. You have vision and see how things can fit together. I don't. For God's sake, I couldn't even explain to Bill what I wanted to do. But you could. You made it clear and simple. So you bring that talent to the relationship. I bring money – which, never forget, I had very little to do with acquiring."

"Well, you took care of Harry. That had to count for something."

"I guess. Sure, I used what talents I had, just as you used yours today with Bill and Mary. That's what I bring to the relationship..."

Toby shook his head. "Wait a minute, Sam. You keep talking about a relationship. Do we have one of those?"

Sam finished his drink in a gulp. "That, young man, is the other elephant in the room." He took a deep breath and just said it out. "Damn it, Toby, I've gone and fallen in love with you. There, I've said it." He grinned. "And I'm glad!"

Toby finished his drink, got up, and took Sam's glass. "I need another. You?"

Sam nodded, wondering if he'd just blown the whole deal.

When Toby came back with the drinks he again sat on the end of the couch, opposite Sam. He looked Sam squarely in the eye and said, "That's quite an elephant, Sam. Now you get to hear my side of all this."

He took a sip of his drink and thought for a moment. "The money thing isn't as important as you think, Sam." He waved off Sam's attempt at a response and went on. "I know I had a very bad night in that restaurant and perhaps I blew it all out of proportion. I'm sorry for that, but I really did think you were in some way trying to buy me, trying to get me to do something… well, I see now that you weren't, but at the time…"

Sam nodded and smiled but wisely remained silent.

"Then there was the painting and the sculpture. I really liked both of them, wanted both of them, but I'd have been pissed as all hell if you'd bought them, especially if you'd bought them for me. I know that's silly and probably self-defeating, but there you are." He looked a little wistful, Sam thought. Then he laughed. "It'd be different today, I guess. I mean now that…" He took a large sip of his drink.

Sam kept his own counsel even though it took a great effort to keep his mouth shut.

"I've got to think about this, Sam. I really do." He looked up and smiled. "And Jumbo, the other elephant, I need to think about him, too. I think sometimes you're all I would ever want in life and then I think…" He sighed. "I don't know, Sam."

"Is it because I'm so much older than you?"

"Don't ever go there Sam. Don't. I've always liked men older than me because they knew so much more than me and could teach me things. Even Jack taught me things, some of which weren't exactly what a nineteen-year-old boy needs to know. So no, it isn't our age difference. It's not anything. Well, except that it's so sudden. I never had a clue…"

"That one's my problem, I guess. But it never occurred to me that I was being subtle. I just didn't want to scare you away."

"Well, you didn't, Sam, you didn't. I just need some time to think, to sort things out." He laughed. "I suppose Denver will be a nice, quiet place to do that." He stood. "For now, I need to be by myself."

He picked up the drink glasses and took them into the kitchen. Sam followed.

"So what..."

Toby smiled. "Tell you what, Sam. I'm back Thursday evening. Why don't you make reservations somewhere for Friday night. If I can't figure this thing out in a week, I'll never figure it out. Okay? No place where I have to wear a tie."

Sam nodded. "I'm sorry to..."

Toby stopped him with a finger across his lips. "Don't ever be sorry, Sam."

A quick kiss and he was out the door.

Sam fixed himself another martini – actually just gin on the rocks – and went up to his bedroom balcony to brood. When that became dull he went to bed.

\* \* \* \*

On Sunday, Sam went down to the pool and swam laps until he couldn't swim any more. Afterward he didn't go into the locker room but showered at home, by himself.

On Monday he called Alistair, in Los Angeles. He also saw Dr. Binns, a physician recommended by one of the men at the complex.

On Tuesday, he drove up to L.A. and met with Alistair in his office. Alistair came out from behind his desk and drew Sam in to a hug. "Good to see you, Sam," he said. "How long has it been?"

"Seems like a long time," Sam said with a grin.

Alistair asked how life had been treating him in Palm Springs, how he liked his new condo and, most of all, how the house was coming. "It must be something, judging from the money you're spending on it."

Sam laughed. "Alistair, to coin a phrase, you ain't seen nothin' yet."

"Well, as long as it isn't frivolous and you're going to get something worthwhile out of it." He looked at the clock on his desk. "By the way, I've taken the liberty of ordering lunch for us in my little dining room. I think you'll enjoy it." He paused for a moment before going on. "But we have an hour or so before lunch is served, so, what can I do for you? You weren't very forthcoming when we spoke on the phone yesterday."

Sam took a deep breath and launched himself into the story of Toby. Everything, including Toby's background, his time with Jack, the age difference, and the fact that he'd fallen in love.

When Sam finished, Alistair smiled. "How long have you been rehearsing that speech, Sam? It was very well done."

Sam blushed. "Last night, on the freeway this morning. Look, Alistair, I don't want you to think this is just some little infatuation that will play itself out in a few months. I really have fallen for this man and I think – I hope – he has done the same with me."

"I'm still not sure as to why you've told me all this. Are you looking for my blessing? Or is it… oh, yes, the boy's background. This is about money, isn't it?"

Sam nodded. "Alistair, I have to make him comfortable. With me, with the money I have, with his place in my life."

"So you want to settle some money on him." He looked up at the ceiling for a moment. "How much?"

Sam shook his head. "I don't know. I don't even know how to do it. That's why I'm here."

Alistair looked at his clock. "Let me think about this for a bit, Sam. Perhaps I can see something here that your love glazed eyes can't. And while I'm thinking, I believe it's time for lunch." He stood. "Shall we?"

They went into Alistair's 'little' dining room where the table was set with heavy silver, German china, and crystal. They were served lobster quiche and a salad of baby greens dressed with vinaigrette.

After sampling both, Sam looked up at Alistair and said, "Where'd you find him?"

Alistair got a hearty laugh out of that. "What tipped you off?"

Sam held up his fork. "The dressing on the salad. No one can make dressing like that but Albert."

"You have a very good palate, Sam. And a good memory, too." He went on to say that when the house in Beverly Hills had been closed up, he simply couldn't let a gem like Albert get lost so he offered him a job managing the kitchen for the firm. Albert had transformed the food from merely good into exquisite and had a job for as long as he wanted. "Unless you're going to try to lure him away to Palm Springs."

Sam shook his head. "That's another thing about Toby. He cooks. Not as well as Albert but I bet he will, someday."

After lunch, which included a chocolate mousse for dessert, Alistair took Sam back into the kitchen where Sam hugged Albert, thanking him for doing that particular lunch. Albert looked very proud that Sam had noticed and remembered the food. It was a brief, but happy, reunion.

Back in his office, Alistair said, "Why don't you approach this as Harry did? Well, not quite, because you'll want to start right away and not wait for his birthday."

"You mean the presents Harry always gave me for my birthdays and Christmas?" He thought about it for a moment. "That might do it. He needs to be in a position that if, for any reason we split up, he won't be out in the cold, as it were. Good thinking, Alistair."

Alistair nodded and smiled. "Thank you. And since it will be in his name alone, and should either of you wish to terminate this relationship, he will have the means to live as he wishes. Also, rather than from the trust, I think you should take the gifts out of your personal account. In that way, he will not have a claim on any assets in the trust until you are ready to make him a trustee."

"More good thinking, Alistair." He paused. "You know, I don't really pay a lot of attention to that account. How much do you suppose it's worth?"

Alistair drew himself up in his chair. "At this firm we do not suppose. We either know or we find out."

Sam blushed. "Sorry. I wasn't thinking."

"Around eight million. Eight million, three hundred and two thousand, fifty-three dollars and seventy cents as of opening of the market this morning, to be exact," Alistair said. "The first gift should probably be in the five hundred thousand range. It will, of course, be his sole property. We'll take care of the mechanics of it."

"Thank you," Sam said gratefully. "How soon?"

Alistair leaned back in his chair and fixed Sam with a very serious expression. "Once you are California Registered Domestic Partners, Sam. That will give some legal standing to your partnership and demonstrate to everyone concerned the depth of your commitment to one another."

Sam nodded. "You think of everything, Alistair. Thank you. I'll let you know if it works out as I hope it will."

"You're really serious about this man, aren't you, Sam? In light of that, I think we should do a background check on him. Like was done on you, just to make sure there aren't any sticky little situations that could come up and haunt us."

"On me? Harry had a background check done on me?"

"Sam, Harry was a man of wealth and importance. You could have been anyone, from a blackmailer to a serial killer to a saint. Of course he did."

Sam smiled. "And?"

"And you turned out to be a sweet kid who couldn't keep a job. Not a saint, mind you, but not evil either." He laughed. "If I'd been in Harry's place I probably wouldn't have hired you but for some reason he believed in you. I now see why."

Sam shrugged. "Well, do as you think necessary but unless Toby's some sort of arch criminal, keep his background to yourself. I want to learn about him by being with him and loving him."

After leaving Alistair, Sam drove by the Beverly Hills house. The front garden was well tended and it actually looked as if somebody lived there. He made a mental note to thank Alistair for seeing to it that it was kept up so well. He also thought he should bring Toby here some day, to see if he wanted to live in it. If he didn't, they'd probably sell it.

On the way back to Palm Springs, he thought a lot about the things Alistair had said, especially about registering a partnership. He found he liked the idea of that. He hoped Toby would as well.

> \* \* \* \*

Back in Palm Springs on Wednesday he went out to the house to see what might be going on. When he got there Bill said he'd found something Sam should see. The something turned out to be a fourteen inch brass plaque inscribed with the words Devá Shaante.

"Found it on the wall by the front gate," Bill said. "It was plastered over, probably had been for years. I guess someone, probably the first owner, named the house and had the plaque made and put on the wall. I wonder what it means?"

Sam looked closely at it. "For that matter, what language is it? I've never seen words like that."

"Well, anyway," Bill laughed, "your house has a name. You should have this cleaned up and we'll mount it when we re-plaster the wall. Outside the plaster."

Sam looked at the plaque critically. "What if it means Whore House in some language everyone knows but us?"

"Well, then you won't lack for company." Bill's tone changed. "Hey, how's it going with that guy you brought around? Mary thought he was great. You going to try to hold on to him for a while?"

Sam smiled. "I'm gonna do my damnedest to hold on to him. Forever."

"Good. As Mary said, he's a keeper." He looked at the plaque again. "Why don't you take this down to the library or something? Maybe they can identify the language."

"Good idea, Bill. I'll do that." Sam replied.

Tom Wacker wandered up along with Tige, who immediately lodged his nose in Sam's crotch. "What's up, gents?" he asked, pulling Tige back.

"Hey, just the man I needed to see," Sam said, holding out the plaque. "You ever seen this before?"

Tom took it and tilted it back and forth in the light. "Can't say that I have," he said. "Where'd it come from?"

"Off the wall, over by the gate," Bill said. "It was plastered over. I think it's a name somebody once gave to the house."

"Can't prove it by me," Tom said. "Jack and Larry just called it 'the place.' I'm sure they didn't have a formal name for it, much less one in some strange language. Let me show it to Dan, maybe he can make something out of it when he finishes his nap."

"Sure, Tom. And if he can't make anything of it then maybe I'll take it down to the library."

After Tom left with Tige, Sam and Bill spent the next hour walking around the house, discussing the logistics of extending the roof eight feet and building new outside walls that would be just like the originals. Sam tucked the idea of the plaque in the back of his mind but didn't think about it much.

# Chapter Twelve

Sam spent the next day worrying about Toby and how he might be feeling. Damn it, I can't let this get to me he thought. A little voice in the back of his head laughed, But you will. You've really done it this time, Sam Davis. You've gone and fallen in love, something you said you'd never do again after Joel.

Damn it," Sam said aloud. "What the hell am I doing?" Not even the little voice in his head had an answer.

Toby called Thursday evening to let Sam know he was home. "We still on for tomorrow?"

"Oh yeah. We have seven-thirty reservations at Shame on the Moon. Come by here for a drink first if you like. Okay?"

"Sure. I'd like that."

Toby called again Friday afternoon saying he'd have to beg off on the pre-dinner drink. "My goal is now to get there by seven."

Sam paced his living room for a very long fifteen minutes but Toby made it by quarter after.

At the restaurant they were hugged by Ginger, the hostess. "Glad to see you back, Sam and Toby. Good to see you." There was a card on their table, again welcoming them by name.

"A class operation," Toby said, passing the card to Sam.

They had the same waiter, Dennis. They ordered Beefeater martinis.

"You haven't told me, how was Denver?"

"Cool, I thought, for May. I didn't get around much, except for some walks in the park across from the hotel." He looked up and smiled. "The paper was well received, though. I got lots of compliments on it."

The drinks were served. Toby touched his glass to Sam's and said simply, "To us."

Sam had a sudden catch in his throat. "Really? There's going to be an us?"

"If you still want to give it a shot, Sam."

Sam let out a breath he hadn't known he was holding. "Yes, Toby. I still want to give it a shot." He slipped his hand under the table and rested it on Toby's thigh. Toby covered it with his own and grinned.

They talked trivia until dinner was served and Sam finally trusted himself enough to say, "So, the thinking went as well as the paper, huh?"

Toby laid down his fork and looked Sam in the eye. "Better. I realized two things, Sam." He held up a finger. "First of all, I guess I had been confusing you with Jack. Not that you're anything alike but somehow I was seeing you as trying to do the same things he did. Thinking it through, I know that's not true. You're you and Jack… isn't."

He held up a second finger. "Second, I realized I had fallen in love with you and I want to be with you."

Under the table Sam squeezed Toby's thigh. "Eat your dinner, Toby. It's the first of so many wonderful dinners we're going to share."

Toby smiled. "Not to mention I'm probably going to need my strength."

They skipped dessert and asked for the check. When Sam paid it he added a nice tip and then, as they were leaving, slipped Dennis a hundred dollars, saying, "Thank you. It's been the best dinner of my life."

When they got home – Odd, I've never really thought of this as home – Sam dug out the Baccarat glasses and poured a little brandy into each of them. "For you," Sam said, holding the drink out to Toby. "The glass, too. I bought them for you."

"That was pretty confident, wasn't it, Sam?" Toby said with a laugh. "And here I thought I was a mystery to you."

"You are. Always will be, probably. But I bought the glasses a while ago and then put them away because I thought you might think... Well, I don't know what you might have thought but I put them away."

Toby held his glass up and studied it. "They're beautiful, Sam. Thank you."

By unspoken agreement they took the brandy upstairs to the bedroom. Standing at the foot of the bed Sam felt suddenly shy and tried to cover it by asking Toby which side of the bed he slept on.

"I guess over there," he said, pointing, "on the left. But I'm probably flexible if that's your side."

Sam went over to the right side and carefully set his brandy on the bedside table. Then he went back to the foot of the bed and took Toby in his arms. "See," he said, kissing him, "see how compatible we are? I've always slept on the other side."

They stood at the end of the bed until Toby finally said it. "Let's go to bed, Sam."

They went to their respective sides and pulled down the spread. Starting to undress, Sam felt a little shy because he was already erect. Glancing at Toby, Sam smiled when he saw that Toby was in the same state.

When they were both down to their underwear, Sam laughed and turned, facing Toby. "Well," he said, "here it is, the whole package." He pushed his briefs down and stepped out of them. "And in case you're wondering," he added, flexing his erection, "this was brought on by you." He climbed into bed and pulled the sheet over him.

Toby grinned, pushed down his boxers and took his hard dick in hand. "Funny the effect we seem to have on each other." He slipped under the sheet and met Sam in the middle.

"You are so beautiful," Sam said, pulling Toby on top of him. "Stubble and all." He touched Toby on the cheek and pulled back, looking at him. "Hey, stubble. Don't you always shave for those meetings?"

Toby kissed him. "I used to. But you know what, Sam? I decided to be me and if anyone really cares then the hell with them. I like me this way."

"So do I. You're very sexy that way. Handsome, just like what's-his-name on that police thing." They held each other for a long time. "Only sexier."

They went back to kissing and Toby gently began to hump Sam, rubbing his dick against Sam's. They quickly lost themselves in the pleasure of it, and in each other. There was no subtlety or artifice about it. The pleasure and pressure built and when they were ready... well, they were ready. They exploded almost at the same time and went to the heights together.

Later, cleaned up, they lay on their sides, facing each other, and Sam gently petted Toby's buns.

"Sam? When's the last time you were tested?"

Sam pulled back and looked in Toby's eyes. "Monday."

"And?"

Sam smiled. "Negative. You?"

"Tuesday." Toby kissed Sam briefly. "Negative, like you."

Sam lifted himself up on his elbow. "Who's going to be first?"

Toby leaned up and put his lips to Sam's. "Me. I want you inside me. Now."

Sam gently turned him. "Like this?"

Toby nodded.

Sam tried to be slow about it but found it hard to control his own pleasure. When it was over and they had both had their orgasms, Toby whispered, "That was wonderful, Sam." And he said it for the first time: "I love you Sam."

They dozed for a short time and then Sam had the pleasure. "You're wonderful, Toby," Sam said when it was over. "I love you. Now and forever."

When they woke at nine-thirty, they used the toilet together, one standing on each side, each frankly watching the other. Once relieved, they got in the shower together.

"See, Toby? This is why we need a big shower at the house. Give us more room to move around. And some grab bars to help me get down on my knees."

He managed it though, even without the grab bars. So did Toby, but with somewhat more grace.

They went to The Rock Garden for breakfast and had champagne with their scrambled eggs. Afterword they went to Toby's apartment so he could get a couple of changes of clothes. Then they went back to the condo, remade the bed and had a long nap. They even managed to get a little sleep.

Toby wanted to cook for dinner so they went to see what Jensen's, an upscale grocery, had to offer.

      \* \* \* \*

Sunday went about as Saturday had except they didn't have to go to Toby's for clothes. The biggest adjustment came on Monday morning when the alarm went off at six-thirty. Sam wasn't at all used to an alarm waking him; he normally woke up when he was ready. Now that he was with Toby, neither of them were getting enough sleep.

"Call in sick," Sam said, shutting off the alarm.

"No, Sam. I have to get up," Toby answered, kissing him. "You go back to sleep and I'll let myself out." He rolled out of bed and went into the bathroom.

Dressed, Toby stood in front of the mirror knotting his tie when Sam appeared, carrying a small tray with two steaming cups of coffee on it. He placed one on the dresser in front of Toby and sipped from the other.

"Good morning," Sam said.

Toby looked at him in the mirror. "You didn't have to do this," he said, lifting the cup. "We have coffee at the hotel."

Sam hadn't bothered with clothes and sat on the bed, leaning against the pillows "I couldn't send you out into the cold, cruel world without a caffeine fix, could I?" He smiled. "Do you know how handsome you are in that suit and tie?"

Toby finished with the tie and turned to Sam. "Do you know how handsome you are, sitting there, naked, on that bed?" His eyes twinkled. "I don't think you should ever wear clothes."

"You want me naked, you'll get me naked." He put his coffee on the bedside table. "Of course, there'll be talk, especially in the grocery store and at the gas station."

Toby laughed. "Well, maybe sometimes." He took a mouthful of coffee and held it for a moment. Then, all in one fluid motion, he swallowed and took Sam's dick in his mouth. Sam groaned and immediately became hard as his dick was heated by Toby's mouth. "There," Toby said when he came up for air, "that'll give you something to think about while I'm slaving over a hot hotel." He picked up his wallet and keys and started to leave.

"Hey, you aren't going to leave me like this, are you?" Sam whined.

Toby grinned. "I am. And you'd better be in the same condition when I get home."

Sam thought about finishing the job with his hand but decided against it because he wanted to save it for Toby. Instead he got up, finished his coffee, and took a shower.

During the day Sam went to a key shop and had keys to the condo and his car made for Toby and then he drove out to Palm Desert where he bought a silver key ring at Tiffany. Late in the afternoon he went to Jensen's and bought things for dinner that needed only to be put in a hot oven for a while. Then he went home, put the food in the refrigerator, showered again, and didn't dress but did spend a little time playing with himself.

When Toby rang the bell Sam opened the door in all his glory. "Well," he said to Toby's surprised expression, "you said you wanted me in the same condition I was in when you left." He flexed his erection. "So here I am, just as you left me."

Toby's clothes ended up in a pile on the floor and the couch substituted for the bed.

And so the week went. They managed to calm down enough to go to the Prime Timers mixer at Sidewinders on Tuesday night where everybody immediately recognized that they were now a couple. For the rest of it they stayed home, got to know each other, and made love. During the day Sam went out to the house, went to the gym – but not to the locker or steam rooms – and shopped for things they could have for dinner which Toby wouldn't have to spend time cooking.

\* \* \* \*

On Wednesday Sam ran into Duane at the gym and on impulse invited Howard and him to dinner Sunday. He'd planned to take them all out but Toby nixed that when Sam told him about it.

"Let's have dinner here," Toby said. "I can put something together and besides, we really need to spend some time out of bed." He said this while he and Sam were having a dinner of seafood pasta – in bed.

"I guess you're right," Sam said with a smile. "Although I sure have enjoyed the past week, having you all to myself in the evening. But," he laid his plate aside, "everything changes, I suppose."

Toby kissed him. "Not everything."

\* \* \* \*

On Saturday morning, after a breakfast of corn pancakes and sausage, Sam and Toby went out to the house. Sam wanted Toby to look carefully at the space that would be the new kitchen and bathrooms and come up with some ideas as to how they should be arranged. Bill said he'd need that in a couple of weeks, to plan for the electrical and plumbing.

When they were standing in the space where the kitchen would go, Sam said, "The only thing I know that I really want is space for a couch and coffee table. Maybe with a reading lamp. Kind of like Howard and Duane have."

"They have a couch in their kitchen?" Toby asked.

"Remember? I told you about that. It's a place where Duane can sit and be with Howard when he's cooking. And, often Howard sits there while Duane is cleaning up. When they have a guest he can be there too so Howard doesn't get left out of the conversation" Sam said.

Toby looked thoughtful. "Sounds like a good idea, Sam. Maybe with a TV too, for watching the news." He looked around and walked over to the big window looking out on the yard. "Probably should go here, where there's light. We can't put cabinets here anyway because the window's too low."

Sam liked the idea. "Will it be near the gin?"

Toby laughed. "Well, if it were my kitchen I'd put the bar…"

Sam put his arms around Toby and said, very quietly, "It is your kitchen."

Toby pulled back so he could look at Sam. "Is it, Sam? Is this thing really going to work? I mean, after a while, after things cool off, will it still work? Will you still want me around?"

Sam leaned in to kiss Toby on the forehead. "You mean when some of the passion wears off? When we can look at each other without getting hard?" He stepped back and smiled. "You know? I think it will. I think we'll turn out to be each other's best friend. But you know what else?" The smile turned into a grin, "I don't think the passion will ever really wear off. I don't think we'll ever lose this need we have for each other."

Toby was still for a long time, looking at Sam. Then he, too, smiled. "You're right, Sam. I don't know how I know, but I know you're right." He laughed and put his hand to his crotch, outlining his erection through his shorts. "Someday this may not always happen when I look at you, but I'll still be in love with you."

Sam fumbled at his waist and let his shorts drop, showing off his own hard dick. "I'll take care of yours if you'll take care of mine."

They did it right there, on the dusty concrete floor and it was better than in a feather bed.

Afterwards they did get much of the kitchen laid out, including a bar for Sam and a couple of TV's for Toby.

* * * *

On Sunday Toby prepared pasta and a salad, things he could put together before Howard and Duane arrived. He deferred to Sam for the dessert, letting him buy some very good vanilla ice cream. He did, however, make a brandied chocolate sauce to go with it.

Sam thought the evening went well. Toby obviously liked the two men and he hoped Howard and Duane felt the same way. Once settled on the patio with drinks, the conversation flowed freely, without any of the tentativeness that so often happens when couples first meet. They talked about the weather, politics, and the Home Owner's Association. Toby shared some stories of things that happened at the hotel and Howard quoted, from memory, some of the weird thoughts his freshmen students had managed to commit to paper.

Over dinner, Toby asked Duane how he first got together with Howard. "If it's not too personal, that is."

Duane laughed. "You know, that's one of the great things about living here. When you've been naked with most of your neighbors – around the pool, in the gym, in the showers – there's very little that's too personal to talk about."

Toby smiled and glanced at Sam. "That's one aspect of living here I haven't experienced yet. But then I've only lived here for a week."

"You'll find out soon enough," Sam said with a grin.

"Yeah," Howard said, "a few Saturdays in the gym and a few Sundays around the pool and you'll know all about your neighbors. All about them."

Toby nodded and went back to the original question. "So, how did you two get together?"

A look passed between Duane and Howard and Howard shrugged. "Well," Duane began, "I've known, I guess all my life, that I'm gay. It was just something I knew."

"Tell them about coming out to your family," Howard said. "That will tell them about the kind of family you come from."

Duane sighed. "Okay, but I don't come off too well here." He looked at Toby. "When I was fourteen or so, and going through the worst of adolescence, I got a stubborn streak in me – about anything and everything. One day my dad asked me to do something, probably clean my room or something, I forget, and I just looked him in the eye and said no. He, rather reasonably I think, asked why. I yelled at him 'because I'm gay, damn it.' He fixed me with a look that

I could almost feel and quietly said, 'Being gay doesn't mean you have to be a prick.' Then he walked out."

Sam stifled a laugh. "Wise man, your father."

"Yeah, he was that. An hour or so later he came into my room and sat on my bed. He said something like 'You okay with this? The gay thing?' I said I was and were they going to throw me out? My dad just laughed and said only if I wanted them to, so I could hate them later."

"That's pretty understanding, don't you think?" Toby asked.

"Well, yeah. But it turned out that I wasn't the only one who'd known, or at least suspected, I was gay. So Dad had done some research, read a bunch of books and was pretty much prepared."

"That's the kind of family he comes from so you can see, any problems with us being together were on my part," Howard said. "Go on Duane, tell them how you seduced me."

Duane laughed. "It wasn't difficult. The day after graduation I went over to his house on the pretext of giving him a thank you gift. He let me in, I kicked the door shut, and kissed him."

Howard held up his hands. "Honest, guys, I didn't have a clue it was coming. But when it did... well, who was I to turn down something I'd had fantasies about for a year or more?" He shrugged. "So here we are, seven years later."

"That's pretty wonderful," Sam said. "I mean, a horny kid who had more on his mind than just getting his rocks off. And he waited, that's what gets to me." He winked at Duane. "Pretty impressive, guy."

Duane blushed. "Not really. I just went after what I wanted. But not until I thought I might actually be able to get it." He turned to Toby. "How about you? You out to your folks?"

"Yeah, pretty much."

"They okay with it? I mean, they didn't throw you out or anything, did they?"

Toby shrugged. "No, nothing like that. We just don't talk about it much." He stood and began clearing the table but Sam stopped him.

"Here now, you cooked, I'll clean up and then we'll have dessert. Anyone want a drink or some more wine?"

"I'll give you a hand," Howard said, getting up.

Later, after Howard and Duane had left, Sam asked Toby what he thought.

"They're nice. I like Howard, he's got a great sense of humor and Duane sure tells a good story." He smiled. "I wouldn't mind seeing more of them."

Sam laughed and made a grab for Toby's crotch. "You will. You'll see all of them."

"You know what I mean, Sam," he said, rubbing Sam's hand against his growing hardness. "But I wouldn't mind seeing all of them, either. They're both sexy guys."

"So are you," Sam said, pulling him towards the stairs. "So are you."

# Chapter Thirteen

On Tuesday they went to a Prime Timers mixer at a place neither of them had ever been. Once they managed to get up to the bar and get a couple of drinks, they checked the place out. It was called The Barracks and had a décor that was two parts military, three parts Western and five parts leather. They both found it kind of fun.

They ran into William and Red on the patio and struck up a conversation.

"Hey, Sam," William said, giving him a hug, "how's it going? You still like the place?"

Sam patted him on the shoulder. "Yeah, we do. It turned out to be a great place to live."

William whispered in his ear, "Do I detect a we?"

Sam pulled back and grinned. "You guys remember Toby, I think?"

Toby, who was shaking hands with Red, smiled and said, "Well, at least Red does." He turned and saluted William.

"How long?" William asked as he let go of Toby.

"Seems like forever," Sam said with a grin.

"Don't mind him," Toby said. "His mind is still in bed."

William asked Sam if he had gotten to known Martin, the man who had committed suicide at Desert Pride.

Sam said he had and in fact had been the one who found him. "It was pretty horrible, I can still see the paramedics pulling him out of that bathtub."

"It was kind of traumatic," Toby added, "finding him like that. You took it a pretty hard, didn't you, Sam?"

Sam nodded. "But the worst part is that I can't get it out of my head that there was something wrong."

"When a guy commits suicide, there's always something wrong," Red offered with a shrug.

"No, I don't mean that," Sam said. "I mean... I don't know. I can't put my finger on it but there's something wrong with the whole scene, some little part of it that doesn't make sense."

Red gave him a brief pat on the shoulder. "Well, it'll come to you. Probably in the middle of the night."

They talked some more and Red went to the bar and bought fresh drinks for all of them. Toby went to help carry them.

"You got plans this weekend?" William asked Sam.

"Memorial Day party at the condo, Monday," Sam answered. "That's about it, I guess. How about you guys? Want us to get you in to Desert Pride for the party?"

"What party?" Toby asked, handing Sam his drink.

"Monday," Sam replied. "Now you'll get to see if we really do have orgies around the pool."

"Sorry, we can't," William said. "I'm working and Red's starting a new project."

"Well, maybe next time." Sam and Toby finished their drinks and decided they didn't need another one so they hugged William and Red and took their leave.

The next day Sam went over to the house and Tom, out walking Tige, stopped by. He told Sam that Dan had found some information about the words on the plaque. He invited Sam – and Toby, once Sam told him they had moved in together – for dinner, so Dan could show off what he'd found. Sam accepted but only for drinks. He said he and Toby would really like to take them out to dinner, as thanks for being such good friends. It would have to be on Friday though, because Toby didn't like to be out late when he had to work the next day.

On Friday, when Sam and Toby arrived at Tom and Dan's, they were greeted with hugs and gin and tonics. "It's only May," Tom said, "but it's already too hot for martinis."

"Bring your drinks into the study," Dan said, "and I'll tell you what I found out about your house."

When they were settled in the den, Dan handed Sam the plaque. Dan had cleaned and polished it, buffing out most of the scratches made when it had been covered over with stucco. He'd also applied black enamel to the lettering, making it stand out.

"My God, Dan, this is beautiful," Sam said, getting up and going over to give him a kiss. "I didn't expect…"

"It's a beautiful piece," Dan said with some pride. "I couldn't leave it as it was. It'll look nice, back on your wall."

"Did you figure out what it means?"

"Actually, I did," Dan said. "I did some searching around on the Internet and found that the words are Sanskrit."

"You're kidding," Sam said. "Sanskrit?"

"Yup. A dead language but nonetheless it's Sanskrit."

"So what does it mean?"

"As best I can tell, Devá Shaante means Peace of God or, depending on context I think, Place of God's Peace or Home of God's Peace. I found it both ways." He looked from Sam to Toby. "No matter. Either will fit the house now."

"I wonder who could have possibly come up with a name like that for a house," Sam said. "In Sanskrit, yet!"

"That's the interesting part," Dan said. "I got to looking at some local history, and found that the house was actually built in 1956 by a woman named Jenks. She taught architecture up at U.C.L.A. and wanted a retreat down here. She designed the place herself."

"But Sanskrit. What do you suppose…"

Dan smiled. "Well, by one account she was also a bit of a scholar, specializing in Eastern philosophy. I suppose that's where she got it. Anyway, she sold the place to a movie producer in '71, when her mother, who by one account hated the heat down here, became ill."

"Wow," Toby said, "a famous movie producer lived in Sam's house." At a sharp look from Sam he amended that to, "lived in our house." He gave Sam a shy glance. "Well, it's hard to remember. I... well, it is. Give me a while, huh?"

Sam smiled. "You've got all the time in the world, Toby."

Dan cleared his throat. "Sorry to pull you off the Famous Homes Tour, young man, but the Hollywood guy never lived in it. Never even saw it, as far as I could find out. It passed through a series of unfamous hands until Jack and Larry bought it. And that's about it, all I can tell you."

"Hey, that's a lot," Sam said. "More than I'd ever be able to find out."

"Do we have time for a little dividend?" Tom asked, indicating Sam's empty glass.

Sam looked at his watch. "A short one," he said. "We're due at the restaurant at seven-thirty."

While Tom made drinks, Toby got up and wandered around the room, admiring things. He stopped at a shelf full of framed pictures and picked one up. "Who's this? He looks familiar."

Dan went over and laughed when he saw the picture. "Well, I suppose he should, seeing as he's sitting in that chair over there."

Toby looked at Sam and then back at the picture. "Well, I'll be. It is Sam. As a child." He showed Sam the picture. "How long have you known these guys?"

Sam smiled. "Not since then. That was taken a long time ago, at Harry's house. He had a lot of pool parties back then."

"Probably to show you off and impress his friends," Dan said. "Certainly impressed Jack and Larry." He turned to Toby. "They always referred to him as The Hunk."

Toby grinned and looked at Sam who shrugged. "Can't prove it by me."

When Tom served their drinks the talk turned to the house and what was going on there.

When they were leaving to go to the restaurant, Toby held the door for Sam. "After you, Hunk," he said.

Sam swatted him on the butt.

They went to Spenser's because Sam wanted Toby to have a good memory of the place. He liked both the food and the setting and wanted Toby to like it, too. Sam remembered to ask for Henry, the kind man who waited on them at their first visit. When they were shown to their table, Henry remembered them.

"Good evening, Mr. Davis," he said with a slight bow.

"Good evening, Henry."

Henry seemed flattered that Sam remembered his name.

"You remember Mr. Litchfield," he said, nodding towards Toby. "And, as you can see, I've brought reinforcements with me." He introduced Tom and Dan.

Henry laughed. "I doubt you'll need actual reinforcements, sir, but welcome. All of you."

The dinner went well and, while Toby still couldn't bring himself to order a twenty-five dollar shrimp cocktail, he enjoyed the meal greatly.

Later, at home and in bed, Toby said, "Are we really going to live in a house named Home of God's Peace? Isn't that just slightly presumptuous?"

Sam snuggled himself closer against Toby's back and put an arm around his chest. "Maybe we should just go for Place of Serenity, then." His hand slid down until it found Toby's crotch. "But there will be a god living there."

"Two," Toby said as he drifted off to sleep.

\* \* \* \*

On Sunday, over a chive, Swiss cheese, and bacon omelet Sam asked Toby if he'd ever been to a naked party.

"Sure. After all this is Palm Springs. You don't have a problem with that, do you Sam?"

Sam laughed. "No Toby. I don't have a problem with anything you've ever done. We're kind of like Duane and Howard, neither of us was a virgin before we met." He stood and leaned across the table to give Toby a kiss. "Everything from your past has brought you to this moment, with me." He sat back down. "I read that somewhere, a long time ago and I've always believed it. We'll have fun."

# Chapter Fourteen

They slept – or at least stayed in bed – late the next day, happy that Memorial Day had come and Toby didn't have to go to work. When they finally did get up they showered, shaved, and went to brunch at Plum.

"Tell me about this party we're going to this afternoon," Toby said, over mimosas.

Sam tasted his drink. "Nothing much to tell," he said. "It's just the complex getting together to enjoy the holiday. A couple of guys named Mark and Jeff like to organize these things and the Home Owners Association pays for them. They had one for me when I first moved there. Good food, too."

"And it's an orgy, right?"

Sam laughed. "Don't get your hopes up. Most of the guys will be naked but... hey, you'll probably get to see more of Duane and Howard."

The waiter appeared and they ordered: a lamb sandwich for Toby and a seafood omelet for Sam.

When he had gone, Toby smiled. "You're sidestepping the orgy question aren't you."

"Not really," Sam said returning the smile. "Not much of anything but a little casual fondling happens out by the pool. More serious stuff sometimes happens in the locker room or the showers." He took a drink of his mimosa and winked. "If you disappear I'll know where to look for you."

"Not to worry, Sam. We're a package deal, remember?"

Sam rubbed Toby's ankle with his foot. "And a very nice package we are."

Before Toby could respond, the waiter served their brunch.

* * * *

They were late getting to the party – for the usual reason – and a lot of the guys were already there. From the very beginning they made Toby feel welcome. Sam and Toby took their clothes off in the changing room, sharing a locker. Toby looked into the shower but found it empty.

"Too early," Sam said. "Wait an hour or two, until the guys have had a couple of drinks."

They went outside and the first people they ran into were Howard and Duane. Sam and Toby greeted them and frankly looked them up and down.

"I see I'm not the only one lucky in the boyfriend department," Howard said to Sam, still looking at Toby.

Toby grinned. "That's double for me," he said, glancing at Sam. "Not only is he handsome and smart, but he has a... well, you can see his attributes for yourselves."

"And very nice ones they are," said Duane with a smile. "You guys up for a drink?"

They all went to the bar. Once they had their drinks, Sam took Toby around and introduced him to as many people as he could remember. He even introduced him to Scotty, the man who catered the party, and Scotty, as was his habit, gave Toby a hug, being sure to push his impressive endowment firmly against him. He then proceeded to scratch his pubic hair, making it flop. Toby seemed to be enthralled.

"Don't even think about it," Sam said quietly as they looked over the buffet. "According to Pete Addison, he doesn't get it on with anyone here."

Toby looked back at Scotty. "There's always a first time."

Sam laughed. "Well, if that first time ever comes, remember, we're a package deal."

Toby ran his hand down Sam's flank. "It'd have to be. It'd take both of us to do him."

"Hey, no fair touching," a blond man behind them said, "unless I get to touch too." He brushed his hand down Toby's side and patted his ass.

"Hi, Pete," Sam said. "We were just talking about you. Toby, this is Pete Addison, who knows everything about everybody. At least everybody here." He turned. "Pete, this is Toby."

Pete put out his hand. "Hi Toby. Welcome to Desert Pride. I wondered when Sam might bring you around."

Toby shook the offered hand. "Thank you. I haven't been here long enough to meet much of anybody."

Pete turned to Sam. "Naughty, naughty, Sam. Are you trying to hide this fine specimen of a man from the Home Owners Association?"

Sam grinned. "And just what interest, Mr. Addison, might the H.O.A. have in Toby?"

"Well, besides being a hell of a good looking man, you need to register him with us. Didn't you read your CC&Rs?"

"What's that?" Toby asked.

Pete turned to him. "It's the Covenants, Conditions & Restrictions; you know, the rules of the place. Your handsome friend here got a copy of them when he closed on the condo."

Sam tried to look innocent. "I did?"

Pete laughed. "You did. But hey, that's okay, nobody ever reads them unless they're on the board and even then most don't. The relevant part says that we have to have an information sheet on everyone who lives here. Also, and this is the important part, your fees are increased."

Sam shook his head. "It costs for him to live here?"

"Of course it does," Pete said. "Let's see, there's potential increased wear and tear on the gym equipment, extra water used in the showers..."

"If it'll save water, we'll shower together," Sam said, with a grin.

"If you let me join you I'll see to it that the water is free. Now let's see, what else? Oh yeah," he waved his arm, taking in the whole party. "These little get-togethers. They don't come free, you know."

Sam laughed. "Okay, you got us there, Pete. Where do I sign him up?"

"I'll be in what we laughingly call 'the office' on Wednesday morning." He patted Sam's cheek. "Bring your checkbook."

They went back to the bar and Sam introduced Toby to Nick and Walt. Nick took an immediate – and obvious – shine to Toby. As they talked, Sam became aware of a tension building between Nick and Walt. At one point in the conversation, Nick put his hand familiarly on Toby's shoulder and Walt gave a very nice simulation of breathing fire and smoke. "Bitch," he said under his breath, put his hand on Nick's neck and yanked him away. "Excuse us," he said to no one in particular.

"What was that all about?" Toby asked.

"Jealousy," Sam said with a shrug. "An emotion I hope never to experience."

"That was kind of heavy handed, wouldn't you say? I mean just yanking him away like that for everyone to see."

"I think," Sam said, putting an arm around Toby's waist, "it's something everyone is aware of already. It seems to happen a lot." He glanced up at the clock. "You want to go inside? I'll bet the showers aren't empty now."

He was right. They stood in the doorway for a few minutes and watched. "You want to dive in?" Sam asked.

"No," Toby answered, running his fingertips lightly over Sam's nipples, "I think I'd rather go home."

Sam's body responded almost immediately. "Then let's go."

"What's this? Leaving so soon?" Pete Addison stood behind them.

Sam turned and flexed his dick. "Yeah, Pete. Something just came up."

Pete followed them into the locker room where he bent down and kissed the head of Sam's dick. "And that, young man," he said turning to Toby, "is something to go home for."

\* \* \* \*

The following Saturday they met Bill and Mary at the house for the preliminary layout of the kitchen and bathrooms. The more they talked and made chalk marks on the floor, the more Mary became impressed with Toby. "You've really thought this thing through, haven't you," she said, marking an outline on the floor.

"I guess I have," he replied. "You know, we've only been together for what? Three weeks? In that short time Sam's really made me feel a part of this. Part of his life, too. I also want to do this thing right because, let's face it, I'm going to be the one cooking in it."

Mary smiled. "Bill's told me about Sam and now I see what he meant. The man isn't afraid to go after what he wants and he does it right. Better hang on to him, Toby. A man like that doesn't come along all that often, you know."

Toby nodded. "I know. But you know what? I think I make him as happy as he makes me. And we're already a team." He stopped and rubbed out a chalk mark with his shoe. "You know what's scary? We each know what the other is thinking." He remade the chalk mark six inches to the right of the old one. "He'll want the bar sink here."

The work went smoothly and they were well along when Bill and Sam came back from the master bath. "When you're finished here bring him along to the bath, will you, Mary? Sam says he can explain better what they want in there."

"Sure," she said. "We're almost finished here. But I need to ask, how difficult is it going to be, putting a grill near the stove?"

Bill turned to Sam. "What kind of grill? Gas? Electric?"

Sam shrugged. "Ask him," he said, nodding towards Toby. "It's his grill."

"Neither," Toby said. "We want a proper charcoal grill, with a gas lighter."

Bill scratched his head. "You mean like outside? Why don't we just put it there, on the patio?"

"Because we like grilled stuff and Palm Springs' winter evenings are often cold," Toby said. "It would be so much easier to have a grill right by the stove where I can keep an eye on both at the same time."

"See," Sam said to no one in particular, "the man knows what he wants and why he wants it." He turned. "So? How much trouble, Bill?"

Bill sighed. "Never mind. I'll work it out. Just mark where you want it."

A few minutes later, in the master bath, Toby pointed to the outside wall which hadn't been moved yet. "When the new wall's built, I think it should be mostly glass block, at least the part that's going to be the shower, right Sam?"

Sam nodded. "Yeah, let in a lot of light. So I can find you."

Toby didn't even blink. He turned to Bill. "Lights, under the block, for night."

They discussed the lights and Bill promised to figure out a way to access them so they could change the bulbs. Then they went to the other fixtures. Toby insisted on a bidet and a urinal along with the toilet. "It's guys who will live here and guys use urinals. That reminds me, we'll want another one out by the pool somewhere."

Bill nodded and said they'd cross that bridge with the pool people.

Later that evening, while Sam watched Toby make spaghetti sauce, he said, "That was a great idea, the urinal. I never would have thought of it."

Toby turned, holding out a spoon of sauce for Sam to taste. "Think of the water we'll save, not flushing a toilet all the time."

"This stuff is wonderful," Sam said passing the spoon back. "That'll let us spend more time in the shower."

Toby grinned. "The spaghetti sauce?"

"No, dummy. The water we'll save by not peeing in the toilet. The spaghetti sauce we'll rub all over each other so we need to spend more time in the shower."

\* \* \* \*

Sunday they went to the pool for cocktails and conversation.

"You know," Toby said as he put his shorts and T-shirt in a locker, "I'm really getting into this naked socializing. It's not like it was when I was at Some Guys or one of the other resorts. This is more for, I don't know, for friendship or maybe comradeship rather than being so sexual." He smiled. "Well, except for the showers and the steam room maybe."

Sam laughed. "That's because whenever you get a group of men together, especially a group of naked gay men, some of them – maybe even most of them – are going to find a place to have sex. That's just the way men are; it's inevitable. It's just that here, the main purpose is, as you say, comradeship. The sex is more play than anything else, an easy release."

"I never thought of it that way," Toby said, "but I think you're right. Maybe one of these days we will try the steam room."

They went outside and at the bar several guys were talking about the web site called OlderButBetter dot com.

"It's really a fun site," a man named Cory said. "There's lots of guys from Palm Springs on it."

"Yeah," laughed another. "That's how I came to be here. I met a guy who called himself SucksIt on that site."

"And he turned out to be Mike Armstrong, right?"

"You got it. He invited me out one time and afterward he brought me over here." He laughed. "I think maybe so I could watch him work. Anyway, I met some really neat guys here and when a place became available, I bought it."

A man named Jose lifted his glass in a toast. "To OlderButBetter," he said. "I met Pete Addison there; oh, and Martin, too. You know, Martin Shields?"

Toby, who had been listening turned to Sam and said, "Isn't that the guy who killed himself? The one you found?"

"Yeah, it is." He put his hand on Jose's shoulder. "You met him on the Internet?"

"Oh, hi, Sam. Yeah, Martin was very big on OlderButBetter. Had lots of pictures of himself there, mainly of his dick and his butt. His profile said he was very versatile and available." He laughed. "His screen name was WhatUWant. He pretty much lived up to it, too."

"And guys hookup there?"

"Sam, don't you even have a computer?"

"Not yet," Toby spoke up, "but we'll get him into the twenty-first century yet. I think."

"Well, when you do be sure to check out that website. It's a pretty cool place."

The conversation turned to cars and Sam and Toby drifted away. "Are we really going to get a computer?" Sam asked as they settled onto one of the wide lounges, in the shade. "Do you know anything about them?"

Toby stretched. "Some. I have one at work, of course, and I had a pretty nice laptop for a while. But I never knew there was something called OlderButBetter."

"What happened to the laptop?"

Toby turned silent for a moment and then gave a little shrug. "I smashed it. With this sledge hammer my dad has."

Sam took Toby's hand in his. "Present from Jack?"

Toby nodded. "It was a stupid thing to do. I mean, just because he gave it..." He stopped and looked into the air. Then, very softly, he said, "I threw away everything Jack ever bought me. It was like throwing him away."

Sam and Toby lay in silence for a long time, lost in thought. Then Toby sat up and smiled. "I'm glad I did. It's part of what brought me here, to you. You want another drink?"

Sam smiled and pulled him into his arms and kissed him lightly. "Maybe just a little wine. What's for dinner?"

"It's Sunday. Fish."

"We always have fish on Sunday?"

Toby grinned. "No."

Sam decided not to go there. "White. Maybe some of that Pinot Grigio."

    \* \* \* \*

Sam and Toby became more and more used to living together. One evening they moved some things from Toby's place to the condo and then another evening they figured out where to put it all. Toby told Sam he kept the place as an ace-in-the-hole, just in case Sam got tired of him. It made Sam happy that he knew Toby was kidding.

On Thursday evening Toby mentioned he would be a little late getting home the next afternoon. When Sam asked why, Toby said they were having a little party at work and he couldn't miss it.

"Why?" Sam asked. "Because it's a party for your birthday or something?"

"How the hell..." Toby shook his head.

Sam laughed. "Lucky guess. But why didn't you tell me it's your birthday?" He took Toby into his arms. "Oh, Toby, there's so much I don't know about you."

Toby kissed him. "You know all the important stuff, Sam. Like who I am and how much I love you."

Sam smiled. "But not... hell, I don't even know your social security number."

Toby burst out laughing. "Sam!"

"Well, I don't. What if you disappeared and I had to call the police?"

"Sam," Toby was still chuckling "I don't think the police would need my social security number to find me."

Now Sam was laughing. "Don't they put it on dogs? So they can identify them if they run away or something?"

"Okay, okay. Remind me tonight when we go to bed, and I'll show you my social security card. That make you happy?"

Sam kissed him. "Won't do any good. If we're going to bed I won't care about your social security number." He hugged him and ran his hand over Toby's crotch. "There's more important things to know, like who's going to do what to whom and how quick can we start."

\* \* \* \*

"Hey, is today really the day," Sam asked the next morning, standing at the toilet watching Toby pee.

"Actually, no. It's tomorrow but nobody works tomorrow."

Sam raised an eyebrow. "Nobody works on Saturday? In a hotel?"

Toby laughed. "It's the accounting department, Sam. Who needs an accountant on Saturday?"

"Well then, if tomorrow is really the day, can we go out to dinner? Someplace nice?"

Toby kissed him. "Yeah, we can."

Toby did get home late but not as late as Sam had thought he'd be. Toby said that it had been a nice party but he'd rather be at home with Sam They never did get any dinner that night.

\* \* \* \*

The next night, Saturday, when they were in the shower, Toby said, "It's Spencer's, isn't it. For dinner."

Sam, who was pretending to wash Toby's back but really used that as an excuse to press against him and touch him everywhere he could, said it was and asked if that was okay.

Toby twisted around and Sam saw – or rather felt – Toby to be in the same state of excitement as he. "Will we be late if we do what you're wanting to do?"

They did it in the shower – a perilous act at best – and of course they were late for their reservation.

At Spencer's they were seated on the patio. Henry waited on them and he had martinis waiting. It was a very good evening.

Over dessert, Sam handed Toby a small bag from Walmart. "I'm sorry, I just didn't have time to get it wrapped," he said.

Toby opened it and inside, in a plastic display box, he found a wristwatch.

"Well," Sam said, "I didn't want to get you anything too extravagant but I did notice that you could use a new watch. Oh, and you'll need these I think." He handed Toby a nail clipper. "To cut the plastic strips and get it out."

Toby took the clippers and began cutting the plastic wires that held the watch prisoner in its plastic display box. He noticed that the Walmart price sticker – $6.93–was still on it. He got it out of the box and slipped it on his wrist.

"Oh, Sam, it's wonderful. And you're right, I do need a new watch. This is perfect." Toby stood, leaned over the table and kissed him. No one in the restaurant seemed to take notice.

Later, in bed and satiated, Toby spooned himself against Sam's back. Just as Sam began to fall asleep Toby leaned up and kissed him on the earlobe. "Thank you for the watch, Sam. I didn't know Walmart carried Rolex."

# Chapter Fifteen

The next morning found them sleeping late. Sam, lying against Toby's back, floated in that twilight state, not quite awake, not quite asleep; that state where his mind wasn't constrained by reality and seemed to roam at will through his consciousness. He idly played with Toby's dick, sliding the foreskin up and finding the flare of the head with his fingers, then pulling the skin back and gently touching the groove just underneath.

The foreskin is such a wonderful part of a man. It slides so easily across the head and hides it, like a turtleneck sweater, a long, soft, warm turtleneck.

Son of a bitch! A turtleneck sweater. He suddenly knew what had been bothering him all along about Martin's suicide.

"Hey, don't stop," Toby said in a sleepy voice. "I was halfway there."

Sam rolled him onto his back and took him the rest of the way with his mouth.

Later, over coffee and rolls, Sam quietly said, "I figured it out. I know what's been bothering me about Martin's suicide."

Toby looked up. "What?"

"It wasn't him."

There was a moment of silence. "But I thought you said that…"

"I did. I looked at him. I watched them lift him out of that tub. But it wasn't Martin."

Toby poured more coffee. "How…"

"Whoever they pulled out of that tub had been circumcised but Martin wasn't. He had a foreskin like yours, one that completely covers the head." He smiled at Toby. "Well, it wasn't as pretty as yours but it was maybe a bit longer."

"But if it wasn't Martin, then who?" He shrugged. "Maybe his twin brother?"

Sam shook his head. "I don't know, but it wasn't Martin. I need to think."

That afternoon Sam said it still baffled him. The man in the tub couldn't have been Martin but Martin had never mentioned a brother.

"Hey," Toby said, "why don't you ask that Pete guy. You know, the one who knows everything about everyone? Maybe the Home Owner's Association knows."

Sam smiled and touched Toby on the arm. "Now I see why the hotel likes you so much. You're not only smart, you remember everything. I'll call him Monday. Now, where shall we go for dinner this evening?"

"I don't care. No really, I don't."

Sam shook his head. "The rule is, if one of us asks a question like that, the other one has to answer. Look at it this way, if I had a preference, I would have asked if you minded that I had my preference. Since I didn't, you not only get to choose, you have to choose. So which is it?"

"Where'd that rule come from?"

Sam laughed. "I just made it up. But it makes sense. One of us has to decide. In this case, I asked first so the decision will be yours. A corollary to the rule, by the way, is that the one who asks has to accept the answer. So, where?"

Toby thought for a moment. "You know, Sam, that is a great idea. Really. If we stick with it we should never have an argument."

"Thank you. Now which will it be?"

Toby thought for a moment. "Spencer's."

It was a good choice. For both of them.

# Chapter Sixteen

On Monday, Sam called Pete Addison and asked him if Martin had had a brother.

"Not that I know of," Pete said. "Or at least none that he talked about. Tell you what though, I'll be in the office Wednesday afternoon and I'll check his information sheet. Okay?"

"Okay! Come to dinner Wednesday evening, say at six? You can tell us about Martin's family status then."

He told Toby about it when Toby got home from work.

"Sure," he said, "what shall we do for dinner?"

They decided on steaks and salad. Sam was assigned the job of finding the steaks and something suitable for dessert at Jensen's.

"If I were you," Toby said, as they were getting ready for bed, "I don't think I'd mention the foreskin thing to Pete. He's going to think you're some kind of nut."

\* \* \* \*

On Wednesday evening, Pete didn't have much information. "We have an information sheet on Martin, but there's nothing in it to indicate he had a brother." He took a sip of his vodka and asked, "What's your interest, anyway?"

"I don't know," Sam hedged. "I guess I was just wondering who our new next door neighbor might be. I mean, if he had a brother the guy might want to live here."

"Well, you're not going to have a new neighbor anytime soon, I think," Pete said. "That's the interesting thing. It seems someone has paid up Martin's H.O.A. arrears, and paid for the next year to boot."

Sam reached for Pete's glass. "Someone? Who pays for a dead man's back dues? And then future ones too?"

"Don't know. That's the funny part. Someone mailed us a cashier's check drawn on a bank in Miami, Florida, with a note telling us to apply the money to Martin's condo fees. Which we did. End of story."

The next day, on a whim, Sam telephoned William, the real estate agent and asked if Martin's condo would go on the market. William said he didn't know but, even though it wasn't in multiple listings, he'd ask around.

\* \* \* \*

On Saturday, they had to go out to the house. Bill had called and said the subcontractors really needed to get started on the new pool. To accommodate Toby, they had agreed to do it on the weekend.

The two guys were like a father and son team. One, the supervisor, was older, somewhere in his late fifty's Sam thought, and the other in his late twenty's, not very much older than Toby. For Sam the odd thing about them was that Joe, the older one, kept himself in really good shape, almost gym-toned while Henry, the young guy, had let himself get soft and just a bit overweight. He found them to be very likable though and they worked perfectly with Toby.

"This shit," Joe said, indicating the existing pool, "has to go. It's got those three fuckin' cracks in it and there's no way on God's earth you're going to save it. So," he looked at Sam, "you can have any fuckin' thing you want."

Sam grinned. "Talk to him," he said, pointing at Toby. "He's the idea man, I just write the checks."

"If all this goes," Toby asked, "what happens to the hole? Does the new pool have to go in it?"

Joe scratched his head. "Not really. If you want the fucker somewhere else, we'll just fill the hole with some shit and dig a new one wherever you want."

"Good. Because not only is that one the wrong shape, it's in the wrong place. It should be over there," he pointed. "Outside the living room and kitchen."

Bill shook his head and turned to Sam, "Mary was right. That boy has vision. I thought from the beginning the pool should have been put over there."

Sam smiled. "Would you have told me that? If Toby hadn't brought it up?"

"Probably. But it's going to be expensive."

"I thought we agreed," Sam said, "that we'd do this thing right or not at all."

Bill laughed. "You're the boss, Sam. We'll do it right."

Sam and Bill walked over to where Toby was talking with Joe. Henry was writing things on a pad and making sketches as they talked.

"The pool shape is pretty important, it seems to me," Toby said. "I think, because of the design of the house, the pool has to be angular as well. But not a simple rectangle. Now Sam here likes to swim laps so we need space for that. Long and fairly narrow, say six feet wide by forty feet long?"

He glanced at Sam who nodded and added, "And it doesn't have to be real deep. Three, three and a half feet, maybe."

Toby went over to Henry, took the pad out of his hand, and began to draw. "Like this, with the main pool here, on the right, and the lap pool on the left with a little waterway connecting them. Like a narrow 'H' with one slender arm for laps and one thicker, shorter arm for lazy swimming."

Joe got out his measuring tape and they roughly laid it out. Toby wanted a seat to run the length and width of the main pool but not in the lap portion. When Joe asked about steps Toby looked at the house, thought for a moment and then said steps should run the full width of the pool.

When he described the handrails, four of them, evenly spaced along the steps, Bill nudged Sam. "That's it! I don't know if I would've seen it, but that's it. Four handrails will mirror the supports for the patio roof. Only they're smaller so there have to be more of them. Perfect."

They spent several more hours working out details.  It was easier when they got to the question of the spa.  Both Joe and Henry were tuned in to Toby by then and so the sketches went rapidly.

The surprise turned out to be the urinal.  Toby wanted a shallow bowl, three feet across, set in the deck and plumbed.  The bowl, he said, would be filled with glass pebbles the same color as the house and needed to have a flushing system.  Henry thought it a great idea and suggested a low sprinkler arrangement surrounding the bowl.  If he felt any surprise at its location, fairly close to the pool and out in the open, he didn't show it.  Joe just snorted and said he doubted he'd ever use the thing.  Bill didn't say a word.

That night they had dinner at the little Mexican place that was fast becoming a favorite.

After they were seated on the patio and had been served their margaritas, Sam said, "You know, that urinal out by the pool is a stroke of genius.  It'll keep people from peeing in the pool or having to traipse through the house to the bathroom.  But why did you put it where you did?  Why not over by where the pumps and filter will be?"

Toby laughed and toasted Sam with his margarita.  "Because I'm a pervert and like to watch guys pee.  Always have, since I was a little kid."

Sam toasted him back.  "Does that mean you're into, uh…"

"Water sports?  No, Sam, I've never gotten into that.  But if you…"

"Maybe someday.  I mean, never say never, right?  But at the moment, no."

\* \* \* \*

Sunday evening, after cocktails around the pool with the guys, they sat in the cool Jacuzzi with glasses of wine.  Sam commented on the number of guys they'd seen wearing cock-rings of one sort or another.  "You ever wear one?" he asked.  "Do you even have one?"

"I'm not much into body adornment or jewelry," Toby replied.

"I've noticed.  You don't even wear a tie clip to work."

Toby laughed.  "But I do wear a pretty fancy watch." He went silent for a few moments and then said, "I used to, though.  Wear jewelry, I mean.

Jack liked me to. He even convinced me to get my ear pierced and wear a diamond stud he bought for me." He laughed again although Sam didn't detect much enjoyment in it. "At least he said it was a diamond."

Sam kissed him. "So what..."

"I left it behind when I left him. After a while the hole in my ear closed up. That was another sign I'd gotten away from him."

They were quiet for a while, enjoying just being together and holding hands.

"How about you? You don't wear any jewelry, either."

Sam added a little wine to their glasses. "Oh, I wore a ring for a few years. It's still around somewhere."

"Why'd you stop wearing it?"

"It... the symbolism had gone. There wasn't any point in wearing it after that."

A long silence ensued which Toby finally broke. "Will you tell me about it someday?"

Sam turned and folded his arms around Toby. "It's not a secret. I'll tell you right now if you want to hear it."

Toby kissed him for a long time. "I'd like to hear it."

So Sam told Toby about his time with Joel, the chauffeur. The only man, before Toby, that he'd shared real passion with. The one man, he said, who had prepared him to love Toby.

Sam finished his story and they went to bed to practice what Joel had taught Sam.

\* \* \* \*

Toby had the Fourth of July off. When they finally got out of bed they went for brunch and then to the house, just to look around again. They were surprised to find stakes and string outlining the new pool.

"Those guys work fast," Sam said. "I didn't expect to see anything before next week."

"And they got it right, just like we said. Even to the urinal," Toby pointed to a small circle of stakes. "I was afraid they thought I was joking."

After an hour or so, they went back to the condo for a nap and then wandered over to the pool where the Forth of July buffet was being set up.

After pouring themselves drinks at the bar, they looked around for Duane and Howard but didn't find them. Pete Addison said he thought they'd gone away for the long weekend. He also advised them to go over and admire the buffet before it got ravaged by the guys. It turned out to be Scotty's usual lavish production and everyone complimented him. The more compliments he got, the more he made his dick sway and the bigger his grin got. He even let a couple of the guys fondle him when they hugged him. Scotty was a happy man.

"Uh oh, here comes trouble," Sam said, nudging Toby.

"Where... oh, Walt and Nick."

"Yeah, and Walt doesn't look happy. I wonder what... oh. Scotty."

Sure enough, Nick pulled Scotty into a hug and quite obviously groped him. Walt, who could hardly miss seeing it, looked ready to explode. When he moved toward Nick and Scotty, Sam said, "Get ready. Here it comes."

And come it did. "You God damned whore," Walt said, loud and low, almost a guttural sound.

He grabbed Nick by the shoulder, hard enough to hurt, and pulled him away, dragging him across the deck. As they exited there was a sound that could only come from a hard slap to a man's ass.

"Jesus, why do they do that?" Sam asked Toby. "And that was no accident. Nick groped Scotty on purpose and he knew Walt would see it. What's with them?"

"I don't know," Toby replied, "but maybe..."

"What?"

"Well, maybe it's some kind of weird sex thing. I mean it looked to me like both of them were on the verge of an erection. You know, when you're puffed up but it hasn't started to rise? I'd swear they were both like that."

Sam thought for a minute. "You know, you may be right. But if you are, they are two sick puppies. Come on, let's forget them and go sample Scotty's buffet."

They finished eating just as the fireworks started. The show came from the city baseball field a few blocks away and they had a perfect view of the aerial displays. Someone turned off most of the lights which created a beautiful effect with the brightly colored sky display reflected in the pool and on the skin of the naked men watching.

When the display finished Sam asked Toby if he wanted to go inside and check out the action in the showers. "And don't forget our rule. I asked and I'm prepared to accept your answer, whatever it is."

Toby thought for a long moment. "You know, Sam, we both know that it's going to happen sooner or later. We, both of us, like sex play too much for us to give it up. But not just yet. Maybe next month, okay?"

Sam reached down and fondled Toby's dick. "Okay. Then how about we go over there, behind the bar, and I blow you?"

Toby went hard in a hurry. When he nodded, Sam led him behind the bar and turned him so he could look out at the men around the pool. Then he slipped down and took Toby in his mouth. It didn't take three minutes before Toby let out a deep, guttural groan and had to hang on to the bar so he's stay upright.

"You liked that," Sam said, standing. He didn't make it a question, but if it had been, he could still taste the answer.

Sam poured drinks for them and when Toby could breathe normally again they went out to socialize. Mark put his hand on Toby's shoulder and asked him if he was all right. "It looked for a minute there like you were going to fall down."

Toby laughed. "I suppose I did. Sam got a little frisky, behind the bar there."

Sam just smirked and said nothing.

When they got home, they took their clothes off again and settled into the patio spa.

"You know, Sam, I've been thinking about it, about going into the showers and playing. I think it'd be fun, but you know what?"

Sam leaned in and kissed him. "What?"

"Well, I think the first time, I'd like to play with a couple, you know, two guys who love each other the way we do. Do you suppose we could ever find that?"

Sam pulled him into his lap and hugged him. "I'm sure we can." He ran his hands over Toby's chest and belly, ending in his crotch. "It'll happen one of these days if we want it to."

\* \* \* \*

Tuesday evening, Prime Timers had a mixer that took place at four different bars along the same block. In the one called Street Bar they ran into William and Red. They talked about the weather for a few minutes before William snapped his fingers and looked at Sam. "Oh, I forgot to call you today. I'm sorry. Not only did I sell a house on Sunday, but I sold two more yesterday and I was up to my balls in paperwork today. Anyway, I did get a chance to ask around about that condo next door to you. And it's the weirdest thing. It's not on the market, it's still in that guy Martin's name and someone has paid off both the mortgages."

"Someone?" Sam asked.

William nodded. "That's the really strange part of it. I was talking to the mortgage company today for one of my clients and happened to mention that place. The guy told me they'd gotten a cashier's check for the payoff, drawn on some bank in Florida. Their only instructions were to hold on to the papers until further notice. No signature, no address, no nothing, just the check. Weird, no?"

"So what happens now?" Toby asked.

"Nothing," William said with a shrug. "My contact said he called the bank in Florida and they told him they had no involvement other than issuing the cashier's check. When he asked who bought the check, the guy at the bank just laughed at him."

"So that's it?"

"Yup, that's it. Oh, but I did ask the guy at the mortgage company to flag the file, to let me know when there's any activity in it. Said I was interested in the property. So, yeah, that's it until I hear from the guy." He shrugged. "Or until the county takes it for taxes."

"Well, thanks for all that," Sam said. "I really appreciate it. And congratulations. Selling three houses in the same weekend sounds like quite a feat. You must be very good at what you do."

Red laughed. "Oh, he is. He's very good at everything he does."

Sam and Toby circulated to a couple of the other bars, talking to people and generally being social. Then they went to dinner.

"You know," Sam said over his linguine with clam sauce, "I really like those Prime Timers' functions. We've met a lot of really interesting guys."

"Yeah, Prime Timers was a lifesaver when I first moved down here. It was kind of an instant family and kept me from that aloneness you can feel, moving to a new place where you don't know anyone."

    \* \* \* \*

On Tuesday Sam went to a Prime Timers lunch at Melvyn's, an exclusive – and quite good – restaurant in an old and very upscale boutique resort. The lunch was informal but it was pretty obvious that dinner would require a coat and tie.

Sam felt sorry Toby wasn't there with him but, as Howard had said, he'd have to get used to that. Toby seemed to like his job and there was no way Sam would upset that.

During cocktails Sam ran into Matt Stevens, the man from the Coroner's Office and bought him a drink.

"How's it going, Matt? You still got the Coroner's Office under control?"

"Hey, they're brighter than I give them credit for."

"I find that hard to believe. They're county government, aren't they?"

"Yeah," Matt said with a laugh, "but somehow they were bright enough to promote me to Supervisor."

"Well congratulations," Sam said, offering his hand. "Let me buy you another drink on that."

Matt shook his head. "They also gave me a hefty raise so let me buy."

While Matt was at the bar Sam had an idea. When Matt came back with new drinks, Sam asked him how much information was kept about the bodies they had to deal with.

"A lot," Matt said. "That's why they need me and the clerks, to keep all that stuff straight and filed properly. We even got a new computer system a couple of years ago so an awful lot of the stuff is in it, pictures and everything."

Bingo. "So you guys take pictures of the bodies?"

"You bet we do. From every conceivable angle. To back up the written stuff. They even take pictures at the autopsies."

"Look, Matt, I don't know if you know it, but I was the one who found that guy who killed himself in my complex. It was a horrible experience and it still haunts me, keeps me awake at night sometimes. I think… I think if maybe I could see the pictures of the guy, see impersonally what I saw in person, well, maybe it'd help me get the images out of my mind."

Matt gave him a strange look but didn't say a word.

Come on, guy. Pick it up. "Could that happen? Could you let me see the pictures of him? Maybe see what they said about him?"

Matt narrowed his eyes.

Damn! He's not gonna do it.

"Well," Matt said after a long pause, "maybe. I mean, if it'll help you get some sleep." A small smile played around his lips. "You have been looking a bit haggard lately, now that you mention it. Sure, I think I can help you. Give me the guy's name and come around at noon Thursday. The clerks will be at lunch then and I can show you around."

Sam thanked him, not too effusively he hoped, and wrote Martin's name on the back of one of his cards, along with the date and location of the suicide.

That evening Sam told Toby about his conversation with Matt.

"You really said that?" Toby asked with a touch of amazement in his voice. "You're losing sleep over finding Martin? Man, that must have been a performance worthy of an Emmy! Especially seeing as how you sleep so soundly they could tear the building down around you and you wouldn't notice until morning."

"Well, yeah, maybe I did overstate it a little. But damn it Toby, I need to see those pictures. Just to prove to myself that the man they pulled out of there was circumcised." He shook his head. "I'm beginning to doubt myself now and I hate that. If I don't do this, sooner or later I will start losing sleep over it."

Toby nodded. "I know you're troubled by this, Sam. See if he'll give you a print or two of the guy. I'd like to see what he looks like." He laughed. "Be sure to get one that includes his face, not just pictures of his dick."

Sam laughed and relaxed a bit. "I'll be sure to do that," he said with a grin.

# Chapter Seventeen

The next day Sam went out to the house and found the pool men hard at work, jack hammering up the old one.

"Won't be long now," Bill said. They'll be digging in a couple of days."

"How come there isn't a dumpster or something out in the driveway?"

"Ah," Bill said with a chuckle, "why drag all that concrete to the landfill and then drag a lot of dirt back here? They'll just fill the hole with it and then put the dirt from the new pool on top. About five feet of it."

"Good. The dirt I mean. Toby wants to plant some sort of orchard there."

Bill looked at the space with a calculating eye. "Yeah, citrus. Have more oranges, lemons, and kumquats than you can shake a stick at." He turned back to Sam. "Keep that man, Sam. Keep him happy, keep him safe, and keep him close. He's got a good eye and good ideas. If I was bigger, had a bigger business, I'd hire him just like that. A little experience and he'd be a firecracker of a designer. Besides that, he's a nice guy."

"I have every intention of keeping him, Bill" Sam said. "But making him a designer? I think the hotel might have something to say about that."

"What do they know?" Bill grumbled.

\* \* \* \*

On Thursday, Sam arrived at the Coroner's Office a half hour early and had to walk around the County Administrative Complex until noon but he couldn't help being anxious. He just had to see some pictures of the man they'd pulled out of Martin's bathtub to set his mind at rest.

At exactly twelve, he went through the glass doors and into the office. Matt was waiting for him at the front counter and took him back into the filing section right away. "I sent them all to lunch a few minutes early," he said as they moved through the office. "Give us a little more time."

He showed Sam the banks of filing cabinets and the console for the new computer system. "We're still putting the old stuff into it," he said, punching a few buttons, "but all the new stuff goes in right away." He typed something into the machine and a copy of a form appeared on the screen, in full color. "Here's the final report on that Martin guy. You'll note that he didn't die from slashing his wrists."

"What? Not from…"

Matt chuckled. "Not a chance. He hardly cut much of anything. Was the water red?"

Sam thought for a second. "Well, it looked sort of pink. And the paramedics put bandages around his wrists when they pulled him out."

"So he wouldn't get blood all over them and the body bag. No Sam, this guy died because he was doped up to the eyeballs with Xanax, Sonata, and alcohol. Looks like he slashed his wrists just for good measure although with that many drugs in him, I don't see how he stayed conscious long enough to do it."

"What… what are those drugs he took? Stuff off the street?"

"No, no," Matt said. "You don't know a lot about drugs, do you?" Sam shook his head. "Well Xanax is a tranquilizer, a pretty powerful one, and Sonata is a sleeping pill, again a very powerful one. Mix a bunch of those up with a couple of drinks and you're guaranteed not to wake up. On top of that he had some water in his lungs but we'll never know if the drugs did it or if he drowned. The slashed wrists certainly didn't."

Sam nodded. "I guess he had become a little bit depressed because he couldn't find a job, and maybe that made him have trouble sleeping but…" But this isn't Martin. How did he get some guy to take all those drugs? "That's a lot of pills to swallow, isn't it?"

"He didn't swallow pills. According to the police report, he'd dissolved them in a rather potent margarita. They found the glass on a shelf by the tub." He typed something else into the computer. "But you're not interested in how he actually did it, are you? I thought you just wanted to see the pictures."

"Uh... yeah, the pictures. So I can get this whole damn thing out of my mind once and for all."

A picture of Martin – or the man who was supposed to be Martin – suddenly appeared on the screen. Its identification data, shown along the bottom, indicated it to be the first picture taken. He hadn't yet been taken out of the bathtub. Sam really couldn't see his face since it was taken from behind and he couldn't make out his dick either. It was blurred, under the water.

"Are there others?" Sam asked.

"Oh, yes. Lots of them. I told you, they photograph everything." He typed another command and a page of thumbnails appeared. "Here," he said, looking closely at the tiny pictures. "we'll bring up a few of these."

Number five hit the jackpot. It had been taken from above, a full body shot, and it clearly showed the man's face and the fact that he had been circumcised. It was obvious, including the change of skin color on the shaft that was somehow emphasized by the lighting.

"Can... can you make a print of that?" Sam asked.

Matt laughed. "You going to put it under your pillow at night? Or maybe out on the Internet?"

"No. I just... I just want to have it, to look at it when I..." He stopped, knowing he was beginning to babble. "I just want it."

Matt shook his head but pushed the 'print' button anyway. "I can't fathom why you want this, but I guess I can give it to you. The department rules say I shouldn't, but what the hell. Anyway, the picture is public property. Just don't go showing it around. I could get into a lot of trouble for this." He went into another part of the office and came back, holding the print out to Sam.

"I owe you for this, Matt. Drinks are on me from now on."

Matt grinned, his good humor returning. "Got to be careful there, Sam. You could be offering a bribe to a public servant." He handed Sam an envelope for the print. "On the other hand, a drink before dinner probably wouldn't count as a major bribe."

Sam laughed. "I'm glad to hear that. Next dinner, whatever you want." He slid the picture into the envelope and looked at his watch. "Can I buy you lunch?"

Matt shook his head. "The girls will be coming back pretty quick, so I think I'd better take a pass on that."

"Then I'd better be getting out of your way." He gave Matt a hug. "Thank you, Matt. I really appreciate this."

That evening he showed the picture to Toby and told him about the drugs in the man's body.

"So, do you think he took the drugs to kill himself and slashed his wrists just for good measure?" Toby asked.

"I don't know. But think about the other possibility."

"You mean someone gave him the drugs to kill him and then slashed the wrists to make it look like suicide? That only works if, one: it isn't Martin and two: Martin had an identical twin brother. And, as far as we know, no one has ever heard of a brother, much less an identical twin brother."

"I know it's far fetched. But the fact remains that the man in this picture," Sam tapped his finger at the appropriate place on the photograph, "is circumcised and Martin was not."

Toby sighed. "Well, I think maybe I need to see a photo of Martin."

"I don't know. That may not be possible. But everyone here has seen it. Hell, most of them have had it. Ask anyone around the pool next Sunday afternoon."

* * * *

Friday, Sam insisted on dinner at Melvyn's because he'd had such a good lunch there with the Prime Timers.

Toby was not happy that they had to wear coats and ties though. "I wear that every day at work," he had reminded Sam several times. "Why would I want to wear it at dinner, too?"

"Because we have to go there and because the food's really good." He brushed Toby's lips with a kiss. "And because you'll really like it, despite the coat and tie, which, by the way, make you look almost as handsome as you do when you're wearing nothing at all."

Toby really did like the place, coat and tie notwithstanding.

Over dessert, which they each ordered rather than sharing one between them, Toby said, "Sam? I think it's time we came at least as far as the twentieth century."

Sam gave him a blank look.

"A computer, Sam. You really need to learn to use one," Toby said.

"Why?" Sam asked.

"Well, for one thing, you could have gone out to that web site, what is it, OlderButBetter? The one Martin used? Maybe you could even find a picture of him there," Toby said.

Sam contemplated that for a moment. "Couldn't you do that? I mean, you have a computer at work don't you?"

Toby laughed. "I can just see my boss now, walking into my office and finding me looking at naked men on the company computer. He may be gay, Sam, but at work he's all business."

"Your boss is gay?"

Toby looked up. "I guess. I mean, he has a boyfriend and all. We never talk about it, but it's pretty much common knowledge."

"Does he know you have a boyfriend, too?"

Toby thought for a moment while the waiter poured coffee. "You know, I really don't know. We don't talk much about personal stuff around the office but he probably does. They all probably do."

Sam ate the last of his crème brûlée. "How?"

"Because, Sam, I've been so very happy since I got back from Denver. It's something I can't hide and they're smart enough to put two and two together."

Sam rubbed his ankle against Toby's calf. "Damn, I love you."

They bought a computer the next day.

\* \* \* \*

On Sunday, they went out to the Las Palmas house to see how things were going. They were surprised to see the digging had begun on the new pool. The dirt that had been dug up was now covering the broken concrete where the old pool had been.

"Man, these guys work fast," Toby said, looking in the hole. "I guess we can't change our minds now."

"You want to? I can stop them if you do," Sam said.

Toby grinned. "I'll bet you would, too. No, Sam, I'm pretty happy with what we're going to get." He paused for a second. "Did you hear that? How easily that we're rolled off my tongue?"

Sam pulled him into a hug. "Yes, and it makes me very happy. Maybe... well, maybe I've got the partner I think I always wanted."

Toby attempted a shrug but couldn't quite pull it off, wrapped up in Sam's arms as he was. "Doesn't matter. You've got me."

In the late afternoon, they went out to the pool at the condo and poured themselves glasses of wine. "You know, Sam, I'm really getting to like this naked socializing. Maybe we shouldn't move out of the condo after all."

Sam patted him on the butt. "With that pool and shower and urinal you designed? No, I think we'll be happy in that house. And we'll have our own naked parties. Besides, I don't think we should sell the condo. That way, we could come here any time we want. We could use the gym, swim in the pool, and drink the wine on Sunday."

"Really? You're not going to sell the condo?" Toby asked.

Sam shook his head. "I've been thinking about it and, like you, how much I enjoy these guys and the whole ambiance of the place. So, unless you feel strongly otherwise, I think we should keep it."

"Agreed," Toby said.

During the afternoon and early evening they spent a lot of time talking with the guys. Sam, and Toby as well, often thought how pleasant the camaraderie was and it was something they really didn't want to give up. In several conversations either Sam or Toby managed to bring up the subject of Martin. Somehow the conversation always led to Martin's dick and, to a man, everyone they spoke to agreed that not only had Martin been intact but he'd had a rather lush foreskin. One man even reminisced over how Martin loved to dock with it, pull his foreskin over the head of another man's dick. By the time they started for home, Toby was convinced. And told Sam so when they went to bed.

\* \* \* \*

During dinner after Toby got home from work on Monday night, Sam asked him what he thought they should to do. "After looking at that picture, I know the man isn't Martin. Maybe it's his twin brother but that doesn't really matter. It's not Martin and Martin's no longer here. What the hell am I supposed to do?"

Toby put down his fork. "Call the police. Dump it in their laps and let them deal with it. That's their job." He shrugged. "Besides, there's really nothing else you can do."

"I guess you're right. They're probably going to laugh at me, maybe throw me out of the police station, but I have to do it," Sam said.

He did it the next day. He called Officer Andy, who turned out to be on vacation and wouldn't be back until the following week. Sam was a little reticent about talking with anyone else so he decided he'd just wait until Andy came back. After all, it wasn't like he had any idea where Martin – the real one – was. When Toby got home from work, he agreed.

Their Internet connection was installed on Thursday but of course it didn't work. The phone company said they'd get right on it.

\* \* \* \*

When Sam went out to the house on Friday, he found trenches jack-hammered into the floor in just about every room, especially in the kitchen and bathrooms.

"What the hell is all this?" he asked Bill.

"New plumbing. Your unshaven buddy moved all the stuff that uses water and gas so we have to put in new lines. New sewers as well."

"Well, why not run them through the walls or on the roof or something?"

Bill led him over to the outside wall of the living room. "This is why," he said, tapping on it. "It's glass, floor to ceiling and almost wall to wall. Can't run plumbing through a glass wall."

"So the layout of the kitchen and bathrooms is really chiseled in stone – or rather concrete?" Sam asked.

"It is now. I hope you're going to be happy with it," Bill said.

Sam shrugged. "I'm only half of who has to be happy with it. And with this kind of stuff, the junior half." He thought for a minute and got an idea. "Bill, could you guys mark where everything goes? Like with chalk or something? I'll bring Toby out tomorrow so he can make sure everything is just where he wants it. Could you do that?"

Bill laughed. "As long as your checkbook holds out, I can do anything you want. I'll put the guys on it right now."

As Sam was leaving Bill came out to the car and handed him a couple of sticks of orange chalk. "It's David's idea. You remember, that workman who was such a big help when we shot your pit cover onto the roof? He suggested we do the layout on the floor in blue and if anything needs to be changed, have Toby make corrections with this so we'll know what to do. Okay?"

Sam thought it was an excellent idea.

When Toby got home that evening he checked the Internet connection and found it still didn't work. He called the help desk number and, after a half hour wait, spoke to a guy who said they were behind and a crew was working nights to get caught up. He said they'd be on line by tomorrow. Sunday for sure.

* * * *

The next day they went out to the house and were pleasantly surprised. Not only had the workmen indicated what each trench was for and where its pipe or cable would come out, they had outlined the footprints of the cabinets, appliances and fixtures as well.

Toby did have a few changes to make but they were minor and probably the result of simple miscommunications.

It was one of those very rare hot, humid days and by the time they'd been in the house for an hour the sweat was dripping off both. They'd taken their shirts off and Sam had lamented the fact that they couldn't take their shorts off as well and work naked. "It sure would be cooler, the sweat evaporating from our skin rather than just making us wet," he said. "But if we take our pants off, sure as hell Andy or Tom or someone will wander in to see what we're doing."

Toby mopped at his chest. "So? You've never been seen naked before?"

Sam laughed. "Well, I guess a few guys have seen me in that state."

"Besides, you don't have to worry about Dan and Tom. They've already seen you naked."

"When?"

"In that picture, silly. The one of you on the diving board?"

"I'd forgotten about that. Yeah, I guess I don't have any secrets from anybody."

"Well," Toby said, running his hand along Sam's fly, "not me, anyway."

When they finished Sam suggested they go next door and see if they could promote a tall, cool drink. Toby concurred.

When they rang, Tom answered the door. "Well, well, well. Look what the cat dragged in, dripping wet. Come in guys, come in. We're out by the pool. I imagine you both need a tall gin and tonic," he said opening the sliding glass door. "Go ahead and get in the pool while I fix them." He turned to Dan who was lying on a lounge. "You ready for a refill?"

Dan nodded and held out his glass. Then he turned to Sam. "Well, go on. You heard the man. Get in the pool and lower that body temperature."

Sam looked at Toby and laughed. "You're right," he said, "there are no secrets." He stripped off his shorts and jumped in the water. Toby followed right behind him.

Once Tom had set out the drinks, he shed his shirt and shorts and joined them. Dan followed and the four of them spent a quarter hour or so in the cool water. When they got out Dan said, "Don't bother with those shorts. Let the air dry you, it'll cool your innards."

They spent an hour, talking and sipping cool drinks. When Sam described what they'd been doing at the house Tom insisted on seeing it.

"But don't get dressed yet," Dan said. "I've got to get something." He went in the house and came back with two things. One was a digital camera and the other was a silver framed photograph.

"I want to update this," he said, showing them the picture of Sam on the diving board. "We don't have a board but I guess it'll do if you just stand over there, at the edge of the pool."

Sam dutifully went to the indicated spot and posed, as if he were about to dive into the pool. Dan took several shots and then asked Toby if he'd mind if he took a shot of the two of them. Toby nodded and went over to Sam and put his arm around his shoulder. Sam did the same to Toby and they looked like a couple of grade school best friends. Dan was delighted. Then they all put their shorts on and went to look at the house.

After the inspection, Sam asked if they'd like to go to dinner and suggested Boscoso. Everyone was agreeable and so, after a quick trip home to change, they all four ended up having martinis and pasta in Boscoso's air conditioned dining room.

When Sam and Toby got home the Internet connection still didn't work.

"Boy," Toby grumbled, "if we handled stuff this way at the hotel we'd be out of business in about seven minutes."

# Chapter Eighteen

Sunday they enjoyed a leisurely brunch at Plum. Afterward Toby, without much hope, tried the Internet again. He was delighted to find that this time he could connect. Once on, he spent a couple of hours showing Sam how to open the browser and how to use the search engines.

"Can we get into that place Martin used?"

Toby showed him how to get there but before they could search for Martin they had to sign up and create a profile. "I think," Toby said, "we'd better just make someone up. If Martin is still using the site, we don't want him to come across us by accident."

"You can do that?"

"Sam, the first, and maybe the most important thing you have to learn about the Internet is that a great deal of it is not what it seems. Especially people, but other stuff too. These sites don't know who you are, so you can be anyone you want."

"Then how do you know what to trust?"

"Instinct mostly. Mixed with a lot of caution and smarts. For example, you never give out any personal information unless you're sure just who is going to get to look at it."

They ended up profiling a rather drab man and gave him the screen name Sucks. They figured that very few of the guys on the site would have much interest in a bland guy called Sucks. For the picture they just put 'Later.' Then they could begin to explore.

Their first search for Martin turned up about fifty hits so they tried his whole name, Martin Shields and found nothing. They tried his screen name WhatUWant but still didn't find a hit.

"Well, that tells us something," Toby said, quitting the search.

"It does?"

"Sure. He's taken himself off the site. Would he do that just because he's decided to commit suicide? I don't think so. A guy with suicide on his mind probably wouldn't think about that, or, if he did, he'd probably leave the information and pictures alone, as a reminder that he was once alive," Toby said.

"You mean kind of like a memorial to himself?" Sam asked.

"Exactly."

"Son of a gun."

\* \* \* \*

The next day Sam called Andy again. He'd returned from vacation and Sam asked him to have a drink with him and Toby. Andy said he couldn't make it until Thursday.

"Well then, it'll just have to wait until Thursday."

"You sound anxious about this, Sam. I could probably break away earlier if it's urgent."

"No. It can wait until Thursday. Tell you what, how about meeting at Spencer's, in the bar. Around six? You have time for dinner?"

"Sure, as long as you're paying. I live on a cop's salary, remember?"

Sam laughed. "Of course I'm paying. After all, you're doing me a favor."

"Well I don't know about that, Sam, but whatever you say. I'll see you guys then."

\* \* \* \*

The next night there was another Prime Timers dinner, this time in the Terrace Room at the Hilton Hotel. Cocktails were served at the pool bar and quite a crowd of men had gathered, standing by the pool, watching and discussing a couple of very hunky young men who were showing off in the water.

"Martini?" Sam asked Toby when they finally got up to the bar.

"I don't think so. This heat calls for gin and tonic. Tall, with lots of ice."

They took their drinks and watched the boys frolicking in the pool.

"Nice, aren't they?" Matthew Stevens, Sam's friend from the Coroner's Office, said.

"Yeah," Sam answered, "but I'm surprised that they're wearing Speedos. Don't most guys their age wear those baggy board shorts?"

Matt nodded. "They wear them to hide their maleness. It's called modesty. I call it fear of an erection."

Sam turned to Toby. "How about it, Toby? What's your take on board shorts? You're the right age."

Toby shook his head. "Never wore 'em. I learned pretty quick that Speedos, like honey, attract a lot more flies."

Matt nearly fell in the pool laughing.

Dinner turned out to be very good.

\* \* \* \*

Thursday evening Sam and Toby were waiting in Spencer's bar when Andy walked in.

He looked around and spotted them. "Hi, men. I was afraid you wouldn't recognize me in my clothes."

Sam and Toby laughed and when Andy realized what he'd said, he laughed too. "I mean my civilian clothes. Not the uniform."

"We'd recognize you the other way, too, Andy," Sam said, finding he really liked the guy.

"Yeah," Toby added. "Come around after the house is finished and we'll prove it to you."

Andy blushed, which only served to make Sam like him more.

They elected to have a drink at the table rather than sitting in the bar.

Once Henry seated them and they ordered drinks, Andy said, "Well Sam, what's this all about?"

"It's about Martin Shields, the man who lived in the condo next door to mine."

"Oh yeah. Committed suicide, didn't he?"

"That's the one. Only he wasn't the one who died."

Andy looked startled. "Huh?"

Toby spoke up. "We think it was Martin's brother, his twin brother, who died."

Conversation stopped while Henry served their drinks and gave them menus.

"Martin had a twin brother?"

"Must have," Sam said with a shrug, "because it sure wasn't Martin in that bathtub."

Andy looked straight at Sam. "How do you figure that? I mean, I saw the body and I saw Martin Shields' driver's license picture. Bad as the picture was, you could tell it was the same guy."

"Or his twin brother," Toby added.

"Twin brother? Where did this twin brother come from?"

"Has to be one because it wasn't Martin in that bathtub. See, Martin wasn't circumcised. The dead guy was."

Andy looked from one to the other of them. "Uh, Sam, can I see you for a moment? Over there?" He indicated the bar.

"That's okay," Toby said with what looked like the beginnings of a grin. "I have to go to the men's room anyway." He got up. "Order for me, will you Sam. In case…"

"We'll wait for you," Andy said. "Go ahead. This won't take long."

Toby left and Andy turned to Sam. "Okay, so how do you know this Martin guy wasn't circumcised? Seeing him around that well known pool? Or in the gym, in the showers, say? Or did you… I mean…"

Sam laughed. "I thought you cop guys were hard bitten and had seen, done, and asked everything."

"Well, we are, and we have. But, I don't know, you're becoming kind of a friend and it's hard to ask a friend some of these questions."

"Okay, Andy. I'll spare you the questions. I know Martin wasn't circumcised because I had sex with him. Several times. Oral sex. And you know what? It's hard not to notice something like a foreskin when it's in... well, you get the idea."

Andy nodded towards the hall to the rest rooms. "Does he know about it? About you and this Martin guy?"

Sam nodded. "There are a lot of things Toby doesn't know about me, but only because he hasn't asked or it's never come up in conversation. Same with me about him. But you know? We – neither one of us – was a virgin when we fell in love. And you know something else? Someday, given the right circumstances – and the right guy – we might... Well, we might branch out once or twice. But only together. As Toby likes to put it, only as a package deal." Sam drank part of his drink. "That's a very long way of saying yes, Toby knows about me and 'this Martin guy.'"

Andy heaved a sigh. "You want to know something? I envy you guys. I really do. I envy the way you can talk about sex, I envy the free and easy way you spread it around and think nothing about it. I envy your attitude, and I probably envy the number of times you guys find someone to get you off."

"That's good to know. Thank you for being... well, for being you. Now, if you'll excuse me for a moment, I'll go and see if Toby needs help."

In the men's room, Sam gave Toby a ten second run down of his conversation with Andy. After that, dinner was fun, almost like three old friends having a meal together and discussing something that was important to all of them.

At the end, over dessert, Andy said, "I haven't any idea where this is going to go, but I'll have a little talk with the lieutenant. I don't know what he's going to say about it, or even if he's going to believe I haven't been smoking something out of the evidence room."

Sam nodded. "Tell him what you need to. Tell him everything."

Andy nodded. "I may have to do that. We'll see. And thanks for the dinner. I've wondered what this place was like."

"And?" Sam asked.

"It's good!" Andy replied with enthusiasm.

\* \* \* \*

Saturday morning, just waking up, Sam slowly rubbed Toby's belly, enjoying the smoothness of the skin and the little forest that ran down to connect with the pubic hair. When Toby quietly groaned and stretched luxuriously, Sam whispered, "You up for some breaking and entering this morning?"

Toby pushed Sam's hand down until it encountered his hardness. "I don't know about the breaking part but I'm sure up for some entering." He rolled up on his side and patted Sam so he'd know just what it was that Toby wished to enter.

Sam kicked the sheet off and reached for the lube.

After coffee, a shower, and a breakfast of French toast, sausage, and raspberry syrup, Toby asked Sam about the breaking and entering thing.

"Well, technically it's not breaking, just entering. I want to get into Martin's condo and look around, see what we can find. Maybe he had an address book he forgot or some letters or something that will tell us about the brother."

"Don't you think he'd get rid of anything that might even imply that he had a brother?"

Sam thought for a moment. "Probably. But what if the brother just sort of dropped in and Martin killed him on the spur of the moment? He might not have had time to get rid of everything."

"You know Sam, there's one thing that bothers me. If it was Martin's brother who was killed, why hasn't anyone missed him?"

"Maybe they have. Maybe even someone called Martin about it. Left a message on his answering machine. We should check that, too."

"And his speed dial numbers." Toby thought for a moment. "So, tell me Sam, just how do we enter without breaking?"

"Because I think I know where a key is. If the gardeners haven't thrown it away."

"Do you think we should wear disguises? Maybe masks?"

Sam laughed. "I don't think that'll be necessary." He thought for a moment. "But you probably should wear gloves, just in case. I don't think we should leave any fingerprints, especially yours, since you've never been in the place."

Armed with latex gloves from under the sink they went to Martin's condo. Sam explained about the fake rock in the little garden by the front door. "I sure hope we can find it in a hurry. You never know who might come along and wonder what we're doing."

Toby looked over the tiny garden. "There it is," he said, pointing.

Sam picked up the rock Toby had pointed out. It was the hollow one with the key inside. He looked at Toby, "How'd you do that? How'd you know?"

"It doesn't fit in with the others. The coloring is wrong and the shape is different from the other rocks." He shrugged. "I don't know. It just didn't look like the others."

Sam muttered something under his breath, took the key out of its hiding place and inserted it in the lock. The door opened.

Toby had a sudden thought. "Do you suppose there's an alarm?"

"I suppose there is but it's not armed. It didn't go off when I found him. And he's not around anymore so who'd even know the code to arm it?"

"Good point."

They went inside and closed the door.

"Hey," Toby said, "it's cool in here. Someone's obviously paying the electric bill."

"Just like everything else." He turned and looked directly at Toby. "I tell you, the man's still alive and somehow paying the bills. I'll bet his brother had money."

They spent an hour looking around the place. They checked his answering machine but there were no messages except one from some guy wanting to know when they could get it on again. The speed-dial buttons were all labeled with people or places they knew and the couple that Toby tried turned out to be just what the label said. They did find an address book in Martin's desk but the page with the last of the R's and the beginning of the S's had been torn out.

Upstairs in Martin's bedroom they found one whole wall covered in framed photographs, drawings and even a few paintings. "Did you ever ask him what this was all about, Sam?"

"No. To tell you the truth, I've never been up here." Toby raised an eyebrow. "No, really. When we played it was always in the living room or out on the patio, in the spa." He looked at the pictures. "Do you see a common thread?"

Toby nodded. "They all have red hair, at least red pubic hair. Those two," he pointed, "are bald."

Sam thought for a moment. "You know, he told me once he had a real thing for red pubic hair, especially if it was a bright, coppery color. And long. He was really into long pubic hair." He stopped and then laughed. "Even mine, which, as you may have noticed, is not at all red."

"Yes, I do believe I've noticed that. But it is long. And silky. And…" he went closer to the wall and looked carefully at a couple of the photographs. "Looks like a guy at work, the Desk Manager." He looked more closely. "But it isn't."

"Then how do you know… never mind."

Toby grinned. "I know in exactly the same way that you know Martin isn't circumcised. Come on, I want to see the rest of the place."

The bathroom was something of a mess with some blood spots on the floor and a lot of water still in the bathtub. They went into the guest room but it looked completely untouched. Then, as they were starting down the stairs, Toby pulled back.

"Let's look in the guest room again," he said. "Like the dead man's dick, something about the guest room isn't right."

Sam watched Toby stand in the doorway of the guest room and let his eyes roam around, looking for something that might not belong or maybe was out of place. It took a few minutes but he found it.

"That book," Toby said, pointing to the dresser. "If it was something for a guest to read then it should be over on the night stand, the one with the light. It's also upside down, lying on its cover. Let's see what it is."

He walked into the room and picked up the book. "Sue Grafton. By the title, a couple of years old." He opened the book, looked at the flyleaf and then ruffled the pages. Then he did it again, letting the book open where it wanted to. It opened at a small white card, used as a bookmark. "Gotcha!"

"What?"

"The brother," he said, handing the book to Sam. "But don't touch the card. I don't know why, but somehow it seems important not to."

Sam looked at a vellum business card carrying the name of Clark Shields. According to the card he was Senior Vice-President of something called Iron Construction located in Natrona, Wyoming. The card also had a phone number.

"Now how the hell did he miss that?" Sam asked, rhetorically.

"Probably in a hurry. Maybe the brother, what's his name?"

Sam looked down at the card. "Clark."

"Yeah, Clark brings his suitcase up here, maybe his shaving kit too, and has the book under his arm. He puts the stuff down and tosses the book on the dresser. He probably wants to clean up. Maybe he's had a long drive or something."

Sam interrupted him. "So how come he's in Martin's bathtub? Can't wash up in the guest bath?"

Toby thought for a moment. "Only a shower in there and maybe he doesn't like showers. Or more likely, he just wants to relax, and where better to do that than in a hot bath?"

Sam finished out the scenario, "So Martin brings him a relaxing drink to go with the bath. The brother drinks it, maybe has another." He put an arm around Toby. "Do you suppose Martin pushed him down, under the water? To hurry it along?"

"I doubt it. The stuff in the drinks would do it quickly enough and why risk a struggle you'd have to clean up? No, I think the guy simply slid under the water because he passed out and couldn't do anything else."

Sam wrote down the information from the card and put the book back on the dresser. "Come on. Let's get out of here."

On the way out they checked the kitchen and found an empty margarita mix bottle on the counter along with an empty pharmacist's pill bottle that had contained Sonata. There was also a half empty tequila bottle, the high proof dark, heavy kind. They were careful not to touch anything.

"Well," Toby said, as they locked the door behind themselves, "now we know how he missed the drugs in his drink. That tequila has a pretty strong taste."

Later, they went to their favorite Mexican place for dinner. They skipped the margaritas and had gin instead.

The next morning they discussed what to do next. The obvious answer was to call Iron Construction in Wyoming and ask them if they knew where their vice president might be. Sam said he'd do that, first thing Monday morning.

"The question is," Sam said, "where the hell is Martin?"

"He may simply have taken over Clark's identity. Couldn't do that at work I guess, but he could call the company and just quit. What're they going to do about it?"

"I suppose. But damn it, Toby, a guy just doesn't up and quit his job and then disappear into the sunset, does he? I mean, where would he go?"

"More importantly, where would Martin go?" Toby said. "But just maybe there's a way to find that out." He was quiet for a few moments and then he grinned. "We haven't a clue where he's gone, so, since we can't go to him, we'll have to get him to come to us."

"And just how might we go about that?"

"The same way you get a fish to come and sample your hook. You use bait. In this case, handsome, redheaded, bait." He started thinking out loud. "We use Zach, my red haired friend at work. We take pictures of him and make up a profile, same as we did for Sucks but we make this one very desirable as well as available and put him up on a couple of sites like OlderButBetter. Sooner or later, Martin is going to come across him and contact him. Bingo, we find our man."

Sam thought for a moment and nodded. "You think that might work? Would the guy at work do it?"

"I don't know, but I'll ask. He's pretty adventurous, so he just might."

Late that afternoon, they decided to go for a swim, to see who might be at the pool. The day had turned hot so there weren't many of the guys there and those who were, were in the water. They went to the locker room to get out of their clothes and found several more guys in the showers.

Outside, they jumped in the pool and found it refreshingly cool. They saw Howard and commented on it.

"Look in the jet tub and you'll see why," Howard said.

They swam over to the place where the spa water poured into the main pool in a little waterfall. It felt downright cold. Toby pulled himself out and went to look. When he did he burst out laughing.

"It's ice, Sam. A big block of ice." He jumped back in and they swam over to Howard.

"You can thank Pete Addison for that," Howard said. "The ice guy comes around every Sunday at noon and throws a couple hundred pounds in the spa. Cools the water down nicely." He looked up and waved. "Well, Duane finally made it out of the E.R."

Duane went into the gym for a few minutes and reappeared in what he termed the uniform of the day: Naked.

"Hi guys. Enjoying the cool water?" he asked, giving Howard a kiss. "I just love it when they put the ice in." He let himself slip under the liquid for a moment and then came up, shaking it out of his hair.

They chatted about nothing for a while and then Howard said, "Hey, you guys doing anything Friday evening? We're grilling some lamb chops, the sweetest, most tender lamb chops you've ever tasted."

"We get them from the Beau Sheep Ranch up in the Sierras," Duane added. "Run by a guy who used to be a biology teacher and his partner. They know what they're doing, at least as far as lamb is concerned."

Sam looked at Toby, who nodded. "I love lamb," he said.

"So, it's a date. Six-thirty, Friday."

They chatted with some of the other guys in the pool before deciding to go home. In the locker room, after getting their clothes, they looked into the showers to see what might be going on. A guy, someone they hadn't seen before, stood with the water beating on the back of his neck. Mike Armstrong knelt in front of him, doubling the pleasure. There were a couple of other guys watching.

"Looks like fun, huh, men?" Pete Addison stepped between them and put his arms around their waists. "You gonna jump in?"

"I don't think so," Sam said, taking hold of Pete's dick. "But you seem to be up for it."

"That I am. It's been a dry weekend so far." He patted them both on the ass. "Think I'd better go get in line."

Pete went over to the man standing under the shower and kissed him.

"You want to join them?" Sam asked.

Toby, who was slowly getting an erection, turned to Sam. "Well, I sure would like to be doing what they're doing but that guy looks like a real pro. Maybe we should go home and practice first. To make sure we know how to do it right."

"I'll let you practice on me if you'll let… well, you get the idea." Sam said.

Toby did.

# Chapter Nineteen

The next evening, when Toby got home, his first words were, "Did you call that iron place?"

Sam nodded.

"And?" Toby asked.

"And I found out how a guy can just disappear into thin air and not have anyone looking for him," Sam replied with a grin.

He told Toby that he'd asked for Clark by name and had been told Clark had retired several months earlier and had left the area. On an off chance, Sam expressed surprise at this and identified himself as Clark's brother. The receptionist transferred him to the woman who had been Clark's secretary. She seemed quite happy – even anxious – to talk about Clark, but admitted, rather wistfully Sam thought, that she hadn't even been aware that Clark had a brother. From her tone Sam wondered if perhaps she'd had designs on the man.

The woman proved to be a fountain of information and told Sam that when Clark had retired, he sold just about everything he owned, including his home, and moved to what she described as 'someplace warm, with palm trees.' She thought perhaps it might be in Mexico but Clark had been a very private man and hadn't talked much about himself, his life, or where he might go.

"Perfect setup," Sam said to Toby. "No one knew much of anything about the man or his life, probably because he was gay, just like his brother."

They went into the kitchen where Sam poured drinks. "You know, it must be hard, being gay in a small town. Especially in Wyoming I would think. She said he traveled quite a bit for the company, so I guess he just kept under the radar at home and… met people when he was on the road." He handed Toby his martini "Sad way to live if you ask me."

"Me, too." Toby sipped the icy fluid and smiled. "Good, Sam. Thank you." He turned silent for a moment while he savored his gin and then said, "You know, I wonder how he came to be circumcised? I mean, especially if they were identical twins."

"She mentioned he had been in the Navy. Maybe that's how."

Toby grinned at him. "You have to be circumcised to be in the Navy?"

"Not exactly, but Harry had wonderful stories about guys having their tonsils taken out and when they woke up they found they had also been circumcised. Harry said it happened as a fairly routine thing in the Navy. He told me he once had to have a little hernia repaired so he wrote 'Leave it alone' and 'Do not touch' on his dick. In ink." Sam laughed. "Harry got kidded in the showers for weeks afterword. It seems he'd written it in indelible ink."

Toby laughed. "Maybe the navy did it but I guess we'll never know for sure."

"Change of subject. Did you get a chance to talk to that redheaded guy?" Sam asked.

"Zach? No. He was off today. I'll try to catch him tomorrow. Now what do you want for dinner?" Toby replied.

"You," Sam said lasciviously.

Toby smiled. "Later. You need nourishment first."

He got both.

The next evening when Toby got home from work Sam said, "I had a phone call today from Andy."

"Oh yeah?" Toby said, "What'd he have to say?

"He said he thought he was going to have real trouble convincing anyone at the station to put a warrant out on a guy just because he isn't circumcised. Especially a guy who's nowhere to be found. In a nutshell, he wasn't very encouraging," Sam said.

Toby kissed him. "Don't worry, Sam. If we find Martin maybe that'll make it easier for Andy to convince whoever he has to convince. And I have some good news on that front. Zach loved the idea. Especially after I told him he'd be helping to track down a murderer."

"I don't suppose he has any pictures we could use, does he?" Sam asked.

"No," Toby replied. "I asked him. But what the heck, Tom and Dan, you know, next door to the house? They have a digital camera. Maybe we could get them to take some pictures of Zach."

"Good thinking," Sam said. "They're up in L.A. until next week but I'll ask them when they get back. I imagine they'll be more than happy to take some pictures of a handsome, naked redheaded man. He is handsome when he's naked, isn't he?"

Toby rolled his eyes. "You'll just have to wait and decide that one for yourself."

\* \* \* \*

On Friday Prime Timers had a mixer at a restaurant called Peter's, located a few miles down the valley and Sam and Toby decided to skip it. A good thing, too, because Toby turned out to be late getting out of his office. When he got home he just had time for a quick shower and a change into shorts, a polo shirt and sandals. He and Sam arrived at Duane and Howard's only a couple of minutes late.

Over dinner, they got onto the subject of Martin. Sam, backed up by Toby, told them the suicide wasn't what it appeared to be. When he said he thought the body had been that of Martin's brother, Howard said he wasn't surprised.

"Why do you say that?" Toby asked.

"Oh, I don't know. Martin was a nice enough guy, but there was something about him that put me off." He laughed. "Maybe because he borrowed money from us and never paid it back. He just ignored the whole question of it."

Duane smiled. "Yeah, he fucked us royally and didn't even say thank you." He turned to Sam. "Have you told the police?"

"Yes, but they aren't too interested. Our friend on the force told us he thought he was going to have real trouble convincing anyone to put out a warrant on a guy just because he isn't circumcised."

"We'll find him, Sam. I'm sure of it," Toby said.

He explained the plan he and Sam had worked out. "So once we get his picture taken, we can put it on a couple of websites and sooner or later Martin is going to find it and then it'll only be a matter of time."

Duane poured more wine in their glasses. "Two things," he said. "Number one, when you write the profile for this redheaded man, make him from out of town. If he's from Palm Springs, Martin may not bite, thinking he's already had him. Number two, have this guy's pictures taken by Jose, you know, the tall Chicano guy who lives over by the other pool?"

"He's good at it?" Toby asked. "We were going to ask the guys next door to the house, but only because we know they have a digital camera."

Both Duane and Howard shook their heads. "You want Jose. Come on upstairs and we'll show you why. He took a couple of shots of us."

"Oh no you don't, Howard," Duane said. "I want to see their reaction too, so you three just sit and enjoy your wine while I clean up."

Cleanup went fast, Sam had to give him that. Fast and organized. In less than ten minutes, it was done. Then they all trooped upstairs to the master bedroom.

"There," Howard said, pointing to a large, framed photograph of himself and Duane. They were standing, in profile, facing each other and holding hands. The more Sam looked at it the more he could see that the two men were in love and were lusting after each other. Not that they were obviously erect but there was something about the way they were looking at each other that said 'I love you and I'm going to have you' and said it loudly. The picture took his breath away.

"Here's another," Duane said, handing them large, framed picture. In this one, Howard stood behind Duane, looking over his shoulder. Duane's hands covered his dick but somehow Sam knew he was hard. The expression on both their faces left no doubt that Howard was pushed up inside him.

"My God, that's sexy," Toby said. "He captured exactly what you guys must have been feeling."

"Yeah," Howard said. "That's the kind of work Jose does. He gets to the very essence of the subject."

Sam tore his eyes away from the picture and said, "I sure hope this Jose will do the pictures for us."

Toby chimed in, "Yeah, and maybe a couple of us. That," he said looking at the picture again, "is art."

\* \* \* \*

On Sunday afternoon Sam and Toby found Jose at the pool, dangling his legs in the water and watching the guys swim and play. The three of them talked for a bit and when Toby asked Jose to dinner he jumped at the chance.

"I hear you're a damn good cook and, boy, could I use a good meal," Jose said.

"You don't cook?" Sam asked.

"Yeah," Jose said, "I can make a few things but it's no fun to cook for yourself, so mostly I nuke something frozen or make a sandwich."

"Well," Toby said with a smile, "you may be disappointed tonight. We're grilling hamburgers."

Sam, Toby, and Jose talked with some of the other men for a while and then Jose disappeared for a bit. Sam assumed he'd gone to have a shower... or something. Sure enough, when he reappeared he had a very satisfied smile on his face.

Over burgers and oven fries, Sam and Toby told Jose what they thought had happened in Martin's condo the night Sam found the body. Then they told him what they wanted to do to find Martin.

Jose, like Howard, said he wasn't surprised Martin might do such a thing. "He was awfully good in bed, but kind of desperate, too. I know he needed money, but Jesus, I didn't think he'd kill for it. You're really sure about this?"

Sam looked at him. "You've had sex with him, right?" Jose nodded. "Describe his dick."

Jose laughed. "Well, let's see. It was pretty good sized, fairly long but not too thick. And it was always clean. I watched him in the shower once, washing his foreskin, although I think a good part of that was just showing off."

"Yeah, well, that's the thing. See, the guy who died up there in Martin's bathtub was circumcised," Sam said.

"You're kidding!" Jose said.

"I'm not. I was there. I saw him and he definitely didn't have a foreskin."

"We think it must have been Martin's brother," Toby said. "His twin brother."

Jose whistled. "You think he killed his own brother? Man, we've got to find him. I mean… his brother? Jesus."

"That's what we're trying to do. That's why we need you to take some pictures of a friend of Toby's." Sam explained about setting up a profile on a couple of websites to smoke Martin out.

"And we want you to photograph him," Toby added. "We saw a couple of the pictures you did for Howard and Duane and they were awesome."

Jose thought for a moment. "I hope your friend is a redhead," he said to Toby. "Martin has a real thing for redheads."

"Oh, he's got red hair alright. Bright red pubic hair, too," Toby said. "So, when can you take his picture?"

"Wednesday would be good. At my place. Unless you want to do it at the pool."

"No. Your place would be better. We don't want Martin to recognize anything," Sam said. "He might get suspicious."

The next day Toby asked Zach if Wednesday would be okay. Zach gave an enthusiastic thumbs up.

\* \* \* \*

On Tuesday, Sam went out to the house. Bill, helping a couple of his workmen nail up sheetrock, took a break to show Sam what they'd done. And they had done a lot. Sam became even more impressed when they went outside and he saw that the new pool was ready for its plaster coating.

"It's bigger than I expected," Sam said, pacing along the lap pool part. "I'm going to have to get into better shape to do many laps in this thing."

Bill laughed. "Oh, I don't know. You must be in pretty good shape now, to keep up with that boyfriend of yours." He thought for a moment. "How come he doesn't shave?"

Sam smiled. "He does shave, every couple of days. He just does it with a number one clipper and then uses a razor on his neck. He thinks it makes him look older and more mature. I think it makes him look sweet and sexy."

Bill shrugged. "Whatever." He turned back to the pool. "The plasterers come tomorrow. It'll be prettier after they finish. Filled with water, too. But you can't swim in it for a couple of days, until the water gets changed. Maybe late next week."

"Won't it be a little cold? Even with this heat?"

"No, it'll be just about right. We're putting in solar heat, remember?"

The solar heat had been Toby's idea after he and Sam saw it at Tom and Dan's, next door. Toby said it'd let them swim nearly all year around and not cost a fortune in gas for a heater.

"It's really coming together, isn't it?" Sam said.

"Sure is. We'll be locking it up in the next day or so. Oh, that reminds me, come on inside."

Inside, Bill sorted through some hardware and handed Sam a key. "Once it's locked up this'll get you in the front door. I know how much you guys like to come out here on weekends. Oh," he said, almost as an afterthought, "after it's locked up the alarm code we'll use will be 9-8-7-1-2-3. You can change it to something else later, after we're out of here."

\* \* \* \*

On Wednesday, after work, Zach changed into a pair of shorts and a T-shirt at the hotel and followed Toby home.  He stood well over six feet tall and, as advertised, he had red hair, cut fairly short.  He also had an infectious smile, green eyes, and from what Sam could see, a very nice body.  If that doesn't smoke Martin out, nothing will, Sam thought as he shook Zach's hand.

Toby served a cold dinner of green salad and shrimp, and Sam decided not only was the Zach handsome, he was also intelligent and spoke well.  He briefly wondered if he should be worried that he was a friend of Toby's but dismissed that as nonsense.  He asked Zach if he would mind company at the shoot.  Zach shook his head.

"Who knows," he said with a laugh, "I might need chaperones."

Jose welcomed them, took them into the living room and made drinks, all without taking his eyes off Zach.

One wall of the living room had been covered with a light blue sheet.  This, Jose told them, would be the background for the pictures.  Later, on the computer, he could change it to any sort of background they might want.

He started by taking a couple of shots of Zach in his clothes, then wearing just his shorts and finally with nothing at all.  Zach didn't seem in the least self conscious about being naked in front of them but neither did he seem to be showing off.  The way Jose and Zach worked together made it appear that they had some sort of silent communication going.

After a couple of close-up shots of Zach's dick and coppery pubic hair, Jose paused and looked at Toby.  "In your profile of him?  Make him married.  Martin is almost as hot for married men as he is for this."  He ran his fingers through Zach's red growth.

Zach didn't flinch but, Sam noted, his dick did begin to fill out.

"Then he needs a wedding ring, doesn't he?" Sam asked.

Jose paused and looked Zach up and down.  "Wait, I think I have something that'll pass for a wedding ring."  He went upstairs and came back with a plain silver band which he worked onto Zach's finger.

Zach held it up to the light and admired it.  "Beautiful," he said.

They did several poses of Zach holding his dick, which highlighted his red growth and brought attention to the ring. Sam noticed Jose seemed to have a large knot in his shorts.

"Can I let it get hard now?" Zach asked. "I don't think I can hold it off much longer."

Jose glanced at Sam and Toby, then back at Zach. "Yeah, now would be good. Do you want some help?"

He didn't wait for an answer, he simply fell to his knees and took Zach in his mouth. Zach's dick cooperated almost instantly.

The look on Sam's face said, Well, that should be enough cock to satisfy anyone, even Martin.

Jose took a couple of pictures and turned to Sam and Toby who were sitting together on the couch. "Uh, look guys, this is going to take a while so if you have something you need to do, just go ahead."

Zach nodded. "Yeah, go on, guys. I'll see you at work tomorrow Toby."

They got the message. They went home to do what Jose and Zach were presumably going to do... only without the camera.

The next day, when Toby came home from work, he kissed Sam and said, "He's still wearing the ring."

\* \* \* \*

The next morning they were laying spoon fashion and Sam pressed his hardness against Toby.

In a low voice Toby said, "We just did that, Sam."

"I know," Sam replied, "but I want to do it again. Can we?"

By way of answering, Toby pushed back, slowly opening for him, still slick from the first time. Sam entered him slowly and easily.

Sam took his time with it, climbing the peak almost to the top and then backing off, knowing exactly where Toby was. It was Toby in fact, who first lost control but Sam sensed it and fell with him in a long spiral of pleasure.

Afterword they lay quietly for a time, still connected and savoring what they'd just done. Without disengaging, Sam pulled himself up on his elbow and nibbled at Toby's ear. "Let's get married."

"Where?"

"I don't know. Canada? Spain? Holland? I just want to be married to you, that's all."

Toby twisted his head around and kissed Sam. "How about here? We can't get married but we can be domestic partners. It's almost like getting married."

"Okay." Sam flexed in him. "But then I want to go to one of those other places and get really married. Maybe all of them." He flexed again.

"Sam? Can you… again?"

Sam moved in him slowly. "For you, again, and again, and again."

The next day, Sam called Alistair.

# Chapter Twenty

That evening, at a Prime Timers mixer in a bar called Ground Zero, Sam asked Toby if he could take Thursday and Friday off for a trip to L.A.

"Yeah, I'm pretty sure I can," Toby said. "What are we going to do up there?"

Sam shrugged. "I talked to Alistair. He's preparing some paperwork and he'd like us up there on Thursday. You know, for signatures and things. I thought on Friday we could go out to Beverly Hills and look at the house. Some guy wants to buy it and we have to decide if we want to sell it."

"We? Wasn't that your friend Harry's house? Did he leave it to you?"

"Not exactly," Sam said dismissively, "but I'm sort of responsible for it. Now come on let's go say hello to some people."

Toby caught Sam by the sleeve. "Wait a minute. What kind of paperwork?"

Sam smiled. "Our domestic partnership." His smile turned into a grin. "Hey, you thought of it first, didn't you?"

Toby sighed. "Yeah, I guess I did. I just had no idea you'd get it done so fast, that's all."

"Hey, my love, no time like the present. Come on, I'll buy you a drink."

Later, at home, Sam said, "If we sign stuff on Thursday, then go out to the house on Friday, on Saturday we could go see your folks. Maybe take them out to dinner."

Toby smiled. "You mean so dad can see who's attached to the dick he always pictures in my mouth?"

"Something like that. You okay with it? I mean, me meeting them?"

"Well, they'll have to meet you sometime. I can't very well keep you hidden away in some closet." He laughed. "Hell, I couldn't even keep me hidden away in the closet. Yeah, let's take them out for dinner."

"Good. How about Spago?"

Toby rolled his eyes. "Do you have any idea how uncomfortable my folks would be at a place like Spago? No, Sam. Definitely not Spago."

"Okay, then where?"

"How about Café Santorini? It's in Pasadena and they think of it as a special occasion restaurant. And this is going to be some special occasion, believe me."

"I'll call Alistair's secretary and have her make a reservation. Seven o'clock?"

"Yeah. I'll call mom tomorrow and let her know we're coming."

On Tuesday, Jose came around with a CD containing Zach's pictures. He also brought Zach, who, Sam noted, still wore the silver ring. "Good pictures, guys. Let me tell you, this man knows how to play to a camera."

Zach blushed a little and said, "It's not me." He smiled at Jose. "It's the photographer."

Jose rolled his eyes but said, "Thank you."

Jose put the CD in the computer and they all could see that Jose hadn't been kidding. The pictures were terrific and they had a difficult time choosing the ones to use. The four of them finally agreed on five of the pictures and then spent a couple of hours setting Zach up on two websites, DaddiesDotCom and OlderButBetter.

Zach was profiled as living in Arizona, married and very horny. They used the e-mail address for an account Toby had set up earlier just for that purpose. Interested guys wouldn't see that address, of course, but the websites would send an e-mail to it whenever someone sent a message to Zach's account.

"Now we just sit back and wait," Toby said when they were finished. "You're going to get a lot of mail and we'll have to sift through it carefully if we're going to find the one from Martin."

"Do you think he'll find me?" Zach asked. "There are a lot of sites out there. What if he never gets on these?"

Toby shrugged. "Then we try some of the others. Don't worry, we'll find him sooner or later."

\* \* \* \*

At seven on Thursday morning, Sam and Toby set out for L.A.

After an hour or so, Toby asked, "Shouldn't we have some sort of agreement or something? I mean, guys with money always do that, don't they? To protect their assets?"

Sam, who was driving, nodded. "Maybe. Alistair said something about an agreement, one to protect you, too."

"Me? What do I have? I'm just a junior accountant."

"You have me, don't you? That's gotta be worth something."

Toby twisted around in his seat so he could look at Sam. "Now that we're getting married I guess I can ask this." He took a deep breath. "Just how much money do you have? Ballpark figure."

Sam glanced over at him. "Are you sure you want to talk about this?"

"Why not? Unless you don't want to."

"You know, Toby, I've been afraid to bring up the subject of money with you. I don't want you to think... well, to think I'm like that guy..."

"Jack? Sam, you are nothing, and I mean nothing like Jack. He was a selfish user who did things only to satisfy his own ego and I doubt he'll ever change." He smiled at Sam. "I have, though. I'm not the affection hungry nineteen-year-old with raging hormones and a dick that's always hard that I was then. I'm learning to think with my head, the big one, and to sort out the emotional parts properly."

"I just don't want you ever to think I'm trying to buy you or make you different than you are. I love you, Toby, with a passion that's so strong it scares me sometimes, and I don't want whatever money I might have to drive you away. That's why I try to be so careful…"

"Like that silly watch you gave me for my birthday? The one with the Walmart price tag? That was a very sweet thing to do and you may never know how much I appreciated it. But I love you too, Sam, and I will not allow something as stupid as money to come between us." He paused for a moment. "That's the long way to say yes, I want to talk about it."

Sam gave a little unconscious shrug. "Okay, we'll talk about it. The first thing you need to know is that the money doesn't really mean much to me."

Toby laughed. "I've noticed."

"Well, it's true. As a kid, I never had any money in my pocket, but I got along okay. Then I went to work for Harry and I didn't really need any money. I lived in his house. He fed me and seemed to always be buying things for me. He…"

"Didn't he pay you?"

"Oh, yes. He paid me very well. But most of it went into a bank account because I just didn't need much of it. He also gave me stocks and things and they went into an account, too. There was a man, I forget his name, who took care of Harry's investments. He also took care of mine."

"So you didn't have to. Does Alistair take care of that now?"

"In a way. Alistair is a lawyer and runs a firm that manages people's money. They pay the bills, the taxes, that sort of thing. They also keep an eye on anyone who has anything to do with the money."

You have any idea how much you actually have?"

Sam laughed. "You're not going to believe this Toby, but I don't, exactly. But let's see, not long ago Alistair said I had something like eight million dollars, give or take."

Toby took a moment to digest this. "Harry left you very well off."

"He did. But you need to understand that he didn't leave me that money. It's money from my salary and the stocks and stuff that Harry gave me over the years. Well, that and the investment savvy of Alistair's firm."

Sam went on to explain about the trust and how it owned everything Harry had. "The trust owns the house in Palm Springs, the one in Beverly Hills and all the investments and cash Harry had. I'm the trustee as well as the beneficiary of the trust so, I guess in the long run, it all belongs to me." He grinned at Toby. "So there you have it, the complete financial story of Samuel Davis."

"That's a little breathtaking, Sam."

"Yeah. But see, Toby? It doesn't do anything for me if I'm alone, if I don't have anyone I love to share it with."

"You could buy a lot of love with all that money, Sam."

"No, I could buy a lot of sex with all that money. Maybe even a few professions of love but nothing more." He laughed. "But believe me, a lot of sex. I tried it for a time, after Harry was gone, when I was kind of at loose ends."

"Was it fun?"

"Not really. Not a whole lot better than I could do all by myself."

"So what do you do with all that money?"

Sam looked over at him. "Well, I leave a lot of it alone, in the account. But I do have a couple of little things I do. I pay Jeremy Scott's salary, for instance. You know, the guy who runs the Desert Aids Help?"

"You pay his salary?"

"Sure. That way, the agency can use the money they'd otherwise have to pay him to solve other problems. I have a couple of guys, too."

"Guys?"

Sam smiled. "Yeah, guys. I don't even know their names but they have AIDS and can't work. So I help them, pay their rent, buy their meds, that sort of thing. That way they can concentrate on staying alive."

Toby shook his head. "The things I don't know about you..."

They got to Alistair's around nine-thirty. His offices took up most of the fifty-third floor of the Aon Center on Wilshire Boulevard and had an incredible view of Los Angeles.

When they went in, a secretary stood and said, "Oh, Mr. Davis. And Mr. Litchfield. Please go right in, he's expecting you."

When they entered his office, Alistair rose, came around the desk and went to shake hands with Sam but Sam was having none of that. He pulled Alistair into a tight hug. "It's been a while Alistair. I've missed you."

"That's very nice of you to say, Sam. Thank you." He turned to Toby. "And you must be Sam's young man." He extended his hand. "Welcome, Toby."

The first thing they discussed was Toby's new account and the five-hundred-thousand dollars in it. Alistair explained the reasoning behind it, which Toby said was silly but was a sweet gesture. Then they went through the partnership agreement, which basically said everything each of them owned prior to signing the domestic partner agreement would remain his own property. Everything acquired afterward would be joint property. Both thought that unnecessary too, but they signed it anyway.

Then came the actual domestic partnership form. They invited Alistair's secretary in to notarize it and then it was done. Sam and Toby were as close to being married as they could get in the state of California in 2005.

"You will join me for lunch," Alistair said after the final signing. Sam nodded, still slightly in awe of what he and Toby had just done.

Alistair had lunch served in his small dining room, the windows of which presented the diners with a view almost to Santa Monica. They were served lobster quiche accompanied by a green salad and freshly made rolls.

"He's still with you, huh?" Sam said when he took his first bite of the quiche.

"Albert? I don't know what we'd do without him."

Dessert was puff pastry swans filled with chocolate mousse. The plates, at least Sam's and Toby's, had Congratulations written in chocolate around the rim. When Alistair poured the champagne Albert came in to offer a toast. He looked very pleased when both Sam and Toby hugged him and told him how much they appreciated the lunch.

After they'd taken their leave and were sitting in the car in the parking garage, they held each other and shared a long kiss.

"I have an idea," Sam said.

"So do I," Toby answered, in a husky voice.

Sam laughed. "I have that one, too, but..." He paused, looking at Toby. "I know neither one of us is really into jewelry but now that we're as good as married, now that we're a family, I think we should have something to symbolize it, what we've done and who we are."

Toby thought about it for a moment. "I think that's a very good idea, Sam."

They went to Tiffany where a well-kept, gray-haired salesman seemed to know exactly what they wanted. They decided on his first offering, wide gold bands with a slight bevel on each edge. They were, as the salesman said, simple, understated, and elegant.

"And what shall we engrave on the inside?"

Sam said, "I never thought about engraving." He turned to Toby. "What..."

"I think I'd like something like Sam, Since August 18, 2005," Toby said.

"Perfect. And mine will have your name and the same date."

The salesman smiled. "A lovely sentiment, gentlemen. Will tomorrow afternoon be acceptable? We will, of course, deliver them."

They agreed and told him the name of the hotel where they were staying.

As they were leaving the store Sam said to Toby, "You know, we ought to take something to your folks, don't you think?"

Toby looked around and spotted a silver Revere bowl. "Mom would love that, as long as she didn't know how much it cost."

Sam nodded and smiled. "I'll never tell. We'll get the glass liner too, so she can put flowers in it."

They stayed at The Mozart in Beverly Hills, a small hotel made up mostly of small one story cabin like structures although there were also a few suites in the central building. The grounds were lush with tropical plants and there were small swimming pools scattered around the grounds. The perfect place for a honeymoon.

Once they were in their bungalow and the sweet faced bell hop who had shown them its features had gone, the fell into each other's arms and spent a long time looking into each other's eyes.

"It's done," Sam said. "You and I are now we."

"Never, in my entire life, did I picture myself as a married man," Toby said. "Thank you."

They slowly undressed each other and made love like it was the first time. After dinner they did it again.

\* \* \* \*

The next day, after breakfast, they went over to the Beverly Hills house.

"My God, Sam!" Toby exclaimed as they drove through the gates, "this isn't a house, it's a mansion."

Sam shrugged. "I guess. When you live in something for all those years you kind of take it for granted."

"And someone wants to buy it?" Toby asked as Sam unlocked the front door. "What's it worth?"

"I don't know. A couple of million, I guess, maybe three. Alistair said the guy wants to tear it down and build something more contemporary."

"Three million for a tear down? You've got to be kidding."

Sam turned and looked at him. "You want to live here? Maybe keep it as a weekend place?"

Toby looked around. "Not really. I mean, if we were going to have a weekend house I'd rather be at the beach or something."

Sam considered. "Me, too. Maybe a villa in Mexico. Or Australia. We could go in winter, when it's summer there."

"Sam!"

"Well, why not? Think about it. But for now, come on, I'll show you around the place. And watch for stuff we should keep, take down to Palm Springs."

They spent several hours at the house, Sam reliving old memories and Toby marveling at the beautiful things scattered everywhere. Furniture, paintings, knickknacks, all of it quite wonderful in his eyes.

When they left, they went back to Rodeo Drive where Sam insisted Toby buy a shirt that had caught his eye. "I don't need that shirt," Toby argued. "It's pretty and all that but –"

Sam cut him off. "You need clothes, Toby. I see what you wear to work every day. You have three suits and one of them is getting just a little threadbare. Now come on."

They went into the shop and spoke to a good looking, young salesman who didn't quite drool over Toby but only by an effort of will. Sam, for his part, kept the salesman busy and out of the changing room and hid the price tags of the things Toby tried on.

In the end, Toby bought five suits – none of which needed further alterations than the length – and seven shirts. Sam picked out a dozen pair of underwear for him, all in deep jewel tones. He also made Toby buy three pairs of Crockett & Jones loafers. "Those are really good shoes," he said, "and your feet will thank you for them a hundred times over. Trust me on this."

When all his purchases were rung up and totaled Toby actually turned pale and when he went to sign the Visa slip his hand shook. Sam made arrangements to have everything shipped to the condo in Palm Springs.

Back at the hotel, Sam took Toby in his arms, kissed him, and said, "You're wonderful, you know that? I thought sure you were going to argue when the guy rang up that stuff, but you signed for them with hardly a flicker."

Toby kissed him back. "I nearly couldn't do it. I couldn't even remember how to spell my last name. Sam, I haven't paid that much for all the clothes I've ever had in my life." He paused and smiled. "But someday I'll get the hang of this, being married to a man with money."

Sam began to undress him. "Don't forget, you're a man with money, too."

"There was so much going on, I never thanked you for that, did I." He started to unbutton Sam's shirt. "The money?"

Sam let him pull the shirt off. "Actually it was Alistair's idea." He opened the button on Toby's jeans and pulled down the zipper. "A good one, I thought."

"Well then, thank you, Alistair," Toby said.

"You're not wearing any underwear," Sam said.

Toby shrugged. "I didn't thank you for keeping that salesman busy, either. I don't know what he would have done if he found out I was," he spread his arms out, "like this. Besides, I thought we might be in a hurry sometime today."

"No hurry, Toby. We have all the time in the world. And as for the salesman, he probably would have fainted when he saw you."

They did hurry, at least getting started. Then it was long, slow, and deeply satisfying.

Both Sam and Toby were lying in that half-light between sleep and awake when there was a knock at the door. "Who the hell can that be?" Sam grumbled as he grabbed a robe and stumbled out to the living room.

He was back a few moments later, carrying a light blue box tied with a white ribbon. "You ready?" he asked.

"Wait. I have to pee."

When he returned Sam was naked again, sitting on the bed and holding the box.

"What is it?"

"It's from Tiffany," Sam said, holding the box out to Toby. "Open it."

Toby took the box and sat next to him on the bed. He realized his hands were shaking just a little as he untied the white ribbon. When he opened the box he found two pale blue boxes, one marked Sam and one marked Toby.

"Do you suppose," Sam said when Toby handed him one of the boxes, "the names on the boxes refer to us or to what's engraved in the ring?"

Toby looked at him as though he'd lost his mind. "Open it, Sam. Just open it."

It turned out that the names described what had been engraved inside the ring, so Sam had Toby's ring and vice versa. Each took the band he was holding and carefully pressed it onto the third finger of the other's left hand. There were no words but each knew what the other was thinking.

"It's beautiful, Sam." Toby said, turning the gold circle slightly on his finger. "Now I can touch you any time I want, even when I'm sitting in that drab office at the hotel. You'll always be with me."

"And you with me. Always." He pulled Toby into a hug and held him for a long time.

They went to Spago for dinner that night. They were late, of course, being otherwise occupied for longer than they should have been, but it turned out to be okay because their table wasn't ready anyway.

Toby couldn't make up his mind, so they had the Chef's Tasting Menu, which consisted of eight courses, each hardly more than enough to savor the dish but, by the time they had finished, more than enough to fill them up. Each offering was accompanied by a different wine, several of which were so good Toby asked the waiter to make a note of its name and year.

Sam had prudently suggested they take a cab to the restaurant so neither one had to drive back to the hotel that night.

# Chapter Twenty-One

In the morning, after an excellent breakfast out on Pacific Coast Highway, which, as a one time native Sam called PCH, Toby asked what Sam had in mind for the day.

"Well, you know, I've been thinking," Sam said. "I want to go back to the house and check something. Then…" he spread his hands, "well, we'll find something to do."

Toby grinned. "Okay, but I want to stop at a drug store before we get to the house. I want to get a disposable camera."

"Oh," Sam laughed. "I thought maybe all those blue cheese French fries hurt your stomach."

Toby gave him a look.

At the house, Sam asked what he wanted to photograph.

"You. On the diving board. Naked," Toby said.

Sam raised an eyebrow.

"It's for Dan. He's so enamored with that picture of you…"

"But he took another one. At their place, remember?" Sam said.

Toby shook his head. "But this will be the real thing. The same place the first one was taken."

Sam sighed. "Okay, if you want to spread pictures of my dick around. Let's get it done."

"It's not like I'm going to put them out on the Internet, Sam. Although…"

They went out into the garden and Sam took off his clothes. "You gotta get naked, too, you know. I need inspiration."

Toby got undressed and Sam climbed up on the diving board, like he was not quite ready to dive. Toby took pictures of him from several angles and distances because, he said, he couldn't quite remember just where the first picture had been taken.

When he was finished, Sam took the camera. "Okay, now you get up there and I'll take a couple of you. I'm not the only one Dan has the hots for you know."

After he'd taken a couple of shots, he put the camera down on a table and sat in one of the cushioned chairs. He waved Toby over.

"Stand right here," he said. "A little closer."

Then he grabbed Toby by the buns, pulled him close and took his dick into his mouth.

Sam gave Toby one of those blow jobs that couples don't do often enough, a blow job that's hard, fast and explosive. When it was finished he stood and kissed Toby.

"I just had to do that," he said. "You were so... so sexy standing up there on that diving board. I couldn't help myself."

"You were pretty sexy yourself, Sam, but I have better self control." He spit into his hand and wet Sam's dick. "However..." He dropped onto a lounge, on his belly.

Sam knew what to do, and he did it well.

When they were dressed again, Toby asked Sam what he needed to do at the house.

"Well," Sam said, "I got to thinking last night. I wondered if anyone thought to clean out the safe in the library. So come on, let's go see."

Sam led the way to the library where he took down one of the pictures, a picture that Toby had decided was a genuine William Keith. Behind the picture was an old fashioned wall safe, just like in the movies. When he opened it he laughed. "I guess not." He reached in and then handed Toby a pack of hundred dollar bills. Being the accountant he was, Toby counted them.

"Ten thousand," Toby said. "Why did you have ten thousand dollars in cash in there?"

"Didn't," Sam said. "Fifty thousand." He shrugged. "What can I tell you? Harry had a thing for cash. Stick that in your pocket and give it to your dad tonight. Tell him to take your mother someplace nice." He closed and locked the safe, leaving the other forty thousand inside.

In the car, Sam said, "If we're going to sell, we have to come back and go through everything, every cupboard, every drawer, every cabinet. Look for cash."

"You mean Harry hid more cash around the house?"

"He didn't exactly hide it, Toby. More like he just put it there, sometimes in plain sight. He just had to have cash around. I think it was because of the Great Depression. He had to have money he could put his hands on."

They spent the rest of the day in West Hollywood. They had a light lunch and then walked around, looking in the shops, admiring the men, and generally enjoying the feeling of being in the center of a gay place. They went back to the hotel around five, to shower, pleasure each other, and get ready for dinner with Toby's parents.

On the way, Sam asked, "Are you sure you want to do this, introduce me to your parents?"

"Why not? I'm married to you, aren't I?"

"Yes, but you know, I'm probably close to the same age they are. Isn't that going to be a problem? At least for them?"

Toby shook his head. "If it's a problem for them, well, it's their problem, not ours." He turned on the seat so he could look directly at Sam. "Just be your normal charming self and everything will be fine. Trust me on this."

When Toby rang the doorbell his mother opened the door so quickly it was obvious she'd been standing just inside, probably looking out through the peephole. Toby hugged her and introduced Sam. A slight look of dismay crossed her face but she quickly hid it.

Inside, Toby introduced his father who didn't wipe the dismay from his face quite as fast as his wife had. He extended his hand anyway.

They all sat in an awkward silence for a moment before Toby said, "Why don't you open your present, Mom?"

She took the box and held it carefully on her lap. "I don't think I've ever had a present from Tiffany's. It's almost too pretty to open."

But she did open it and was thrilled with the Revere bowl. "It's so… I don't know, classical, I guess is the word. Thank you, both of you."

Toby looked at his watch and said, "We probably should go. There's a lot of traffic out there."

They took Sam's car, but Toby drove since he knew the area. His mother sat next to him with Sam and his father sharing the back seat.

"Toby tells me you work for an insurance company, Mr. Litchfield," Sam said by way of making conversation. "It must be interesting work."

"Sometimes," Toby's dad answered. "For one thing, it's title insurance, and searching title to land can be quite engaging." He paused for a moment and then laughed. "But mostly it's boring. Same old thing over and over. What do you do?"

"Well, uh, at the moment I'm restoring a Mid-Century Modern house with Toby's help," Sam said proudly.

Mr. Litchfield considered for a moment. "You going to turn it? Must be good profits in work like that, if you know what you're doing."

"No, sir. We're going to live in it."

It took a moment for the ramifications of that to sink in.

At the same time, in the front seat, Mrs. Litchfield spoke more directly. "He's a little older than you, isn't he?"

"A little. Nineteen years, to be exact. He's forty-five."

Under her breath she quietly said, "Almost my age." She turned to Toby and said, "Are you sure about… this?"

Toby patted her on the knee. "Yes, Mom. More sure than I've ever been about anything."

At the restaurant they were seated right away. Sam had a moment of panic when Mrs. Litchfield ordered iced tea but then Mr. Litchfield ordered bourbon on the rocks. When both he and Toby ordered Sapphire martinis, Mrs. Litchfield changed her mind and ordered a cosmopolitan.

They made small talk for a little while, discussing the menu and the wine list, then ordered. When the alcohol began its work, the talk, in an oblique sort of way, turned to Sam and Toby.

"So, Sam, you and my boy here are going to live together in that house you're doing?"

"Yes, sir. We are."

Mr. Litchfield took a sip of his bourbon. "Look Sam, let's cut the sir crap. The name is Gill, and I'm not a hell of a lot older than you are so just call me Gill, okay?"

Mrs. Litchfield went just a little pale and took a gulp of her cosmopolitan but didn't say anything.

"Thank you, uh... Gill. I appreciate that."

Mr. Litchfield waved Sam's thanks aside and looked at his son. "You okay with this? You want to do it, live with him?" Toby nodded. "It's not going to be like with that other guy, is it?"

"You mean Jack?"

"Yeah, him. This guy," he gestured at Sam, "isn't going to hurt you like Jack did, is he?" He turned back to Sam. "You see, Sam, Toby is my son. I don't always agree with him or even understand him, but no one's ever going to shit on him again like that other guy did. Not if I can help it."

Mrs. Litchfield turned a shade paler, but the server's arrival with the salads saved her from having to speak. Sam caught the man's eye and gestured for another round of drinks. No one at the table objected.

They ate their salads in silence until the new drinks were served.

Sam said, not exactly to Mr. Litchfield but more to the entire table, "My intentions toward your son, sir, are to love him, to honor him, and to care for him. I intend to do that to the best of my abilities for as long as he will allow me to do so."

Mr. Litchfield snorted. "Sounds to me like you're marrying him and you can't do that. At least not in California."

"Well, we can get close to it anyway," Sam said by way of clarification. "The state denies us the right to marry but it does allow us many of the same responsibilities and privileges."

Mrs. Litchfield took a deep breath. "It's called domestic partners, honey," she said to her husband. Looking back and forth between Toby and Sam, she asked, "Is that what you're planning? A domestic partnership?"

Toby sighed and put down his fork. "It's a done deal, Mom. We signed the papers Thursday." He looked back and forth between his parents. "You have a son-in-law named Sam."

Mr. Litchfield looked at Toby with hard eyes. "You wanted this? To... whatever it is... with this man?"

Toby never wavered. "Yes. I love him. More importantly, I also like him."

Mr. Litchfield put down his fork and finished his wine. When Sam refilled the glass, Mr. Litchfield looked up and smiled. "You'll really do that? Love him and honor him and take care of him? Forever?"

"I will."

"Then I'll be happy to call you son-in-law." He looked at his wife. "And you, honey? What do you think?"

She ran her hand over her eyes. "It's a lot to take in so suddenly. But yes." She looked at Toby. "You'll do the same? For him?"

"I will."

She turned to Sam. "Then welcome to the family, son-in-law." She seemed about to burst into tears but managed to control herself. "I think I'd like another drink."

After dessert, complete with celebratory champagne, Sam said, "If you're ready, they probably need the table." He stood and the rest followed suit.

On the way out Toby's father, walking next to him, said quietly, "Are we stiffing them for the bill?"

Toby laughed and assured him they weren't. "It's Sam's way. He doesn't like having a bill presented at table, at least not when it's a celebration."

Outside, while they were waiting for the valet, the manager came up and thanked them, saying he hoped to see them more often. In the car Toby sat in back with his father while his mother sat up front with Sam.

"Thank you, Dad. Thank you with all my heart," Toby said.

"For what?" asked his father.

Toby replied, "For loving me the way you do. For raising me the way you did. For understanding."

Mr. Litchfield turned in the seat and looked at his son. "Toby, I don't pretend to understand you, hell, I don't even know what you guys do to each other – and I don't want to know – but if he," he nodded at the front seat, "if he means what he says and he makes you happy, well, that's enough."

Toby took a small package out of his inside coat pocket and handed it to his father. "Sam wants you to take Mom someplace nice. No, don't open it now. When you get home."

\* \* \* \*

Sam was unusually quiet as he drove them back to Palm Springs, at least until Redlands, when he put his hand on Toby's thigh. "Well, my love, it's certainly been a heady three days, hasn't it?"

Toby laughed. "Almost more than I could take in." He turned towards Sam. "Do you suppose it'll last? Oh, not the part about us; that'll last forever I think. I mean my folks. I wonder if, right now, they're having second thoughts about welcoming us into the family."

"They might have second thoughts," Sam said, "but you're their son. Somehow that'll make it all okay. Even the part about me. They'll balk at it a little I suppose, but in the end they'll be just fine with it."

They stopped at the house on the way into town, but found it locked up and Sam's key was on the dresser in the condo. Sam noted the wall had been given the finish stucco coat and the plaque with the house's name, Devá Shaante, had been set in it.

"Peace of the gods," Sam mused. "Perhaps it will be so." Then, "let's go see if Tom and Dan are around. Maybe we can talk them out of a drink."

Tom and Dan were indeed around and were all too happy to serve cocktails They were also kind enough to notice the new rings.

"Well, well," Tom said, taking Sam's hand in his and touching the band of gold. "I assume, since this matches the one Toby's wearing, that they mean something?"

Sam nodded. "We became partners. Signed the papers and everything. Best thing we ever did. A little scary but still the best thing."

Toby laughed. "He exaggerates, Tom. The scary thing we did was to have dinner with my parents."

"Now that I've got to hear about," said Dan, so Toby told the story, to everyone's amusement, including his own.

When he finished, Sam said they'd stopped by to see the house but, as he had forgotten his key…

Tom interrupted. "Yeah, Bill thought it was time to lock the place up. But we have a key if you want to see what they've done."

A lot had been done. Most of the sheetrock had been nailed up and the interior doors had been hung.

Tom observed, "About time to pick out some colors and maybe buy some furniture, huh?"

"That's Toby's department," Sam said. "If it was just me I'd paint everything white and have some store fill the place with stuff to sit on." He glanced at Toby. "And a bed. A big one."

Toby laughed. "But he's not going to do that." He turned, "Are you Sam?"

Sam thrust out his hands, palms up. "It would never cross my mind." He smiled at Tom and Dan. "Even if I thought I could get away with it."

Tom and Dan invited them to stay for dinner but Sam declined. He was anxious to get to the Sunday cocktail party around the pool and show off the new rings and he figured Toby felt the same way.

The first people they ran into at the pool were Howard and Duane, who noticed the new rings right away and immediately knew what they meant.

"Well, I do believe congratulations are in order," Duane said as soon as he saw them. "Look, Howard. We have newlyweds in our midst."

Mark and Jeff, who were standing nearby, came over to see and before they knew it Sam and Toby were surrounded with well-wishers and, they realized later, a couple of cases of jealousy. A very satisfying evening.

At home, Toby checked for e-mail at each of the sites they had put Zach on. There were a couple but none of them appeared to be from Martin.

"It's been long enough that we should check this daily," Toby said. "After all, we don't want to let our man get away."

# Chapter Twenty-Two

The next day, at dinner, Toby said he'd run into Zach at lunch. "He's checking the e-mail every day so he could see who, out there, wants his body." Toby laughed, "I said, 'You never can tell. There might be some good ones hot for your body.' Zach said it was too late. He couldn't handle any more than Jose at the moment."

Sam chuckled "See? It never rains but what it pours. Is Zach living with Jose yet?"

"Don't know," Toby said, passing the garlic bread. "They weren't at the pool yesterday and I forgot to ask today."

"I'll bet he is," Sam said with a wink. "Oh, I went out to the house today and Mary said you and she need to get together about the paint, and right away. The guys want to start as soon as the floors are in and that's probably Friday."

"Okay. I'll call her. Maybe take an afternoon off work."

Sam grinned at him. "You already know what you want, don't you? This is just a formality."

Toby laughed. "You have to at least look like you're considering different things. If you don't, nobody thinks you've given it any thought." He shrugged. "So we'll go look."

Sam just shook his head.

"Oh, by the way, I had a call from Dad today," Toby said.

"Good. What'd he want?" Sam asked.

"Well, he said it was just to thank us for the dinner. But what he really wanted was to know if you're an embezzler, a thief or a counterfeiter." Sam raised an eyebrow and Toby laughed. "The money, Sam. Remember when you took that pack of money out of the safe and told me to give it to dad? Tell him to take Mom someplace nice?" Sam nodded. "Well, I did."

"And he thought…"

"Exactly. I told him not to worry, you're multi-talented." He laughed. "I also told him to take a hundred dollars out of the pack and put the rest in his bank account."

"Why…"

"See, if it's ten thousand or more in cash the bank has to report it. If it's less, the bank doesn't. And they won't ask any questions because they don't actually want to report it. That takes time and makes for red tape which nobody wants." He shrugged. "Oh, and he said thanks for it, too."

* * * *

After dinner Wednesday evening, Sam found himself a book to read while Toby was on the computer.

"Bingo!" Toby exclaimed softly.

Sam looked up from the page he was reading. "What've you got?"

"Martin," Toby said.

Sam closed his book and went to see. "That's him alright. I'd know that dick anywhere."

"Here," Toby said. He selected another picture and brought it up. A full body shot, both face and dick. Definitely Martin.

"He send Zach an e-mail?" Sam asked.

Toby nodded and brought it up.

*Man, you're just what I've been looking for all my life. Please take a look at my profile. It's not as good as yours (who took those pictures?) but I hope it'll spark some interest. Please, take a look and come back to me.*
*Clark*

"Well, would you look at that?" Toby said, pointing at the signature. "I think that's pretty bold, don't you?"

"Not really," Sam said. "I'll bet he's just taken over Clark's life. Why not the name, too?"

Toby thought about that for a moment. "Yeah, makes sense when you say it like that."

"You going to answer it?"

"Not yet. Have to check with Zach. I don't think both of us should be answering. I mean, it's a question of style. Even a heavily horny guy ought to be able to tell when it's two different people e-mailing him." He brought up Martin's profile again. "Hey, look here. He says he's in Florida. Miami."

"Yeah, but that could be a lie too, couldn't it?"

Toby shook his head. "Doubtful. If you're looking to hook up with guys why would you say you were someplace you weren't? We did it because Palm Springs might make him suspicious, but your average guy who wants to get his rocks off wants you to know where those rocks are." He went through Martin's profile pictures slowly. "He sure is a hunk," he said, turning to Sam. "No wonder you liked to fool around with him."

"Yeah," Sam said, patting Toby's shoulder "There was just one thing missing." Toby looked up and Sam kissed him. "I didn't love him."

Toby took Friday off and went to the paint store with Mary. Afterwards they met Sam and Bill for lunch at The Rainbow.

"This man is so amazing," Mary said as drinks were served, beer for the men, ice tea for Mary. "He knew exactly what he wanted." She turned to Toby. "I don't know why we bothered looking at all those samples."

Toby took a swallow of bubbly liquid. "Well, you never know. There could actually be something new out there." He looked at Sam. "But there wasn't."

That night Jose and Zach came for dinner. Afterward they drafted an answer to Martin:

*Hi, Clark –*

*Checked your profile and all I can say is WOW.  We need to
spend some quality horizontal time together!  I would just
love to take your – no I won't tell you.  I'll wait until I can
SHOW you.  But man, what an – well, what an everything!*

*This is going to take some arranging, as all good things tend
to do.  You're in Florida and I'm in Phoenix.  But we'll think
of something.*

*E-mail me back if you're still interested.*
*Zach*

*PS: You asked who took the pictures.  It was my wife.  I think
she masturbates to them when I'm out of town.*

They agreed that if anything would get to Martin, that e-mail would.
"So what's the rest of the plan?" Jose asked.

"I think we have to get him to Palm Springs somehow," Sam said.
"Somewhere that Andy can see him, make the comparison to the coroner's
picture."

Zach's eyes lit up.  "How about we get him over here for a weekend
of debauchery at Some Guys?  This Andy guy could certainly see him there,
all of him."

"Good thinking, Zach," Toby said with a mischievous grin.  "Maybe
we'd also get to see all of Andy.  He is a good looking man."

"Wait a minute," Sam said with mock seriousness, "he is also an
officer of the law.  Besides," he grinned.  "You're taken."

The e-mails flew thick and fast for the next week.  First Martin wanted
him to come to Miami.  Zach said he didn't think he could manufacture a

reason for that. He said that he traveled a lot on business but always west, not east. His wife might get suspicious if he did something different.

Then Martin wanted to come to Phoenix, but Zach nixed that telling him that he and his wife were quite socially and charitably prominent in the town and his policy was never to have that kind of meeting within a hundred miles of home. Never.

Finally Martin set his own trap. Could Zach get to Palm Springs? If he could, Martin knew a gay, clothing optional resort called Some Guys where they could spend a weekend of bliss.

Zach e-mailed back:

*SexySkin –*

*It WAS meant to be. I have to be in PS on Saturday morning the 17th to do some paperwork with a client. I can tell my wife I'm staying over to check out a couple of real estate developments so I can stay until Monday morning. That would allow us the whole weekend, unless you get tired of doing – well, what we're going to be doing a whole lot of.*

*Let me know.*
*RedHotForYou*

He attached a picture of his hard dick lying across his palm.
\* \* \* \*

The next Saturday, when they were at the house, Mary asked Toby what they were going to do about furniture. "You going to go with straight edge mid-century chrome?"

Toby laughed. "Not hardly. It's going to be more like mid-century comfortable. Sam needs a comfortable reading chair and something to put his feet up on. I think that calls for fabric, something in a geometric pattern maybe." He put his hand on her shoulder. "It may be a great restoration, Mary, but it's also going to be a place for people to live, Sam and me people for example and if we aren't comfortable, what's the point?"

She nodded. "Makes sense. You got a lot of furniture picked out?"

"Some," Toby said. "Not much. Sofa. Dining set. Bed."

"There's a new shop that just opened up. They specialize in mid-century stuff and have a great inventory. Want to go shopping?" Mary asked.

He did.

\* \* \* \*

The next day Jeff and his partner dropped by to make sure Sam and Toby would be at the Labor Day buffet at the pool. "Scotty's doing it and it promises to be a good one," Jeff said. "You have to come."

"Yeah, and I'd skip lunch if I were you," Mark added. "You know how carried away he gets. I'll bet he's been cooking since Wednesday."

That evening another e-mail from Miami came through.

*HotRedMan.*

*It's all set. The room is confirmed and the guys are expecting us Saturday the 17th. I have plans for you, some involving raspberry jam and red pubic hair. So we'll ignore all those other guys, at least until later. Then – well, we'll see what develops, won't we?*

*Now I have to go read War And Peace. Anything to keep my mind off you.*

*And my hand off my dick!*
*ForeverHard*

*PS: Can I have one of those pictures of you? The ones your wife uses? Please?*

"Now there is a horny, desperate man," Sam observed, reading the e-mail again. "What do you suppose he's going to do with the raspberry jam?"

Toby laughed. "I have no idea, Sam." He paused and thought. "But I was once with a guy who did some very creative things with a can of pizza sauce." He attempted a leer. "Wanna try it?"

Sam kissed him on the nose. "Only if it's the kind with extra basil. You going to answer that?"

"Nah, I'll leave that to Zach. He and Jose are really getting off on this, I think." He turned serious. "Shouldn't you be talking to Andy pretty soon? The 16th is only two weeks away."

"Right. I'll call him Tuesday."

\* \* \* \*

The Labor Day luncheon turned out to also be a celebration of Sam and Toby's new status as domestic partners. And, as usual, Scotty had out done himself with the buffet which included an ice cream cake set over a bowl of dry ice. On top of the cake were two naked groom figures complete with the appropriate anatomy. Everyone could tell they were grooms because they were holding hands and wearing top hats. The guys loved it.

At one point in the celebration Walt Wentworth came to congratulate them and admired their rings. He asked where they got them and when they told him he let out a low whistle.

"Man, you must love each other just one hell of a lot to go to Tiffany's. That's one expensive store."

Sam grinned. "Love knows no bounds, Walt."

"Yeah, and no budget, either. But they are beautiful." Walt glanced across the pool where his partner Nick was talking to Mike Armstrong. "Shit!" he said almost to himself. Then, to Sam and Toby, "Gotta go."

Walt gave Nick a hard slap across the butt and dragged him out the gate by his arm.

"What was that all about?" Toby asked of no one in particular.

"Jealousy, fear and, to some degree, I imagine, sex. Or lust," said Ben Smith, who happened to be passing by. "Sometimes I really wish they'd stop but of course they won't. This is the only place they can get so convenient an audience."

"You think they do it just to get attention?" Toby asked.

"Yeah, but not ours. I think they do it to get each other's attention. And I wouldn't be surprised if by now they weren't slapping and cursing and fucking like minks."

"Gives tough love a whole new meaning, doesn't it?" Sam said with a grin. "Oh well, to each his own I guess."

"You guys up for some food? I see our newest resident over there sampling the buffet," Ben said, nodding towards Zach who fed Jose one of the tiny appetizers that were Scotty's trademark.

"He's living with Jose now?"

"Moved in Saturday. Charlie and I gave them a hand. Seems like a nice guy. Handsome, too, with that bright red hair. We didn't see that on Saturday. You know him?"

"Yeah," Toby said, "I work with him. And he is a nice guy."

"Good. He'll fit right in. Besides, we need more handsome guys to dress up the place."

Privately Sam thought there were lots of handsome guys dressing up the place but he kept it to himself.

\* \* \* \*

On Tuesday morning Sam called Andy and invited him for six o'clock drinks in the Blue Bar at the Hyatt.

When Andy asked what the occasion might be, Sam simply said, "We found him."

Sam felt very much at loose ends the whole day. He worried Andy would think they'd gone too far or maybe feel they were usurping his job. He went out to the house but found himself in the way of the painters although they were very nice about it and didn't say anything.

He went next door but Tom and Dan weren't home so he finally went back to the condo gym and worked out for a couple of hours.

At six sharp Sam found Toby at the bar. A few moments later Andy came in.

"So you found him, did you? Where? And maybe how but I'm not sure I want to know that," Andy said.

"Don't worry, Andy. We didn't cross any real lines," Toby said.

"Uh... new ring?" He looked back and forth at Sam and Toby. "They mean what I think they mean?"

"Yeah, I decided to keep him," Toby said with a laugh. "I just couldn't let him go." He shrugged his shoulders. "What can I say?"

"Nothing. The expression in your eyes, both of you, says it all." He took a sip of his drink. "So what'd you do to find our man? Oh, and where, exactly, is he?"

They explained about Martin's fetishes for red pubic hair and married men and the website and profile they'd set up. "Then we just let it sit and marinate," Toby said.

Sam added, "And he walked into it with his eyes wide open, as they say. He's in Miami but, to save you the trouble of explaining all this to the Miami police..."

"A difficult job at best," Andy interjected, "considering a foreskin – or the lack of one – is our main evidence."

"Anyway," Sam went on, "Martin suggested Zach meet him right here, in Palm Springs."

Andy looked warily at Sam. "Where?"

"Even better," Toby said. "At a gay resort called Some Guys. Which, just to frost the cake heavily, is owned and run by friends of ours."

Andy sighed. "How the hell do you guys fall into shit like this?"

"It's the power of clean living, Andy. You ought to try it sometime." Sam looked at his watch and changed the subject. "I'm hungry. You want to come to dinner with us? We're buying."

Andy held out his arm. "Twist."

They went to Spencer's.

Henry saw them come in and immediately ushered them to the bar. "Your table isn't quite ready, sir. Please, have a drink, on us. It shouldn't be long."

"You had this planned all along, didn't you?" Andy said when their drinks were served.

Sam shook his head. "I just thought of it, back there at the hotel."

"You have a standing reservation? I'm impressed!"

"Hardly," Sam said, raising his drink. "We have an understanding waiter." They touched glasses. "To Henry, the best waiter in the world."

When they were seated and had ordered an appetizer sampler, Andy said, "There is one little thing. I talked with the chief about this – he thinks it's funny by the way, or maybe he thinks foreskins in general are funny, I don't know. Anyway, he says it would sure be helpful to have fingerprints for both of them. That way, if we should catch one of them we'd know which one it is."

Toby shook his head. "But the foreskin…"

"I know, I know," Andy said. "But the chief thinks fingerprints are better."

Toby tried the coconut shrimp with obvious pleasure. "But I thought identical twins had identical fingerprints. I mean, they have the same genetics, don't they?"

Andy ate a lobster pot sticker. "Well, yes and no." Sam looked pained but Andy went right on. "They are identical at the start but since the two babies can't be in the same place at the same time, outside things like skin and fingerprints get subtly changed depending on where they rest, what they rub against and so on. So, by the time they're born there are little differences all over the skin. It takes an expert to spot them but they're there."

They were silent while the busboy removed the appetizer dishes and Henry served the main course. Once each had sampled his dinner and pronounced it excellent, Andy went on.

"Getting this Martin guy's prints should be easy. They'll be all over his stuff. It's the other one's that's a problem."

Toby stared off into space for a moment and suddenly snapped his fingers. "No it's not." Andy and Sam both looked at him. "The business card, Sam. The brother's business card in the book." He turned to Andy and began to choose his words very carefully. "Uh, there's a book on the dresser in Martin's guest room. Clark's business card is in it, as a bookmark. I don't think, uh, anyone else has touched it."

"And you know this how?"

Toby smiled. "Common knowledge, Officer. Common knowledge."

They finished dinner while Andy contemplated the extent of 'common knowledge.'

* * * *

The rest of the week passed in a flurry of e-mails from Martin and a flurry of deliveries of furniture, rugs and house wares to the house. Toby, and sometimes Sam, had been spending a lot of their free time searching for just the right pieces to go in the house and had been surprisingly successful at it considering the stuff in the stores.

Over the weekend they went up to the Beverly Hills house because Toby thought the Oriental rug in the den would be perfect in their new living room. While they were there they also went through a lot of drawers and cabinets, looking, as Toby put it, for hidden treasure. They found a lot.

"Harry really did have a thing about cash, didn't he?" Toby asked, stuffing another packet of bills into a shopping bag. "What are we going to do with it? I mean, put it in the bank or what?"

Sam thought for a moment. "No, I think we should do what Harry did. We'll spread it around the cupboards and drawers in the house and use it as we see fit. Besides, if we haul it off to the bank it'll just cause problems for the bank staff."

"That's my Sam," Toby said with a laugh, "always thinking of the other guy."

"Well…"

Toby took him in a hug and kissed him lightly on the mouth. "No, I mean it. You are a very kind man. And I love you for it." His hand slipped down along the curve of Sam's buns. "Among other things."

Sam thrust his crotch into Toby's. "We got time for a quickie?"

Back in Palm Springs the e-mails were becoming almost desperate and Zach was greatly enjoying his position as lust object. "Jose and I are having fun doing all the things he says he wants to do with me. And believe me, he's very creative."

Jose laughed. "So creative he says he gave himself a wet dream the other night. Maybe you guys ought to hold off for a day, let Zach find out what the guy can really do."

"I don't think so," Zach said. "You're doing just fine. Any better and I don't think I'd survive it. Besides, he'll need all that creative energy in jail. I'm sure he'll find lots of willing guys in there."

\* \* \* \*

Andy called on Wednesday to say they had found a couple of good fingerprints on Clark's business card. "And you were right. They don't match the ones all over everything in Martin's condo. Everyone agrees. They're from different people. We also tested a few things around the house, that tequila bottle for example and the drug bottle. Turns out the only prints on them are the same as all the other ones in the house. It looks like our suicide never touched them."

"So we're going ahead with it?" Sam was elated.

"Yeah, we're going ahead with it. The chief isn't too happy about doing it in a resort, what with all those other people there, but I assured him there wouldn't be much in the way of danger. I mean, if the guy's naked he can't very well have a gun on him, can he?"

"Not one that hurts when it shoots," Toby said with a laugh.

They also, of course, talked with Roger and Bob at Some Guys. Like the chief, Roger wasn't really happy about the whole plan but Bob thought it would be exciting and convinced Roger to go along with it.

\* \* \* \*

Martin arrived about ten in the morning and checked in. When he did, Bob told him that Zach had called and said he'd be in around eleven.

"Good," Martin said with a grin. "That gives me time to take a shower and check out the guys. See you at eleven."

As soon as Martin went to his room, Bob made a phone call. "Your man is here," he said.

"We'll be there right away," Toby said. "Thanks."

When Toby, Sam and Andy walked in Bob told them Martin was out by the pool and would be coming to the office at eleven to meet Zach.

Sure enough, at about ten to eleven Martin wandered into the office.

"Martin!" Sam said in a loud voice as the others gathered round. "Martin Shields, my old next door neighbor."

"Sa..." He caught himself. "Sorry sir, you're mistaken. My name is Clark. Maybe you know my brother or something. His name was Martin."

"No," Sam said with a grin. "Your brother Clark is circumcised. That handsome thing of yours," he reached out and ran his fingertips along Martin's dick, "still has all the skin it was born with."

Martin seemed to lose focus as he pushed Sam's hand away. "What do you mean... circumcised? Clar... I mean, my brother? Who are you?"

By this time Toby, Sam and Andy had virtually surrounded Martin, although he didn't seem to notice. Neither did he seem aware of the two uniformed police officers who had joined them.

Sam's voice turned gentle. "I know because I found him, Martin. In your bathtub. Dead."

Martin faltered, nearly losing his balance. He stared at Sam, his brow furrowed. "But my brother... he wasn't circ... was he?" Martin stammered.

"You'll have to come along with us, sir," one of the uniformed men said, taking Martin's arms and handcuffing him. He threw a robe over Martin's shoulders to hide his nakedness. Andy nodded and they took Martin away.

That evening Sam took them all to Spencer's for dinner; Sam, Toby, Andy, Zach, Jose, Roger, and Bob. They all looked to Andy for information since he'd been in on the questioning down at the police station.

"You know," Toby said, "in the office at Some Guys, he acted like he really didn't know Clark had been circumcised."

"As far as we can tell, he didn't," Andy said.

"But, even if Clark had never told him, how could he miss it when he was... well, when he was murdering him?"

"Look," Andy said, "you're killing someone, you're killing your brother for God's sake, are you going to take time to look at his dick? Especially when he's your identical twin brother. Everything looks like you. You don't check because you don't have to, you know. Besides, you're kind of busy."

Over the salad, Sam wondered what Martin had been doing since the murder.

"Being his brother. I gather he spent a couple of days up in L.A, drunk. Then, when he sobered up, he went through Clark's papers and found Clark had just bought a condo in Florida. So he went to Florida. No one there really knew his brother so he simply became Clark. Not difficult when you've only dealt with real estate people and a few bankers. And you look just like him."

"Except for his dick."

"Except for his dick, but no one down there knows about that."

By time for dessert, they'd grown tired of Martin and the conversation turned to Sam, Toby, and their house.

"It looks like two weeks from next Saturday," Toby said when asked when they would move in. "At least, that's probably the first night we'll be able to sleep there."

"We'll miss you at Desert Pride," Jose said.

"I doubt that," Sam said, between bites of chocolate soufflé. "We're not giving up the condo, at least for now. So Pete Addison will still have to let us in for Sunday cocktails and we'll still be using the gym."

"Well, if you decide to rent it out, keep me in mind," Andy said with a smile.

"You?"

"Sure. Why not? I clean up okay, don't I? Just a thought."

Sam shook his head but let it go.  "We'll do that, Andy." .

# Chapter Twenty-Three

The next Friday, Toby had lunch with Mary, and when Sam asked how it'd gone he said "Weird. She wants me to quit the hotel and go to work with her."

Sam grinned. "I thought she might do something like that. You want a drink?"

"Gin," Toby replied. "On the rocks. Skip the vermouth." He paused for a moment, thinking. "What do you mean. you thought she'd do that?"

"It only makes sense," Sam said, handing Toby his drink. "She's been very impressed with you, Toby, with the way you see things and put things together. Hell, I'm impressed, too." He kissed Toby on the nose. "But I may be prejudiced." He went about fixing his own martini "Look at it this way. You brought that house together – had really good ideas about it." He touched the rim of his glass to Toby's. "What's the offer?"

They went out to the patio and sat at the umbrella table. "Partnership," Toby said. "Some kind of design thing with Bill as preferred builder." He looked up at Sam. "What the hell do I know about designing stuff? I'm an accountant, for God's sake. A junior accountant!"

Sam grinned and leaned back in his chair. "Which would you rather do, Toby? Figure out how to make a kitchen exactly the way it ought to be or figure out how much to charge for a room to make it profitable?"

Toby actually thought about it for a few moments and then laughed. "The kitchen, of course. Room rates are boring. But Sam, do you really think I could do it? Design someone else's kitchen?"

"Toby, what I think doesn't make much difference because, as I said, I'm prejudiced. I think you could do anything you set your mind to. The opinion that counts here is Mary's. If she thinks you can do it, I have no doubt that you can." They sat in silence for a few minutes before Sam added, "Look, why don't you push it to the back of your mind and let it percolate for a couple of days? The answer will come to you, just like the answer to my problem with the scene in Martin's bathtub came to me. I guarantee it."

Toby smiled. "Okay, Sam. As long as you guarantee it."

"Another thing I can guarantee? There's some pasta primavera over at Boscoso that is desperate to be eaten. Let's go and help out, okay?"

\* \* \* \*

On Tuesday morning, Toby said, "You were right, Sam."

"Huh?" Replied Sam.

"You sure you don't want to go back to bed? I can have coffee at work, you know." Toby asked.

Sam shook his head. "Yes, I'd like to, but no I can't. I have to be over at the house at eight. They're delivering the bed. Maybe, after they set it up, I'll just – "

Toby shook his head. "Oh, no, you don't, Sam. The first time that bed gets used, it'll be us using it."

Sam grinned. "Okay, maybe I'll just put the sheets and spread on it. Get it ready for... you know." Just to prove that he was paying attention, he added, "Now, what was I right about?"

Toby suddenly looked serious. "That if I just put it away, my problem would solve itself. You know, about what I'd rather do, the kitchen or the room rates?"

Sam nodded. "Who won?"

Toby smiled. "The kitchen, of course. But you knew all along that it would, didn't you?"

Sam had the courtesy not to gloat. "All I knew was that it was a decision you had to make for yourself. So..."

Toby smiled. "Well, I need to talk to Mary some more before I give notice at the hotel but... I want to give it a shot. I figure I can always go back to being a junior accountant if it doesn't work out."

\* \* \* \*

For the next ten days, Sam divided his time between checking progress on the house and shopping for things he felt competent to pick out, things like linens and towels. Toby, who had finally given his notice to the hotel, devoted most of his time to the hotel so there would be as few loose ends as possible when he left.

Toby's boss, knowing that he was moving into a new place, gave him the last two days of the week – the last two days of his employment – off, and by Saturday morning things were very much under control. So much so that Toby started to hang the few pieces of art they had brought from the condo.

"No, wait," Sam said, seeing what Toby was doing. At Toby's questioning look he smiled and said, "There's a couple of other things coming and you should wait, see where they should go."

"Other things? What other things?"

Sam was saved from answering by a UPS truck pulling into the driveway. The driver came to the door with a large, flat package. "Litchfield? Toby Litchfield?"

Toby nodded. "That's me."

"Sign here," the driver said, leaning the package against the door frame and then holding out an electronic clipboard.

Toby signed, the driver pushed the package towards him and left.

"And just what is this?" Toby asked, indicating the package.

"Open it and see," Sam suggested with a smile.

When Toby got through the heavy paper, the bubble wrap, and three layers of cardboard, he looked up at Sam and grinned. "The William Keith painting from the house in Beverly Hills. But how'd..."

"I saw how much you liked it when we were up there, so I called Alistair and asked him to have it shipped down here."

"Well, it's perfect, Sam. Thank you." He hugged Sam and gave him a kiss. "Right there," he said, pointing at the north wall of the living room. "That's where it'll go."

"Uh… could we wait just a little longer?" Sam ducked his head and studied his shoes.

"Okay, Sam. Out with it. What've you done now?" Toby asked.

Again, Sam was saved by the arrival of a delivery truck. Two men got out, and one came to the door. "Okay, guys," the man from the delivery truck said. "Where do you want this stuff?"

"Let's see it, first," Toby said, giving Sam a hard look and accompanying the man out to the truck, which the other man had opened.

Inside, fastened to the truck wall, were the Case Paul painting and the near-life-size sculpture of a naked man Toby had admired that morning they had gone to buy paintings.

Toby turned to Sam, who had followed them out. "Pretty sure of yourself, weren't you, Sam?"

Sam put his arm around Toby's waist. "The most uncertain man in the world," he said, "but you said they were good pieces, and I thought they might make a pretty good investment, whether or not – "

"They are, Sam. They are." Toby gave Sam a squeeze and then turned to the delivery men, all business. He directed that the sculpture be taken to a spot by the pool.

By late afternoon they'd done all they'd planned to do and, in unison, pronounced the house livable. To celebrate they made use of the new, very big, glass-block shower, where they ended up blowing each other on the tile floor.

Later, at dusk, they sat contentedly by the pool, drinking champagne. "That shower is wonderful," Sam said, with a great deal of enthusiasm. "It's big, bright, and even the floor is warm." He thought for a moment. "How is that? I thought it'd be cold – or at least cool – lying on the tile."

"I asked Bill to put some heat cables under the floor," Toby replied. He stretched and grinned at Sam. "So your handsome feet won't get cold in winter."

They cooked lamb sausage on the grill and ate it with green salad and tiny, roasted potatoes. Afterward they took their wine and wandered through the house, taking great satisfaction from all that they – and especially Bill – had done.

Then they went to bed and made love for a long, long time.

# About the Author

Greg Bowden was born in Southern California and grew up on the Central Coast. He loves to write and has more than fifty stories and five books to his credit. He is a member of Prime Timers of the Desert, lives in Palm Springs, California with his partner of forty-two years and a Wirehair Fox Terrier named Winnifred.

E-mail: psgreg357@gmail.com

Also by Greg Bowden:
Available from Nazca Plains Publishing:

323 Kearny
Brothers
The Folks on Taylor Circle

From MLRPress:

Devils Shaft

From Silver Publishing:
Angel's Quest

Also available from Amazon.com and several local retailers.

www.ingramcontent.com/pod-product-compliance
Lightning Source LLC
Chambersburg PA
CBHW051629260626
47170CB00004B/1098